From Havram to Abraham

From Havram
to Abraham

E. WILLIAM PETTER

The Shortest Journey Is a Detour Series

RESOURCE *Publications* · Eugene, Oregon

FROM HAVRAM TO ABRAHAM

Resource Publications
An Imprint of Wipf and Stock Publishers
199 W. 8th Ave., Suite 3
Eugene, OR 97401

www.wipfandstock.com

PAPERBACK ISBN: 978-1-6667-1535-4
HARDCOVER ISBN: 978-1-6667-1536-1
EBOOK ISBN: 978-1-6667-1537-8

JULY 22, 2021

To my beloved wife Connie
Without whose Love, Support, and Editing,
I would not have been able to write this novel

Chapter 1

Smithsonian, Washington, DC—Present

Doctor David Scortun answered the intercom buzzer on his phone, "Yes, Nancy?"

"A Mister Ian Maccleith is here for his appointment, Doctor."

"Please show him in."

The man at the door was about ninety, spry, moving as nimbly as someone half his age. His jacket's left sleeve was pinned to his shoulder; he'd obviously lost his arm. His full crop of white hair was streaked with residual scarlet strands. He carried a wooden box in his right arm. "Thank you for meeting with me, Doctor."

Dr. Scortun replied, "My pleasure, Mister Maccleith. Please have a seat. This is the artifact?"

"Just Ian, Doctor." He placed the box on the desk in front of the doctor, removed the top, and took a chair. The doctor peered inside: resting there was a fourteen-by-sixteen-inch clay tablet on white faded cloth. Every square inch contained a signet ring impression.

"There are 187 impressions, Doctor. The remaining 43 are on the backside. The newest ones are in English, but the older ones elude me. The ephod has been a family heirloom for hundreds of years. I've finally decided it might have some historical value—187 generations goes back a long way. If it has historical value, it wouldn't be proper to keep it closeted. So I've brought it for your evaluation."

The doctor scanned the impressions. He could identify most of the scripts: cuneiform, ancient Canaanite, Egyptian hieroglyphics, Aramaic

Block Script, Greek, and Latin, but not being an ancient language expert, couldn't read any of them.

The doctor had a quizzical look, "Ian, you said ephod. The only ephod I know of is the robe the ancient Jewish high priest wore, not a clay tablet."

"I know, Doctor, I can't explain it either. But our family has called the tablet an ephod for at least seven generations—not the garment. You are welcome to give it any nondestructive tests you want. If it helps dating or identifying provenance, you may use a few grams of the cloth or wood. I know I don't need to tell you to treat it reverently. It's valuable, at least for our family."

"Thank you, Ian, we'll do that. Let's move it to the credenza until some-one can take it to the lab."

David moved the ephod to the credenza, shook hands, and Ian left.

The doctor picked up his phone. "George, could you please ask Jerry to bring a high-resolution camera to my office. I need some close-up pictures of an artifact to email to some scholars."

In twenty minutes, he was examining a picture of the first seal impres-sions on his screen. He minimized it, changed to his Rolodex, and emailed a copy of the first ten cuneiform impressions. Picking up the phone, he called, "Irving, got something interesting and just sent you pictures. Got a few min-utes to give me a first impression?"

"Sure. Let me put you on speaker. Give me a minute to open them . . . O.K, got them. Opening the first. The name is Havram. The second is . . . Oh my God!" Silence for two minutes, broken only by the click of computer keyboard keys. Finally, "You aren't going to believe this. First, this style of cuneiform is archaic; these symbols date to 1800 BCE or a little later. It's unlikely a forger would know them. The impressions appear made by signet rings, the type used for bullae. The first three are Havram, Abraham, Isaac and—care to guess the next two?"

"You aren't going to say Jacob is one of them, are you?"

"Jacob is the fourth; Israel is the fifth."

David let out a long, slow whistle.

"David," said Irving. "Before you do anything else, I'd recommend you get that tablet to the lab under lock and key."

****

IN THE FIELDS AROUND NINUWA—ANCIENT NINEVAH

July 1752 BC

As Havram was returning to camp after his day's watch over the herds, his father met him, "We just got news. A few days ago a locust swarm devastated croplands in a ten-mile swath north of us. Whoever's in that path has lost their crop and needs a substitute food source. We don't want them looking at our sheep and goats. We're breaking camp and moving the herds. I need you and Jurael to scout the trail for five miles west going straight for Dag Sünbül. We need to put at least fifteen miles under our belt before tomorrow night."

"Yes, Father," Havram replied. "If you could please have Jurael get us some water and food skins, I'll feed Nanos and we'll be on our way within ten minutes."

Just after noon the following day a runner caught up with the two men.

"Havram, change of plans. I'm to replace you. You're to join your father on the trailing side of the herds."

Havram's head fell as he slowly shook it, saying to no one in particular, "Vintage Father. Gives you no background. Tells you what to do, but not why, so when conditions change, you don't know how to adjust." Since sixteen-year-old boys in the Aramean culture didn't question their father's decisions, his comments fell just short of breach of respect. He finished with a huge sigh.

Jurael, ten years older, had been listening, arms crossed on his bow. "Havram, you're still young. You're always thinking, always questioning, but sometimes you don't pick up on the clues and therefore make snap judgements. Your father's told us what's happened. The villagers have found us, so this is no longer an exercise in caution. The two of you have the best bows and now Terrah needs that power behind the herd more than he needs it in front. Trust him. Your father is the brains of this band. He knows what he's doing. Have faith in your father."

Havram thought a minute, then turned to face Jurael, "You're right. Father doesn't change his mind without circumstances altering. Whatever it is, it must be bad." He pulled his waterskin band across his chest to move the weight higher onto his back, turned, and left.

In an hour, he had passed the herds and joined Terrah a quarter-mile beyond. A quarter-mile further were four men trailing the herds. Havram asked, "Farmers?"

Terrah nodded, "Yes. I recognize one of them. I've sold him wool and sheep for sacrifice several times. He's an elder in a village on the locust path."

Havram realized they had been spotted, but what was the danger? How much threat were four farmers when they had eight men?

An hour later, Havram noticed two of them leaving, heading to their village.

"Father," he said with hope in his voice, "Good news. Two of them are leaving. They've given up!"

"No, Son, it's not good news. Since the elder remained, it means they haven't given up. They are returning for reinforcements. They've decided to kill us and steal the herd. They've lost their crop and face starvation before they reap their next. Desperate farmers with a family to support will do *anything* to avoid *that* fate. Always remember, farmers belong to a different ethnic and cultural group. They are Akkadian Chaldeans; we are Arameans. Neither trusts the other. In Chaldean eyes, we are less than fully human. In times of desperation, it's fine to lie, cheat, steal and kill us. They consider this a desperate time with no alternatives. Every man from the village will arrive at noon tomorrow for the battle."

How does Father know all this? Havram steeled himself for what he would say next, "If it's them or us, let's confront the two men and force them either to stop following us or kill them outright."

Terrah shook his head, "If we turn back, they will also. They'll keep their distance and continue trailing us until the rest of the villagers join."

"Then, let's veer the herd and lose them in the wilderness."

Terrah smiled, "Havram, you've been around sheep so long you no longer notice the smell. Horse droppings almost smell good. Cows are readily distinguishable, but not bad. Pig droppings are horrible. Sheep are worse. Sheep are so foul a blind man could follow a three-day old trail from smell alone. We can't lose them."

"Isn't there anything we can do?"

"Yes, we can chose the battlefield. We can be at the wadi at Dag Sünbül at noon tomorrow."

What is the wadi at Dag Sünbül? Why noon tomorrow? Nothing made sense. But, Havram knew that even when Terrah seemed to make no sense, he knew what he was doing and had formulated a plan. Havram fell silent.

An hour after nightfall Terrah and Havram joined the camp. They would sleep in the open tonight to get an early morning start. The women had dinner cooked and waiting for them, but Havram didn't immediately join them for the meal. He had one chore to perform—the runt came first.

Hanah was waiting for him at the edge of camp with a small bowl in her arms. Havram went straight to her.

"Nanos?" Havram asked.

She jerked her thumb towards the herd.

Havram heard the runt. Over the residual normal bleating of ewes and lambs locating each other and settling in for the night was one distinctive, higher-pitched sorrowful voice. *"Where are you?"* it asked.

Hanah reached out with the bowl, "I've milked one of the goats for you." She smiled and headed back to the campfire.

"Thank you, Hanah," he called after her. Turning towards the herd, "Nanos, Nanos."

The bleating changed voice, *"Here I am. Here I am."* A gap in the taller sheep's bodies formed a trail as a smaller body forced its way slowly to the edge. Finally, Nanos—the runt—appeared and skipped straight towards Havram, her tail wagging in delight.

Havram put the bowl on the ground and Nanos went straight for it, lowering her head to the bowl. As she slurped the milk, Havram petted her head. The tail wagged more vigorously.

Terrah stood arms crossed over the top of his bow, "How much longer?"

"She's seven weeks old now. With most lambs, I'd say another week, but she still wants two bowls a day. With her small size, I'd say probably two or three weeks until she's fully weaned and on her own. Next week I'll cut her back to one bowl a day."

"I still say you should have let her perish. That's normal for sheep."

"I know, Father, but I was there at her birth. I knew it would be a huge chore, but I didn't have the heart to let her die. That's just not who I am."

Terrah didn't say a word, but his manner voiced his thoughts. *But, that's life. It isn't fair. It's normal for first pregnancy ewes to only accept one from a twin birth. She can't feed both, so the rejected one dies.*

"I know, I know. That first two weeks about killed me. Every two hours she cried and head-butted me for food. But, now she's eating more grass. She'll soon be on her own. And, she no longer wants to sleep next to me; she's realized she's a sheep and not a person. It's been worth the struggle. The herd has one more female."

Terrah smiled and nodded his head. His face radiated his pride.

When Nanos had licked the bottom of the bowl clean, she headed for the herd and sleep.

The two men joined the camp for dinner.

As the two lay down for sleep, Havram tried one last time to pump Terrah for information. "Why won't the farmers just let us go in peace?"

Terrah propped himself on an elbow, "Put yourself in the farmer's sandals. What happens when your family starves to death? The children die first because they have less fat reserves. As their father, you have to endure their slow death, knowing your wife goes next and you last. Better a quick death in battle. Next, it's a small village of a dozen houses, so they'll have somewhere between twenty to thirty men. They believe they outnumber us over three to one. Those aren't bad odds if everything is equal. Only we know that, in this case, it isn't. They also believe their chances are nine in ten of winning the battle and only one in three of surviving starvation. And, the farmers will have made a pact to care for the family of anyone killed. Last, if they lose the battle, yes, their wife and children will be sold into slavery. But, at least they will survive. What would you do?"

Havram thought for a minute. "Yes, I see the logic. But, what can we do?"

"Win, of course. They don't know about our bows. All we need is to control our pace to be at the wadi when they arrive. Until then, they need to believe they have the initiative. Enough. We need a good night's sleep so we'll be fresh in the morning." Terrah pulled his robes over him and in thirty seconds was snoring loudly.

Havram lay on his back, staring at the stars. *Good night's sleep? My stomach's knotted tight and the knots are churning. It may be my last night. How can I sleep?* But, the day's stress finally overcame the stomach and he dropped off.

Havram woke before dawn to the sounds of the camp rising. Terrah had left to attend to whatever. Havram sought out Hanah. She had the goat's milk in the bowl. "Hanah, if I don't make it back tonight, please cut Nanos back to one bowl in the evening for the next two weeks, then wean her."

"I'll do that, Havram, but please come back. We'll all miss you, not just Nanos."

Havram smiled and nodded. "Thank you for everything."

Heading to the herd, he called, "Nanos. Nanos."

He couldn't see her head bob as she heard him, but he recognized her voice as she answered, *"Here I am. Here I am."* As she left the herd, she skipped to him, lowering her head to the offered bowl.

Havram petted her head. As he put his mouth next to her ear, he could feel the air from her wagging tail whoosh past his face. "If I don't make it back tonight, don't forget me."

Before leaving, Havram and Terrah loaded four quivers of arrows each. They trekked to where they'd been the day before. They couldn't see the two farmers still sleeping a quarter mile away, but they knew they were there.

As the morning crept toward noon, the two men's pace slowed, allowing the camp to get further and further away. Dag Sünbül loomed above them. The two entered a wadi eroded by mountain runoff. Ten-foot steep walls closed in on both sides as the wadi floor slowly rose to meet the mountain.

Havram turned and walked backwards for a few steps. The two men still followed a half mile behind. He took solace in the bow in his hand and the arrows in the four quivers each carried.

When he grabbed another look, a gasp escaped his mouth.

"What's wrong, son?" his father wanted to know.

"More men from the village have joined those following us. There's more than twenty." Havram blurted out, his voice tinged with apprehension. "Father, we're outnumbered."

Terrah said nothing. In another hundred paces, he picked a spot where swift mountain run-off left no scrub growth, turned to face the oncoming men and removed his quivers.

Terrah spoke in a moderate tone, untouched by any hint of apprehension. His calm manner displayed complete confidence. "Twenty-six men just joined the two following us. There were four men yesterday when they started trailing us. Two left, leaving the ones you saw this morning. I sent Michel to follow those who left. They went to their home village. This morning every man joined them. These are the ones who arrived, so twenty-eight oppose us. That's why I moved the flocks."

"But, Father, you also sent the other men away. Now it's just the two of us."

"Son, just the two of us is precisely why these men continued following. It's also why they haven't asked for help from their neighboring villages. They don't want to share our herds with their neighbors. They believe their greater numbers will ensure success, despite only having two swords and three bows. The rest carry clubs or farm tools. So yes, your first impression is correct. They do outnumber us.

"But, your first impression is also mistaken. They may outnumber us, but they don't out-power us. You keep forgetting the weapons we carry are not ordinary bows. Our bows come from Ur. There are no yew trees here. Each of these bows is worth thirty men. Their bows only fire a hundred twenty-five yards, ours three hundred twenty-five. Their effective range is seventy-five yards, ours two hundred. Therefore, we have the power of sixty men. Our bow-power out-numbers their twenty-eight men by two to one. These villagers have remained confident because they aren't aware of the power of our weapons.

"Always remember, we were born with a bow in our hand. This is what we were born for. This isn't my first battle, and it won't be your last. Now, Havram, it's time for archery; just like we practice it."

Havram removed his quivers and the two of them bent to their task. In the soft silt of the wadi floor they carefully arranged their arrows. Each arrow stuck point-down, upright, four inches apart, in a straight line pointing to the approaching enemy, six feet separating the two lines, one hundred arrows each. They retraced their steps to the beginning of the line of arrows, one arrow strung in their bowstring, waiting.

When the leading rank of men got to three hundred twenty-fifty yards distance, Terrah raised his bow high, drew it all the way back, and fired. Three hundred yards downrange, the arrow stuck into the wadi bed in front of the enemy. The arrow warned, "Better think twice."

The enemy leader walked up to the arrow. Pulling it from the ground, he glared contemptuously at them, and then broke it in two over his knee. His face proclaimed the answer, "You're buzzard meat."

The enemy leader turned to his followers. Brandished his sword in one hand and the broken arrow in the other, he encouraged everyone to steel themselves for battle.

Terrah took time to counsel his son, "Their leader is confident; and that works to our advantage. Our greatest danger is if their men lose their nerve for battle. We need them to be confident and determined as they begin their attack. Remember what I told you: success in battle is more mental than physical. This is your first battle, so expect to be nervous. It's normal. I'm going to give them twenty-five yards with no arrows. That will allow them to gain confidence. They'll start to spread out towards the wadi walls. When I give the nod, aim for the men nearest the walls. We must goad them into a tight group in the center. When the leader gets to two hundred seventy-five yards distance, I'll signal to begin rapid-fire. Don't aim for the leaders; aim over their heads at the group behind them. At this range, don't aim for a kill. Any hit is a win. We don't want the leaders to know how many wounded they've taken until too late. At a hundred yards, aim for the kill. Begin with the leader and anyone carrying bows or swords. After that, keep firing until no one remains standing."

Havram trusted that Terrah knew what to do. Terrah's calming words reassured Havram's brain that all would be well, but his gut wouldn't agree. It wanted to tighten into a hard ball.

Terrah put his hand on Havram's shoulder and nodded reassuringly. They needed no words. They were comrades-in-arms. Both turned to face the enemy.

The first twenty-five yards the approaching men took was the longest period of time Havram had ever experienced.

His heart began racing.

Thirty enemy paces.

Two hundred heartbeats.

As his father predicted, the group began spreading.

Their men thumped their weapons into their open palms.

Fortifying resolve, increasing confidence.

When they completed the first twenty-five yards, Terrah nodded his head.

Havram aimed at the far-left man.

He knew it was too far for an accurate shot, but he hoped for a lucky hit.

Anxiousness affected his aim and his nervousness made his aim jittery.

He watched the arrow all the way.

It missed, but the man jumped and moved to join the central group.

Havram noted the arrow had achieved its intended result.

It forced the enemy into a tight group.

It wasn't that he'd doubted what his father told him.

It was just the unavoidable first-time jitters.

His confidence began improving.

His father's prediction must be right; they'd live through this.

He began calming down.

"Begin!" Terrah directed, his voice as calm as if this was a practice session.

Two arrows flew downrange, into the center of the group.

Havram bent down, inserting the next arrow onto his bowstring.

He rose, pulling back on the bow as he stood.

He began his aim even before he was standing.

When fully upright, it only took another half-second to fire.

String an arrow. Rise and aim. Fire.

String an arrow. Rise and aim. Fire.

Six seconds each arrow.

Round after round, the pair loosed one arrow every three seconds.

Havram was no longer thinking.

His mind reverted to target practice.

Nervousness vanished in the mindless mechanics of motion.
He no longer realized his targets were men.
They were merely targets.
He was no longer thinking; he was doing.
He was a death machine.

From three to two hundred yards distance a hundred-twenty seconds
     ticked away.
The enemy advanced one hundred twenty paces.
Thirty arrows flew downrange.
Only three found their mark; all wounded.
A one-in-ten hit ratio.
The enemy leader assumed that hit ratio would remain constant.
That would mean twelve wounded total for his force.
A successful attack.
His misunderstanding proved a fatal mistake.
He didn't expect the hit ratio to rise exponentially.
From two to a hundred-fifty yards the likelihood of a hit rose to one
     in four.
The arrows struck eight.
From a hundred-fifty to a hundred yards, the ratio rose to one in three.
The enemy lost five more.

Six enemy decided they wanted no more, turned and fled.
They discovered two shepherds had circled to straddle them on the
     wadi walls.
Each fired from a different sidewall.
The last four approached from behind.
There was no escape.

The leader suddenly realized he only had twelve men standing.
Realization of their danger gripped him.
He called for a charge; his remaining men broke into a run.
Brandishing weapons they yelled at the top of their lungs,
"Death to the shepherds."
A hundred yards distance.
But the arrow's successful hit ratio was up to seventy-five percent.
Terrah and Havram switched aim to the sword carriers and archers.
Terrah dropped the leader first.
Sixteen arrows dropped twelve men.
The last man fell at fifty yards distance.
Havram didn't realize there was no enemy left until he rose to fire …
and discovered no targets.
Three hundred seconds had ticked past.

Three and a third minutes of elapsed time.

Three and a third years of emotional stress.

Havram's brain kicked in as targets disappeared. "Father, we won. It's over."

Terrah shook his head, "Yes, we've won, but it's not over. Collect a quiver of unused arrows. We must ensure every enemy is dead. Assume everyone is wounded. Center shot in the chest—and get no closer than five yards before firing."

They collected a quiver-full of twenty-five arrows from the unfired ones still poking into the wadi floor.

As they started to the wounded lying on the ground, screams and moans overwhelmed Havram's consciousness. Many reached out to them, pleading for help.

No help. No quarter.

The wounded saw they were executing everyone and realized their fate.

When Havram reached his eighth man, he stopped. He looked to be a sixteen-year old boy, no older than he was, shot in the stomach, writhing in pain, grabbing onto the shaft of the arrow with both hands. "Father," Havram pleaded.

When Terrah approached, Havram pointed, "Father, he's just a boy, no older than I am. I can't do this. Can't we spare him?"

Terrah drew his bow and shot the boy center-chest.

"Son," Terrah explained, "This world is dangerous. It's also cold and ruthless. It's full of heartless men who would kill you for the lunch you carry.

"You need to remember two facts. First: he chose to be part of the band that attacked us. He wanted to be a man. If you want to be a man, you must be ready to live or die as one.

"Second: these men come from an honor culture. If we allow even one to escape and tell their village what happened, their honor code would compel neighboring villages to band together for vengeance. It doesn't matter that they attacked us first. Tribal honor demands total annihilation. If five villages banded together, they would destroy us. I'm sorry, Son, but we can't allow any witnesses to escape. We must kill all wounded."

They resumed their executions.

Minutes later one man, shot in the leg, but otherwise unhurt, was lurking. He'd seen what was happening and realized his danger. He snapped off the end of the arrow in his leg and held the shaft in one hand, pointing out of his chest. He covered a knife in his other hand, playing possum. As Havram approached, he readied himself.

When Havram stopped and started to withdraw an arrow from his quiver, the man jumped up and started towards Havram as fast as his wound allowed. Resolve and rage flooded his face—if he had to die, he'd take at least one of them with him.

Havram froze in unanticipated fright.

Five feet away the man raised his knife to stab. His body shook as the tip of an arrow protruded from his lower chest. The blow forced the air out of his lungs. He gasped for air that wouldn't come, stumbled, fell at Havram's feet, shuddered and died.

Terrah stood ten yards behind the man, "Havram, you need to fix your arrow before you approach your man." Terrah's tone of voice was as calm as asking someone to pass the bowl of couscous at dinner.

Havram discovered he was shaking.

When they'd executed the last man, Terrah explained that one last task remained. If the dead all had arrow-wounds, it'd be obvious that shepherds were responsible. Shepherds used bows; soldiers and villagers used swords. Neighboring villages would go on a warpath against all shepherds. They must erase every trace of identity.

Terrah and the men removed every arrow, then thrust a sword into the wound. This masked their cause of death by arrows. They beheaded or slashed others. The evidence must suggest everyone died in hand-to-hand battle with another village. They carried away every farm tool, as if the victors considered them valuable. Last, they piled the bodies in a heap. Arrows cause internal bleeding while swords cause bleed-out. Moving the bodies would mask the lack of bleed-out.

There was one issue Terrah did not discuss with Havram. The villager's families knew they were going to attack shepherds, not other villagers. Would they believe another village had attacked them as they returned? Would they suspect shepherds were responsible after all?

To be on the safe side, Terrah wanted enough distance for safety no matter what they decided. They kept moving west.

Havram ate little that night. Eating was a chore. The food had no satisfying relish.

It was for times like this that a king opens the beer barrels for his soldiers. Alcohol deadens emotional nerves so a man can stretch the healing over a longer time. But they didn't have alcohol.

Terrah ate in silence. Havram needed to face his fears, beginning with emotional trauma.

When he lay down to sleep. his experience caught up to his emotions. *Now I understand why we practice archery so much. It isn't to get better at hitting the target, though that certainly helps. It's to give your body muscle memory. It ensures you can still function when you're scared out of your wits. Your body knows what to do, even when your brain can't control it.*

Several times during the night Havram awoke in a sweat, heart racing. The sight of the sixteen-year-old boy haunted his dream. The night seemed endless.

The nightmare angst began bleeding over into the day. He knew: for shepherds, there was always a future battle.

Can I spot warning signs earlier? This was almost too late. What more can I do? How can I recognize the signals indicating farmers around me have been pushed to the danger condition?

The next morning, Terrah motioned for Havram to remain after everyone had eaten breakfast. "Did you get much sleep last night?" He wanted to know.

"No, Father, I kept waking up during the night. The sight of that young boy haunted me. He was no older than I am."

"My experience was similar. It's normal. You will come to experience peace. But, it takes time. Remember, we didn't start this fight, they did. Once they refused our warning, we had no choice. Dying resulted from *their* decision. By choosing to attack, they chose the possibility of dying.

"Now the important subject. You told me yesterday they outnumbered us, and I didn't answer you. I have taught you about power, but understanding in your mind is different from experiencing in your gut. You've had time to reflect about yesterday's battle. What was wrong with your statement that they outnumbered us? Describe how power decided yesterday's battle."

"Father, I think I understand what you want me to learn. They had twenty-eight men and we had two. But, power isn't about numbers. If both sides had swords, numbers equals power. If both sides had bows, numbers equals power. But, they had swords and we had bows. All weapons have a power range. Sword power range is a maximum six feet. Swords have no power outside that range. Saying it differently, swords have no power when you are seven feet away from each other. On the other hand, bows have no power at three feet—that's too close to wield the bow. Their archers had no power because our bows had a longer range. They never closed to their effective range of seventy-five yards because we killed them first. The sword fighters never had power in yesterday's battle because we killed them before they could close to sword-fight distance. The lesson: they had greater num-bers, but they had no power. Fighting a battle isn't about numbers; it's about power. Am I right, Father?"

"Yes, son. That's what you need to know for now. There's more. For ex-ample, our two bows are worth thirty men against a mob, but only twenty-five against a disciplined enemy. Well done, my son.

"You have grown to display the capacity to understand what you are seeing. Six months ago you wouldn't have understood the lesson about power. You have matured. That doesn't mean you are fully mature, only that you are ready for the next stage in your life.

"Where am I leading? You face your most important decision. Who are you supposed to be? What will your profession be? Where will your life lead?

"I can give you some guidance. What you want—what you feel—is not as important as who you are. Who you need to become is the decision. Two questions should serve as your guide. First, what is your greatest desire; your greatest goal in life? The second is its opposite, what is your greatest fear? The answers to these questions will decide your future." Terrah paused, "And, Havram . . ."

"Yes, Father?"

"What's important isn't the decision itself. What's important is the *why* of the decision. That's what I need to hear. In the normal cycle of events, you shouldn't decide for another six months or even two more years. But, yes-terday's battle *hastened* the timeline. The decision is now upon you. Spend time today thinking about these questions. After breakfast tomorrow, we'll discuss your answers and what they mean. This is a man's first decision. This is a doorway which will close behind you. Once you pass this threshold, there is no return to boyhood."

That day was an emotional turmoil. *I'm not ready to be a man! Am I climbing the hill to manhood? Or, is Father pushing me into a fast-flowing river and over its falls into oblivion?*

Certainty and doubt chased each other in circles about his head. Yes-terday's battle and its sixteen-year-old boy. His mind was a category-five tornado.

That night was worse. Several times he awoke in a cold sweat, his chest tight and his muscles tense. The slain body of the young boy lay before him. But Havram's head was on the boy's shoulders. Waiting for his sweat to dry, Havram gazed up at the tent's black ceiling, wondering. *What will happen the next time? With shepherds, there's always a next time. Who am I now? I know I'm not an innocent, adolescent boy anymore. But, I'm not a man yet.*

I'm caught in the middle. I'm neither. Sometime during the battle, I crossed over my soul's dark line. I can never go back. Who am I now? I don't know.

But, Havram did know one fact. Father was right. There was no return to boyhood. He'd killed how many? At least ten men. He could never completely erase the battle from his memory. He must endure its anguish, waiting for the memory to become bearable. But, the angst of knowing he would face the same battle every ten or so years began weighing on him.

Father implied I had a choice. That means I don't have to be a shepherd. I can choose something else. What does he have in mind? I've always wanted to be a servant like him and my brother Harran, but I don't understand what this means. Should I say that? But, he wants to know why. *I don't* have *a why.*

Do servants fight battles? Father has never mentioned it. But then again, Father never talks about his battles. If I go into the unknown, I may fall into a sinkhole.

If I remain a shepherd, there will be future battles. But, I have my bow. That gives me an advantage. And, shepherds lead comfortable lives—good lives. Is staying with the known better than jumping into the unknown?

For Havram, the last two days were too much, too fast. Instinctively, he knew he must answer the two questions his father had asked. But, as long as the answers remained inside his head, they weren't real. He wouldn't have to face them. They could change. But, he also knew, as soon as he uttered the words, he would voice them into being. They would become his reality, and he must live with them.

What should I say? What must *I say? What is my greatest goal? What is my greatest fear? Why?*

Chapter 2

Smithsonian, Washington, DC—Present

Doctor David Scortun wasted no time in getting the box into the lab vault. He accompanied it himself; this was potentially too valuable to allow any chance mishap. Returning to his office, he directed his secretary to hold all calls, put his feet on the desk and rested his head on his index fingers, and thought.

Havram, Abraham, Isaac, Jacob and Israel. Abraham through Israel were Biblical patriarchs, but he couldn't remember a Havram. He opened his online computer Bible to Genesis, chapter 11. Thinking Havram might be Abraham's grandfather with the father's name missing proved to be a fruitless thought. Abraham's father was Tarah and his grandfather Nahor. Neither remotely close to Havram. So how did Havram fit into this puzzle?

After a few minutes, he felt forced to perform a simple cross-check. *I don't know about Havram, but Abraham dated to the period 1800–1700 BCE. I wonder?* He opened a desk drawer and withdrew his calculator. 2000 CE + 1750 BCE = 3750 years total. 3750 years ÷ 187 names = 20.05 years each generation. Given some firstborn children were females, that's too high a frequency. But given some younger siblings succeeded older deceased ones to family leadership . . . no, this is about the right number of names to put this specimen at the right time range for Abraham.

Doctor David Scortun made a mental analysis. *What's unusual about this set of circumstances? This artifact is looking genuine. But serious questions remain. Why would someone create a large clay tablet for small bullae? Why so thick? They couldn't predict 4000 years of use.*

The signet impressions must be a secondary use. That suggests a differ-ent original reason for the large size. . . . Maybe it's only a clay coating. . . . A specific gravity test: that would confirm the tablet being all clay. A low reading would suggest a void; a high reading something heavy inside.

Dave called in two lab technicians. "Gentlemen, warm up the Coordi-nate Measuring Machine; I think an accuracy of a thousandth of an inch will be enough for a preliminary measurement. Measure a hundred data points, paying special attention to the edges; I need to know the exact number of cubic centimeters making up this specimen. It's probably too heavy for the 1/1,000th gram scale, but the 1/10th scale should give us enough precision. Get me a rough calculation of its specific gravity. We need to discover if it's fired or unhardened clay, or something else. I need the answers before the end of the day. If this turns out as I'm beginning to suspect, we'll have to run more tests tomorrow."

In the end he was so excited he couldn't wait; he went downstairs to the lab. The technicians had finished measuring and were transferring data into the shape-generator program. The enter key confirmed the tablet was an almost exact box-shape. Two minutes later they had the weight. Thirty seconds on a calculator gave them the specific gravity.

It was ten minutes to find the correct specific gravity tables. As Doctor Scortun expected, the density was too high for clay. Something made of metal or rock was inside.

He needed a time slot for an x-ray test. Excitement gripped him; this promised to be one of those rare moments scientists live for: discovering something never seen.

Being the director helps. There was no x-ray time slot available, but he wangled an agreement with another group for the morning. They only ex-pected to use half of their time slot—they had scheduled more than needed "just in case." They would grant him any unused portion.

****

FIELDS WEST OF DAG SÜNBÜL

July 1752 BC

The following morning Terrah and Havram sat on their tent mat.

It was a man's tent; strictly utilitarian. There were no traces of a woman's touch; the little enrichments that make a place into a home. No children's playthings to trip over, nothing to add beauty or charm, nothing to add a pleasing scent. Havram's mother had died during his childbirth and, although Terrah had remarried, for some unexplained reason his wife had never joined him.

Terrah's men claimed his wife stayed away because she couldn't stand his snoring. The circulating rumor was that once Terrah's snoring had wakened a hibernating bear. The clearly exaggerated detail was the bear was sleeping in his cave a mile away from Terrah's tent.

Terrah asked the first question, "Havram, let's start with your greatest fear."

"Father, for this question, I can give you a ready answer and the reason. You remember about a year ago, we stumbled onto an abandoned wooden shepherd's bowl laying in a field?"

"Yes, I remember."

"His bowl is a shepherd's most prized possession. He carries only one. In the field, he eats every meal from that bowl. No one loses their bowl. That means someone killed the shepherd, probably for his flock. Like the villagers. Only this shepherd didn't prepare. His bowl was laying askew. Its bottom rotted out. It had weathered fifty years or more. No one remembers who that shepherd was. No one remembers his name. It's as if he never lived. His life was a waste."

Terrah nodded understanding.

"You remember the trip when you, Harran and I went to Cha-tel Hyuyuck? It was so old doors weren't invented yet. You climbed down a ladder from the roof. It was so old no one remembers its people's name. But, they left a legacy. They were the first to build permanent buildings. Before them, people lived in tents. They invented something, giving everyone a better life. They made a difference." Havram paused, taking a large breath, "I don't need anyone to remember my name, but I want my life to make a difference. I want to leave the world a better place. I'm afraid if I just live the life of a shepherd, my life will make no difference. It will be a rotting shepherd's bowl on history's plain."

Terrah nodded, "You have made a good argument. You have thought this through for some time, haven't you?"

"Yes, Father, I have."

"Now, the second question. What is your greatest goal in life?"

"I want to become a servant, like you and Harran."

"A noble goal. Now, why?"

"I don't know why, Father. I've never questioned it. Harran is our family's fourth generation of Servants. I don't know what else to do."

"Havram, that's not enough. Becoming a servant has three preconditions.

"First, it must be your passion. We often misunderstand passion. Your passion is more who you are than what you want. Who you are eventually drives what will satisfy you. That determines what you *should* want. They must align. We need to discover if you have that passion. If you don't, you will not be successful. The best you can hope for is mediocre. We'll come back to passion.

"Second, you need to have an aptitude, the raw skills. It's not enough to be able to think. You need to use fact-based reasoning. I believe you fulfill the basics, however, your skill needs developing. You don't understand what that means yet. However, I can teach you the mechanics of reasoned thinking.

"Third, you must hear The Divine calling you." Terrah paused to stress what came next, "Havram, I am the servant assigned to Ninuwa. The Divine called me to be a Servant of the Light. I believe The Divine has also called you."

"Father, I don't understand. No one has called me."

Terrah smiled. "You can't hear this calling with the ears; you feel it in the heart or understand with the mind. The word is discernment. It's a tug on your innermost being. When it calls, you can't rest until you answer it. Sometimes a person doesn't understand their experience. They are too involved for objectivity. Others see their life change and help them understand their call. Only when they show you, can you understand. When you answer your call, it will change your life."

"But my life hasn't changed."

"Actually, it has. I have seen it. I hope I can help you understand. Think back to when you were eight years old. Remember playing with all the boys? What games did you play?"

Havram's face took on the gentle smile of pleasant memories, "We played Kick the Stomach into the Goal, Hide and Seek, Races, Throw the Rock, many games."

"Did you enjoy them?"

"Oh, yes."

"Do you still play them?"

"No."

"Why not?"

"Oh, I don't know. It just isn't fun anymore."

"Do your former playmates still play games?"

"Yes."

"If they still like playing games, why don't you?"

That stopped Havram in his tracks. He had never thought about it. "I don't know. Father, do you think there's something wrong with me?"

"No, I think it's something right. But, I need to ask a few more questions before you will understand. Now that you don't play games with the rest of the young adults, what do you do with your time?"

"I spend it alone or with men tending our herds."

"Why?"

"First, I want to learn to become a man. But, I want more. I want to learn something no one else in the world knows. Only me. I want to do something new. Something no one else has done."

"That's the answer that shows The Divine has called you. Let's summarize what you just said. What was common about eight-year-old games? They required moving your body. You started playing those less often after you turned ten and, when you were thirteen or fourteen, you stopped. What took its place? Thinking. You started using your brain instead of your body. When you were fourteen you fully transitioned from doing to thinking. You concentrated on using your brain."

"Father, now that I think about it that way, you're right. I never realized it. It just started being fun to learn and I started to learn everything I could from the men. After I learned what they could teach me, I started to try understanding the sheep and goats—why they do what they do. I wanted to prepare myself for manhood and tending the flocks and herds."

"I understand, because I followed a similar path to manhood as you did. So, let's look at what this path means. To make a point, I will present this as black and white. Men are divided into two categories. We will call them thinkers and doers. Most men are doers. They're the farmers, herdsmen, laborers and so on. Thinkers are the leaders. The king uses thinkers for his army's officers and doers for his soldiers. You are a thinker. You having this skill isn't surprising; it runs in our family. I am a third-generation servant; my father and grandfather were also servants. Your older brother Harran also has the skill, and that's why he's a servant."

Havram's eyes opened wide; it was obvious he had never looked at the world like this before, "Then that means . . ."

"Yes, Son. Servants have to be thinkers, and good ones. Hard problems are beyond an average man's skill level. You have unknowingly prepared to become a servant. That's what I have seen and you have missed. That's why I know The Divine has been calling you. Not understanding the call is inexperience, not lack of ability. Yesterday you evaluated what happened in the battle and why we prevailed. You displayed a basic skill in solving hard problems, but you lack training in how to use and improve your skill.

"But I didn't do anything exceptional. That wasn't surprising. The answer just made sense."

"You *should* be surprised. Most people aren't logical and don't have common sense. It's rare. However, you have servant ability. You confirmed your call.

"What remains is to discover your passion. How do you want to spend your life? Let's assume you have two choices: you can remain as a shepherd or become a servant. What would your life be like?

"How will people in the greater community treat you? As a shepherd, the farmers won't hate you—they will loath you. You are different—an outsider. They will not respect you. They will tolerate you for your wool and meat. But, they will cheat you, lie to you, do everything they can to take advantage of you without a pang of conscious. They tolerate you as resident aliens. You are a necessary evil. Nothing more. As a servant, you will be loved—you will be hated. You will be envied—you will be despised. You will be trusted—you will be distrusted. You will be looked up to—you will be looked down upon. You will be friendly to all, but have no real friends.

"What will be your home? Belonging to a shepherd family, you will always have a tent for a home. You will never be rich. But, it's a comfortable living. As a servant, you will never have your own home. The community you serve will lend you a place to live for a while. You will live as a resident alien, usually tolerated, but often resented as much as appreciated.

"What does a shepherd's future hold? A plague of locusts or a year of drought will happen every ten years. Farmers will band together to kill you without hesitation or remorse to steal your herds. You will have no recourse but to kill them. Then, like we did, you will leave before their neighbors rise against you. As a servant, the council will reassign you every five or ten years. Each time, you must leave everyone behind. Every assignment starts anew.

"A servant experiences aloneness. Your duty is calling a tyrant a tyrant—and you will be as welcome in his city as a leper.

"You indicated that you desire to make the world better. As a shepherd, will you contribute? Shepherds have no opportunity. To use your metaphor: they leave life as a rotting bowl on the plains of history. For a servant, if they are good, they will enrich the community they serve. For the called, being a servant is the most rewarding occupation on earth."

As Terrah talked, Havram's eyes grew wider. His jaw dropped, although he managed to keep his mouth closed. It was obvious he had never considered the whole panorama of effects his decision would create. The opportunity would open some doors, while others would close.

Terrah stopped. After a few seconds, he tilted his head slightly to the side and his eyebrows raised.

Havram couldn't speak. It wasn't certainty and doubt running in circles outside his head; now it was his head itself spinning. He looked down at the hands cupped in his lap. His eyes wouldn't focus; there were four out-of-focus hands. He looked at the tent ceiling. It wasn't a ceiling; it was a blur. He couldn't distinguish how faraway it was.

Terrah understood. "Havram," he said gently, "Let's finish this in the morning." He rose and left the tent. Havram needed to face himself.

Before, Havram didn't know that he didn't know. He had lived in a protected bubble. Terrah had just popped that bubble. Now, Havram knew that he didn't know. The world was larger than imagined—and swirling. It had to stop spinning before he could think clearly.

Terrah was snoring loudly, but that wasn't why Havram couldn't sleep. He was used to the snoring.

He lay, eyes open, staring at the tent ceiling. Terrah's words roiled in his mind, his thoughts boiling over, spilling out.

You will be loved—you will be hated. You will be envied—you will be despised. You will be trusted—you will be distrusted. You will be looked up to—you will be looked down upon.

You will never have your own home. The community you serve will lend you a place to live for a while. You will serve as a resident alien, usually tolerated, but often resented as much as appreciated. The council will reassign you every five or ten years. You will have no friends. When reassigned, you leave everyone. Every assignment starts anew. Yours will be an aloneness life. Your duty is calling a tyrant a tyrant—and you will be as welcome in his city as a leper.

For the called, it's the most rewarding occupation on earth.

I don't feel called. Even if I am, I'm not sure I want to answer. I'm not sure it's what I want.

I may spend years trying to become a servant, and never make it. Do I want to waste a significant portion of my life trying for something beyond my reach? It's safer to remain a shepherd. I may never reach high enough to touch heaven, but no one will throw me out of their city. Shepherds always have a community caring for them.

What do I want?

Then an epiphany hit him.

Wait a minute. What did Father say? This isn't about what I want, it's about who I am. But . . . who am I?

Then he remembered what he'd said in answer to his Father's question of why he hadn't let Nanos die. He'd said that he couldn't let her die because that just wasn't who he was.

So what am I called to be? On one hand is not letting my own sheep die. On the other is helping the city I'll be assigned to as a servant become better and giving their citizens a better life. Who am I?

Chapter 3

Smithsonian Laboratory, Washington, DC—Present

Doctor Scortun, a lab technician, and the box on its cart waited as patiently as someone who can't wait. True to form, the group finished an hour early. The two men and box rushed into the x-ray chamber, removed the tablet and placed it onto the table.

Rounding the x-ray shield, they adjusted the x-ray intensity to "clay" and pressed the button. The screen showed a twelve by twelve inch blackness inside the light gray tablet on one side and a short rectangle beside it. The specific gravity test was correct. There was something inside the tablet that was so dense the x-rays wouldn't penetrate at low power level.

Turning the setting to maximum, they pressed the button again. Now the "clay" disappeared, but the object inside the tablet was a dark gray with small, lighter gray circles. He counted them: fifty-seven. Fifty-six formed a large circle with the last off to the side.

He left the x-ray room with a printout of the screen in his hand, its image on his thumb-drive and questions in his mind.

Back in his office, he closed the door and started thinking. *Fifty-seven, fifty-seven, what could fifty-seven mean.* No answers. He dredged up Google on his computer and entered "57 holes." Meaningless results such as shooting three holes-in-one with a score of 57.

He frowned: *My mind is hitting a brick wall.*

Doctor Scortun lifted the handset and called Ian Maccleith, "Ian, David Scortun of the Smithsonian here. Have some interesting news for you.

We've sent the first five seal impressions to a renowned cuneiform expert. The first five names are Havram, Abraham, Isaac, Jacob, and Israel. Excluding the first name, the rest are Biblical—and in order. If this is genuine, the tablet dates to 1800–1700 BCE. That makes this tablet not only of great historical value, but possibly of critical value for what it can tell us about Abraham's genealogical tree.

"I know you already approved taking a few grams to radiocarbon date the garment and box, but I wanted to let you know it's time. We'll use a few grams from the sewn-up backside of the garment and a sliver of wood from the inside box lining. I'd also like to send the garment out for pollen testing. That's nondestructive, but may answer where the cloth was made. Do you have any issues we need to be aware of or guidance you may have?"

Hearing the affirmative answer, he continued, "Thank you, Ian. We'll begin work. When we get the preliminary answers, probably in about three or four weeks, we'll let you know what the labs found."

Hanging up, he pressed the phone's intercom button, "George, David. First: we have a 'go' on getting samples of the cloth and box for radiocarbon dating. I suggest we use Beta-Analytics, but don't pay extra for a rush job, just use a regular three-week test schedule. Next, it's been so long since we needed pollen analysis I've lost track of who's at the Boston University Pollen Lab. Please call them and arrange to get the garment analyzed. Please let me know who's in charge and a phone number. We may want to call them after we get the results. I know I don't need to tell you to send it in an air-sealed bag. . . . Right, thanks."

****

FIELDS WEST OF DAG SÜNBÜL

July 1752 BC

Finally, he drifted off to slumber, more from exhaustion than any sense of peace. It was sleep, not rest. As he slept, the pieces of the puzzle started falling into place in his mind. When he opened his eyes, his world had stabilized. His old-world was 250 pieces of a 1,000-piece puzzle, just a quarter of the whole picture. Now all 1,000 pieces had solidified into a coherent picture. His world made sense again.

"Father," he said as everyone sat down for breakfast, "I need to become a servant. It's in our family's blood; it's who I am. I won't be a whole person until I do."

Terrah's face formed a gentle satisfied smile, "I'm happy for you, Son. But, now comes the hard part. Ten man apply for every training opening. Only thinkers apply, so these people aren't ordinary. You have to beat out nine other men to earn admission. Becoming a servant is this world's greatest challenge. Only the good apply. Only the best succeed. You must excel to succeed. You're either all-in, or you're not in at all."

"Nine other men—all older and more experienced than I am? Can I possibly be good enough?"

"I won't make light of the challenge ahead. And even if you don't make it on the first try, there are still four more years ahead of you when you can apply. Remember your brother Harran? He didn't make it the first time. I can teach you the basics. You'll have to study. But, if you work hard, you have a good chance. What is your passion? Are you willing to give it everything you've got?"

In their tent after breakfast, Havram confronted Terrah. "Father, you never told me until just now that I have to beat out ten men to be able to go to Ur. What is going on?"

"Son, I didn't tell you because it wasn't time yet. First, you had to decide your path in life. If you decided to remain a shepherd, explaining the competition would waste our time. Only now should I explain what's ahead."

Havram thought for a few seconds, then reluctantly agreed it made sense, even if he didn't like it. "All right, what is going to happen and what do I need to do?"

"First, I'll tell you what doesn't happen. You can't just show up at Ur. It doesn't happen that way. The Region's Selection Committee selects two candidates per year. The Regional Director also has an option to appoint one applicant. On average, at least ten applicants compete for each opening. Let's hit some high points.

"When can you go? You can apply once each year, starting at two hands plus five and continuing until three hands plus three. You are just about to turn two hands plus five, so you will probably be the youngest person applying in our region.

"When does the board meet? The week after the fall equinox. However, the exact dates vary. It cannot happen on a new moon day. Second, the Committee schedules two days so there is enough time to examine all applicants. I am sending Jurael to present your application and learn the dates. We'll know in a few days.

"What questions will the board ask? I can give you only general guidance. All questions will evaluate how you think. Some are numbers questions, others "what/why." The questions vary each year. The committee will have three judges, one of whom is usually the Regional Director. His actual title is the Region's Melchizadek. All applicants answer the same questions. There are four rounds of five questions each round. Each round will eliminate applicants until only two remain.

"So, we have about a month's preparation time. Some applicants have more than a year. They have a head start. However, your advantage is innate skill. I believe in you." Terrah reached out and put his hand on Havram's shoulder. That spoke far more than words.

Terrah leaned back and reclined, propped up on one elbow. "Havram, let's begin with some examples of 'what/why' questions. What do the judges want? Anyone can describe what they see. Not everyone can evaluate what they see and extract only the few key characteristics. Key characteristics are 'what.' They explain the observations. Reasons explain 'why.' The board wants to hear 'why.' This reveals your reasoning ability.

"Let's begin by talking about hunting. Lions successfully bring down a gazelle about one time in twenty attacks. How do lions hunt gazelle?"

"They select an animal, usually the young or the old, sneak up on it and attack."

"Can lions run faster than gazelles?"

"Yes."

"Please explain why a lion sneaks up on its prey before attacking. Explain a lion only being successful one time in twenty. If a lion's successful kill rate is one in twenty, why does the lion select the young or the old to hunt? Why not hunt the biggest animal?"

"Father, I don't know; I can't explain."

"We'll come back to the lion and gazelle. Let's go to the next example. How does a pack of wolves hunt gazelle?

"The wolf pack leader selects an animal and the pack runs down the gazelle and kills it."

"Is the gazelle faster than the wolf pack."

"Yes."

"If the gazelle is faster, explain a wolf pack running down a gazelle."

"I don't know; I can't explain."

"Remember the two categories. You explained 'what.' That's first. Then I asked 'why.' You didn't know and don't know how to figure it out. The Council evaluates your 'why' ability. Ordinary people can tell 'what,' but it's a servant's task to figure out 'why.'

"There is a method to these questions. Central to his calling: a servant first asks 'why,' then uses 'why' to understand 'how' to improvement the world. Solving 'why' gives you innovation; you can invent something no one else has ever done. 'What' only yields incremental improvements for existing solutions.

"Let's review the lion and the gazelle. A lion's advantage is being faster than gazelles. But—only just a little bit faster. However, lions only run a hundred yards, then must stop to catch their breath. Gazelles run a quarter mile at top speed. Lions must sneak close enough to overtake a gazelle within a hundred yards. If the gazelle detects the lion sooner, it always outruns the lion. The gazelle's weakness is, while grazing with its head down, it can't see slow motions more than twenty yards. If the lion sneaks slowly while the gazelle is grazing, and freezes when the gazelle raises its head, it remains invisible. If the gazelle can't see the lion, it won't run. When the lion gets to twenty yards, it attacks at full speed. If it can cover ten yards, half the distance, before the gazelle understands the danger, it will overtake and kill the gazelle within the hundred yards. Otherwise, the gazelle escapes. A young or older gazelle can't run as fast, so attacking these improves the lion's changes of a kill. We call this style 'attack hunting'

"Now, what did I just do? I identified each individual part of the puzzle that together make up the whole problem. First, you identify all the separate pieces, then find how each works, and last how they fit together.

"There is an old mantra you can use to help remember. When the gazelle awakes each day, it knows it must run faster than the fastest lion or it may not live to awake tomorrow. When the lion awakes each day, it knows it must run faster than the slowest gazelle, or it may not eat and have the strength to run tomorrow. Now, I have explained innovation, try solving the wolf pack and the gazelle."

Havram thought before answering, "The gazelle always runs faster than a wolf, so attack hunting won't work. A gazelle can't run farther than a quarter-mile. However, wolves run all-day. So even though wolves can't outrun gazelles, they run fast enough so they don't lose sight of the gazelle within a quarter-mile. So the wolf pack runs until it overtakes and kills the gazelle. Have I explained it, Father?"

"Exactly, its name is 'persistence hunting.' Excluding minor types, such as trapping, attack and persistence hunting are the two hunting styles. Now, what style hunter are we?"

Havram immediately answered, "We sneak up on prey like a lion, so we must be attack hunters."

Terrah gently chided, "Havram, you made a snap judgment; you didn't take time to think the problem through. Fact 1: Do we run faster than the gazelle?"

"No."

"Fact 2: How often does our arrow go through the gazelle's heart and kill it immediately?"

"Perhaps one time in ten."

"Fact 3: If the arrow doesn't kill the gazelle immediately, how often does the gazelle die within a hundred yards?"

"We must run to keep the gazelle within sight until we overtake it. Father, you are right, I made a snap decision. You don't need to ask for a fourth fact. We are persistence hunters."

Terrah smiled. He didn't say anything; smiling was the approval message.

Havram continued thinking, and his thoughts led him to a question, "Father, I have always thought the purpose of the arrow was to pierce the heart. If true, any shape or size arrow would work. Now, I'm thinking if an immediate kill chance is only one in ten, then nine times the arrow misses the heart. We still run down the animal by persistence hunting, implying the arrow has another purpose."

Terrah's smile broadened, "You have progressed beyond my expectations. You are right; the arrow cuts an animal's artery, so the animal will start bleeding out internally, weakening the animal so we can overtake it."

Havram's mind was now fully into examination thinking. "That explains the arrowhead's size. If smaller, it penetrates deeper, but hits fewer arteries. If larger, it penetrates less, and hits fewer arteries. The arrow size we use seems a happy medium yielding the best chance. Am I thinking correctly?"

Terrah's smile morphed into astonishment, "Havram, you are exactly correct. Each different arrowhead type we use has a different purpose, and therefore a different size, shape, or material."

Terrah thought for a minute, then nodded his head. Havram had a real shot at being selected. "Havram, you've made a good beginning. Now it's time to get to work."

The next two months were a whirlwind. As well as showing Havram how to think, Terrah had to teach the rudiments of occupations Havram didn't know, such as farming, metalwork, and sword fighting. No one could anticipate the questions the judges would ask until the competition, so no one could know in advance what background knowledge he needed to have.

Havram progressed rapidly, but the same thought was always on the two men's minds: rapidly enough? Was he prepared? Would Havram be ready in time?

The night before they left on the trip to Assur, Havram was so worked up he couldn't fall asleep. He needed his rest. But, trying to command sleep wouldn't work.

I feel like I'm a young male mountain goat with first-year horns, trying to challenge the ten-year-old head of the herd in one-on-one battle.

I have significant weaknesses, but can my strengths offset my drawbacks?

I don't have a smooth speaking style, but am I intelligent enough to say what matters?

I haven't learned enough, but can I compensate with wisdom?

I don't have experience, but can my thinking ability counterbalance?

Do I have enough guts?

In two days—I'll know.

Chapter 4

Smithsonian, Washington, DC—Present

As anticipated, three weeks later Doctor Scortun held an emailed initial test report from Beta-Analytics. The results: the cloth: 1750 BCE +/- 45 years; the wooden box: 1725 BCE +/- 45 years.

His mind raced: *1725 to 1750. That fits the estimated dates from the number of names and the cuneiform style. Think. This is starting to look real. It's too many independent data all in agreement. If it's real, the evidence should fit a pattern. Do I have enough evidence to form a pattern, or do I need more evidence?*

No, I don't have a clear pattern. I need more evidence.

After calling Ian and reporting the test results, he punched intercom on his phone, "George, David again. Let's set up a CT Scan on that tablet. . . . Right, I'll hold. . . . Next time slot on the machine is in ten days? Make it happen. Thanks."

****

ASSUR

September 1752 BC

Havram could see Assur in the distance. The city sat on a tall limestone cliff in a sharp bend of the Tigris river. It was significantly smaller than Ninuwa.

Instead of ashlars, the walls were mudbrick, reddish brown in the afternoon sun. He wondered. Ninuwa's walls used ashlars. Good, thick, hard stone. Why build walls with mudbrick? Mudbrick was soft and vulnerable to piercing. Then he realized. Two sides of the city were tall rocky cliffs surrounded by the river, one side on the old river's bank and one on the new. Only on the landward side were walls approachable, and these walls had a steep switchback road leading up to the city gate. Even ashlars wouldn't make the city more impregnable. The steep road leading up to the city's high walls made it unassailable.

Landscape defends Assur, not soldiers.

He wondered how many years laborers had hauled mudbricks up that road, but dismissed the thought. Sitting at the hub of the north-south and east-west trade routes, the city had been wealthy. It's wealth afforded the labor.

Then a second thought hit him. The city today was small. Why? Before Hammurabi, Assur had been the largest city in Mesopotamia. Then he realized the limestone hill restricted the size of the original city. At its heyday, the city sprawled onto the surrounding countryside. When King Hammurabi had conquered Assur and forced the caravan trade to divert to Babylon, the wealth supporting the sprawl evaporated. Havram looked closer. Farmers on the plain had taken apart many abandoned ramshackle huts to reclaim land for farms.

These abandoned huts are Assur's rotting shepherd's bowl on the plains of history.

When they reached the city gate, an official was waiting for them. He knew Terrah by sight because he approached Terrah with an attendant in tow. "Terrah, welcome back to Assur. It's been a long time."

"Sha-ila. You're right, it's been a few years."

"And you must be Terrah's son, Havram. Welcome to Assur."

Havram bowed, "Thank you. It's a pleasure."

The official consulted his papyrus, then turned to his attendant, "Show them to their room. Number 27."

Terrah recognized the importance of the number. Second story, not the top floor, so it was cooler. An odd number, so it had a river view. Being a servant helps get the best rooms.

The attendant bowed, "Follow me, please." He turned and started toward the old palace.

On the way, Havram noticed every building was mudbrick. The guard shack. The temple buildings. The bakery. The palace. He asked himself, *Why mudbrick?*

Havram understood as soon as they entered the palace building. The outside remained in the lingering heat of summer's last grasp. The inside was cool. Havram didn't have the words for it, but he understood the mud-brick resisted absorbing heat. The sun slowly heated the outside, but delayed its penetration to the rooms inside. Then he realized the resistance to heat transfer would work both ways. If cold outside, it wouldn't release heat from the room. The interior remained a moderate temperature day and night.

As they traversed the halls, he noticed wood paneling lined every floor, every wall, everything except the ceiling. Havram marveled at the lavish wealth, ostentatiously portrayed in its wood. There were no local forests. Wood logs had to be floated downriver from forests more than a hundred miles upstream. The paneling didn't have a voice, but it screamed wealth. This palace cost a fortune to build. The palace's intent was to inspire awe—and he was awed.

That evening, they ate dinner in a large dining hall. There were no tables or chairs. Eight bowls, spoons, and cloth napkins on the floor made circular tables. Everyone sat tailor position or with legs crossed. The waiters placed the platters and bowls on the floor and people served themselves.

After everyone had eaten, excess meat remained. Havram wondered about the leftovers. He never discovered the answer, but he imagined a row of poor in a line outside the kitchen, waiting for whatever remained. Just in case, he avoided overeating.

The Regional Director wanted the applicants nervous, but confident. The dinner was the best way to achieve that goal. Conversation was brisk. Everyone was an applicant or their companion. In Havram's group were three applicants. They were also nervous. For the oldest, this was his last year of eligibility. He wasn't just nervous, his anxiety level was almost panic.

Havram realized why the region wanted all the applicants to meet the evening before. So they could discover the others were just like them. Everyone felt apprehension. No one had any advantages. His unfounded fears of competing against a cadre of geniuses were baseless. He realized he *could* beat these men.

When Havram and Terrah returned to their room, Terrah asked, "Feeling better about tomorrow?"

"Oh, yes. I had imagined going up against a lineup of geniuses, but these men are just like me."

"That's right. You are on equal footing with all of them. There may be one or two in the crowd who are smarter than you are. However, I can tell you that no one is better prepared."

Havram let that thought gel for a minute, then let out a long, slow exhalation. His worse fears were as baseless as his childhood monsters in the night.

Terrah waited for the exhalation. He hadn't known exactly what Havram's sign of relief would be, but he knew there would be something—and had been waiting for it. "I can give you one admonition of guidance for tomorrow: be faithful. You will not be in charge—nor will the judges, no matter what they believe. The Divine will actually be in charge. No matter what happens, The Divine's guiding hand will be in it. No matter what happens, remain faithful. If you are faithful to The Divine, He will be faithful to you. This does not necessarily mean that He will do what you want or what you expect, but it does mean that He will do what's best for you and best for His plan for this world."

Havram absorbed the wisdom, and nodded assent.

Terrah finished, "Let's get some rest. Tomorrow will be stressful."

Only when he lay down to sleep, his worst fears laid to rest, did Havram realize that his entire pattern of thinking had changed. Two months ago he would not have seen the city as he had today. He would not have evaluated the city defenses. He would not have noticed the mudbrick's value.

He would have concentrated on what he was doing—his own small world—and never have seen the rest. Let alone be able to evaluate the implications of his observations. Yes, he was ready for tomorrow.

If everyone in the competition was like the other two contestants at his table, he felt confident. But, the contest still lay before him. Did other tables have a genius? Was he good enough to beat them?

The competition began with all twenty-two applicants in the council chamber. The applicants stood in front of a small dais with three chairs. The door behind the dais opened and three men took their seats.

The man in the center opened the proceedings, "Men, my name is Nohra. I am the Melchizadek, the Regional Director for the Servants. Mirhbandoq is to my right. Eshoa is to my left. We will be your judges. We expect the competition to take a day and a half. There will be four rounds. The fourth will select two candidates to represent the region. For each round, we will ask five questions. There will be no talking between applicants except at meals. We will immediately dismiss anyone violating the rules. Questions?"

There weren't.

Attendants led all but the first two applicants to their rooms. An hour later, an attendant fetched Havram and took him to the waiting room. Five minutes later an attendant ushered him to the council chamber. The door closed behind him.

Eshoa asked the first question, "You are the Commanding General for the King. The King has learned that two opposing kingdoms are thinking about joining forces and invading your kingdom. They will invade if their army outnumbers yours by two to one. They each have one thousand men under arms. How many men does your army need to avoid invasion?"

Havram thought for a minute, *Should I give them the answer they want, or the correct answer? I don't know what they expect. No, I shouldn't give them the answer I believe they expect. If The Divine has called me, I must remain faithful to my calling. I should do what's right, whether it's what they expect or not.*

Finally, his mind made up, he replied. "Eshoa, your question has two answers. A number's answer is one thousand and one men. However, that's not the military answer. Simply adding numbers of men doesn't give you the army's power. For example, a common swordsman's power assignment is three, each archer two and each spearman one. You need half the power of the opposing armies plus one."

That confused Eshoa. He leaned over and whispered to Nohra. Nohra thought for a minute and announced, "We need a minute to confer." The three men rose and disappeared through the door behind the dais.

Havram sighed and stared at the ceiling. *There's no way they just accepted my answer. Either I succeeded or they think I'm a blithering idiot. Either way, I can't undo what's done. For better or worse, I remained faithful.*

It was a full five minutes later when the three men reappeared. Nohra spoke to the attendant. "Fetch the commanding general. If you can't find him, fetch the most senior officer you can."

The attendant disappeared. In ten minutes he reappeared with a grizzled old man in his late forties.

The general turned to Havram, "What was the question, Boy?"

Havram told him.

The general turned to Nohra, "That right?"

Nohra nodded.

"Okay, Boy, what was your answer?"

Havram told him.

"Where did you learn this, Boy?"

"From my father, General."

"What army is your father in?"

"He's not. He's a servant, General."

"How old are you, Boy?

"One moon ago I turned two hands plus five."

"How many battles have you fought, Boy?"

"Just one, General."

"Tell me about it."

Havram recounted the battle with the villagers.

"The two of you killed twenty-eight men?"

"Almost, General. A few tried to flee, but we sent our men behind them to prevent escape. Father and I only killed about twenty-four."

The general turned to face Nohra. "Nohra, this boy is . . . No, this *man* is right. He gave you the correct answer. Battle isn't about numbers. It's about power. It's about using the power you have and using tactics to deny the enemy the power they have. This man and his father had power. The tactics they used denied the villagers their power. Power is why they lived and the twenty-eight died. Nohra, this man is wise beyond his years. If you don't select him as a servant, I want him for an officer in our army. I need good men like him."

Nohra sat speechless.

After a short pause, the general continued, "Do you need me for anything else, Nohra?"

Nohra shook his head, "No, thank you for coming on such short notice."

The general nodded, turned and left.

After a short pause to gather their thoughts, the examiners asked the remaining four questions. But, it was a matter of form. The judges decided at the first question. However, Havram answered all questions successfully.

For the first competition, each judge received twenty-two stones in a bag, ten black, twelve white. A black was a yes vote, a white was a no vote. Each contestant sat with a basket in front. The judge grabbed one stone from his bag, either black or white, for each man, reached deep into each basket, and dropped it. No one could tell the number of blacks received until tallying everyone's votes. Havram was one of five to receive three blacks. Four applicants had two black and seven had one. Those with one had a run-off selecting the last.

That afternoon repeated the morning. Havram was one of three getting three blacks. Two contestants receive two each, removing the other contestants. Five candidates progressed to the third round.

At dinner that night, Havram was ecstatic. The sight of Ur before his eyes was real.

"Father. Two rounds—all black. I can do this!"

Terrah cautioned him. "You can't think victory is certain. The first day merely separates the also-ran. This coming day is the challenge. You can't lose your competitive edge, strategy counts now."

Terrah didn't define strategy—and Havram was too enthusiastic to listen to the wisdom or the warning.

In the elimination from five to three, Havram received a wake-up call. One contestant received three black. Havram and one other received two. He advanced, but he realized he was vulnerable.

To begin the final round, Nohra called the three remaining contestants to appear. "Men," he began, "the judges will select two of you. One will go home. But, the one who goes home shouldn't think he lost. If we had three allotments, all deserve to go. But, we have two. The unsuccessful man should not lose heart. Another opportunity may lie ahead.

"Now, this round changes rules. Each contestant will receive three bags in his basket, one from each judge. Each judge will have one bag of five black stones for first place. In a second is three black stones for second place. The last has one black for third place. Each judge will award one first, one second and one third-place bag. The two contestants with the most black stones will represent the region at Ur. Questions?"

The three remaining were the cream of the original contestants. There were no wrong answers given to any question asked. That left the decision to judgment.

The final count: the oldest anxiety-ridden contestant at Havram's first dinner had eleven black, the second man nine, and Havram seven.

Nohra asked the two winning contestants to step forward. "Gentlemen, speaking for the region, I would like to congratulate you both. I realize it's been a grueling experience, but a rewarding one. We wish you well and look forward to the day in two years when you return with a tablet in your robe."

Shock overtook Havram while Nohra congratulated the other two men. He knew he was still standing, but he couldn't feel his feet on the floor. He felt as if he was looking through a thick fog. Nohra's voice appeared muffled. It sounded like cotton stuffed Havram's ears.

Nohra closed, "Gentlemen, you are dismissed. May The Divine keep you in the palm of his hand."

It was over. Havram could hardly put one foot in front of the other. Terrah was waiting for him in their room. Terrah didn't ask how the competition ended. One glance at Havram's face revealed the answer.

Havram blurted out, "Father, do you mind if we skip lunch and just go. I'm not hungry."

Terrah knew not to try perking up his son's spirits. It was too early. Havram needed to get over the experience of feeling dead before he could return to normal. Terrah would wait. At times like this, the best words are your presence beside him. "Of course, Son."

They had already packed after breakfast. Each slung their traveling bag over his shoulder and they headed towards the city gate.

Sha-ila was waiting for them at the gate. Terrah didn't need to hear what Sha-ila would say. He could read the circumstances for their omen. But, Havram was still enveloped in grief.

Sha-ila moved to intercept them, "Terrah, Havram, could I please have a word with you?"

"Certainly, Sha-ila," replied Terrah.

"If you don't mind, Nohra would like to see you."

"Certainly, Sha-ila, lead on."

Sha-ila led them back to the council chamber. The three chairs had been moved to the floor. Nohra rose from his and motioned for Terrah and Havram to sit in the vacant two. Sha-ila disappeared.

Havram was grateful for the chair. He wasn't sure he had the strength to remain standing.

Nohra began, "Havram, the committee owes you an apology."

At that Havram's head recoiled. This was too much, too fast. *Was this real?*

Nohra continued, "Havram, you have been the victim of a conspiracy. Mirhbandoq's nephew was an applicant. That disqualified from being a judge, but he failed to disclose his conflict of interest. Last night he convinced Eshoa that, if his nephew survived the cut to three, each would award the other's favorite with their second-place vote. That collusion resulted in your third-place finish.

"First, I assure you neither man will judge again. They put their interests ahead of The Divine. They were not faithful.

"Next, you were faithful to your calling. The judge's answer to the first question about the number of soldiers was wrong. The person presenting that question didn't verify his answer was correct. He intended an answer of one thousand and one—which you reported as the numbers answer. Then you continued, giving the real military answer. If I hadn't been there, the other judges would have ruled your answer incorrect. You answered correctly despite knowing they might misinterpret you. You remained faithful, despite the possible result.

"In short, if there had been no collusion, you would represent the region. Use this to learn. Over half the candidates at Ur do not complete the two years training. Mirhbandoq's nephew won't last three months. That's half the collusion's result. I will correct the other half. You should be a regional candidate. However, as Regional Director, I chose one man at my discretion. This year you are that man. I hereby appoint you as my representative at Ur. This corrects the mistake's second half. Always remember: being a servant requires faithfulness, even when it's not worldly wise. The Divine always remains faithful.

"Will you accept being my representative?"

This overwhelmed Havram. His broken world was whole—because he had remained faithful.

The realization hit him. *I'm in the doorway to my new world. If I take one step, the door will slam shut behind me. No matter what happens, there's no going back.*

Havram took a deep breath and opened his mouth to speak, but no sound came out. After another, he managed a squeak, "Yes, Nohra, I accept."

Both Terrah and Nohra wore huge smiles. After a minute, Havram's world slowly righted itself inside his stomach, and he added his own smile.

Chapter 5

Smithsonian, Washington, DC—Present

Finally the CT scan results arrived. If anything, it was more confusing. Doctor Scortun felt as if he was driving a car deeper and deeper into the fog. He couldn't tell where he was or where he was going.

The evidence wasn't contradictory, but it didn't help make sense of the whole. Fifty-seven holes formed in a large circle of fifty-six with the last to one side. That matched the x-ray evidence. The scan added hole depth information, but having depth knowledge didn't add extra meaning. The x-ray rectangle was halves of a cylinder, split down its length. Their diameter fit all 57 holes.

David scratched his neck. What did that mean? Why semicircular cylinders? Why split lengthwise?

Most confusing, the large block was in three pieces. From one hole were three breaks at right angles to the top surface. Each break penetrated from a single hole straight to the end of the block in different directions. The starting hole had a small missing chip. Someone positioned the block so the cracked pieces fit exactly. He rechecked the x-ray. Yes, now that he knew where to look, they were on the x-ray, but so faint that, unless you knew they were there, you wouldn't notice them.

There is no pattern to the evidence. What to do?

He finally gave up and left for home. Maybe a good night's sleep on the problem would help.

The sleep didn't help, but he did awake with a renewed determination. He needed to wait until 8:00 AM in El Paso. He would wait no longer; by now he dialed Ian's number from memory, "Alice, may I please speak to Ian?"

After a short wait, "Ian, let me bring you up-to-date." David told him of the latest developments. "From the density measurements, we're almost certain the large object inside the tablet is stone. To advance we need to perform some intrusive analysis. Here's what I recommend:

"We'll use an ultrasound knife to extract the cylinders from the edge. Then we'll drill a 1/16th inch diameter hole 1/16th inch deep into the stone's edge, keeping well clear of the holes. That will give us enough material for an isotopic analysis. We'll filter-vacuum every microgram of material. Hopefully, that may enable us to pinpoint what quarry the stone came from. Then we'll subject every piece to Bragg Refractive Diffusion Scattering to discover any possible surface materials. When finished, we clear-epoxy the stone drill-section and stone dust back in place. The cylinders go back into their original position. We'll lather the residual clay and dust into its original position. Finally we'll low-temperature bake the piece into an original-strength condition. When finished, you won't be able to tell we'd disturbed the piece.

"Our intent is to make a 3D printed replica for public display. In a display case the top- and bottom-side signet impressions will live on the top-shelf. Underneath will rest the stone and cylinder pieces. Would you give us permission to continue? . . . Thanks, Ian. We'll make it happen. . . . Oh, sorry. How long? I assure you we're not going to rush this. We want to do it once—do it right. Expect four to six weeks, but depending on what we find, we may need up to three months. I'll keep you posted as we carry out the major steps. . . . Right. Thanks again."

****

IN THE FIELDS APPROACHING MARI

October 1752

After leaving Assur, Terrah moved their herds further west along the lower foothills. In two months, Terrah wanted to leave for Bagdad by going south and skirting Mari.

After breakfast the second day after rejoining the herds, the two men reclined in their tent. Terrah started, "It's time to take the next step in your growth as a servant. At the end of your two years at Ur, there will be two tests. The first test regards this world. The Divine has given us a less than perfect world. He did this on purpose. A servant's primary purpose is being His stewards in this world. He wants us to fix everything that's broken.

"Yes, that's a huge challenge, and we won't be able to do everything in our lifetime. He knows we need the challenge; it's necessary for our growth. To make the world a better place, we must invent. Your first test: can you do that? You need to invent something. That will be your improvement project. That means either fixing something that's broken or improving something. The Council at Ur will evaluate your project. Only successful projects result in an ephod tablet in your robe.

"The second test regards The Divine. We need to learn more about Him. Can you advance our knowledge? Who is He? What is He like?"

"These two may sound easy, but they are the hardest tasks in the world. The council does not expect perfection. They do expect growth."

Terrah paused to evaluate the effect his words were having.

Havram blurted out, "That sounds like The Divine wants us to jump up and touch the sky."

Terrah smiled, "An apt description. That's how it feels. We can't do it ourselves. He needs to help us. Being a servant is going on a journey. We won't reach our destination in our lifetime. In fact, no one can discern our destination, and that's all right. We aren't in charge, The Divine is. As long as we're faithful as a people, He'll lead us there."

Terrah paused and took a large breath, "It may surprise you to discover we are not the first people to worship The Divine at Ur. Many years ago another people lived there, a dark-skinned people we call the Ancients. We've lost their language, and no one remembers their name. The Divine gave the Ancients a problem to solve and a clue to solve it. This world has two lights in the sky. The greater provides daylight and the lesser moonlight. We never say the words in our language for those lights. Ignorant men have used those names for their gods. For example, the city of Haran's name for their moon god is "Sin." These lights provide a problem: periodically their light dwindles. We call that darkening an eclipse. Why does this happen? When does this happen? The Divine gave the Ancients this problem to solve. Could they predict when an eclipse will happen? He wanted us to control the event, not the event control us.

"The Divine gave the Ancients a clue. He gave them The Road. The Road showed when days would begin shortening and when they'd begin lengthening. That was enough. The Ancients solved the problem of the eclipse; they devised a method to predict when an eclipse would happen. They laid out a square using ropes and set out a circle of stones. But that technique only works at one place on earth—at The Road. Go two hands worth of miles north or south and it no longer works."

That news puzzled Havram, "How did they do that?"

"Good question, but we'll get to that at a later time. First, we'll examine what we can discover about The Divine from this small clue. The Divine isn't the lights, nor is He the God of the lights. The Divine uses them to point to Himself.

"Now we ask: who is The Divine? The short answer is: We don't know. What is His character? We don't know. What does He want from us? We only begin to understand. Let's start with His name. In the language of the Servants, God's name is 'Fod-ef.' It translates word for word into the Semitic 'He be.' Correcting for grammar, we say 'He is.' But, it isn't usual to say His name, instead we use His title, 'The Divine.' What was He telling us by our solving the puzzle? He placed us on earth to solve the world's puzzles; we would say its problems. In essence, He wants us to make His world a better place.

"To understand the history, we need to finish the story. The Ancients stopped innovating; they stopped solving problems. They did not continue to make our world a better place. So, when the Servant people arrived, The Divine allowed the Ancients to die out. Disease killed everyone within one generation. Since then, the Servant people have continued solving problems. Therefore, The Divine has blessed us. We have prospered."

"Wow," Havram said, "That's a lot—all from one road."

"Yes, I agree. That's the story's *beginning*. Our question is solving its application *today*. The Divine called the Servant people to Ur to replace the Ancients. The Servant people came to recognize The Divine as God, and spread His religion over the known world. By predicting eclipses, we prove The Divine controls eclipses. The Divine is God. That's how our family came to worship The Divine and become Servants. He calls us to serve humanity and solve the world's problems.

"To explain, let me give you an example of a project. This is my proposed project to earn a seat on the council at Ur. Here are three different types of arrows." Terrah placed them on the mat before Havram.

Havram opened the tent flap to allow more light so he could better examine the arrows. Two had the standard inverted "V" arrow-shape with the point towards its flight direction, one made of flint, the other bronze. Another two were bronze, but a shape Havram had never seen. Looked at from the end, both tips were one-half-inch square narrowing at the end to a pointed tip. Looked at from the side, each had a thin, one-half-inch long edge of copper brazed onto a brass base. Havram picked up the two square arrows and examined them closely, but couldn't understand why they had such a different shape. Terrah silently allowed him time. After a few minutes, Terrah asked Havram to put the arrows down.

"OK, Havram, you've looked at the arrows. That's the 'what.' Can you tell me 'why' they are each different?

"No, Father. I have failed already, and I've barely begun."

"No, Havram, you haven't failed. I told you that you need training. I had given you a hint before in the hunting questions when we started your training. Each different arrowhead type we use has a different purpose, and therefore a different size, shape, or material. Your not picking up on that simply demonstrates that you aren't ready yet. That's why candidates for servant need the two years of training at Ur. Let's begin by examining an arrow's characteristics. Why are they different?

Havram thought for a minute, "Father, you said size, shape, and material. You have two of the standard, familiar arrowheads the same size and shape, one flint, the other bronze. I didn't know we even had any arrows with bronze arrowheads."

"We don't use bronze. The villagers we killed carried those arrows."

"Let me make a guess. Since we could use either kind, but only use flint, that means that flint has advantages farmers wouldn't understand or need. Flint is harder and has a sharper edge. That implies flint penetrates flesh deeper than bronze. Am I correct?"

"Yes, but you need to understand why. Bronze is a softer material, therefore it deforms. Deforming explains its shallow penetration. So flint is a better material targeting flesh."

Havram picked up the two square-tipped arrows. "You just said flint is the better material for targeting flesh. That explains why we used flint-tipped arrows when hunting. But your statement and these square arrowheads must mean there are other target categories needing different shapes or materials."

Havram continued to amaze Terrah for his ability to notice clues and think quickly. "Yes, Son, you have never seen an arrow like this before. This is my invention; one I hope will earn a Council seat. Why the need? Archers have proven so powerful against infantry the larger city-states have developed protection against arrows. The first protection is chest armor of hardened cattle-skin. Normal flint and bronze arrows won't penetrate. The second is a shield woven of reeds. This flexes when a flint or bronze arrow hits it and bounces the arrow backwards. Again, the arrow won't penetrate.

"I am claiming my invention defeats both types of protection. I am making an extraordinary claim, and extraordinary claims need extraordinary evidence. You need to see this evidence to understand and believe. Therefore yesterday afternoon I had the men erect a test range to prove the claim."

The two men grabbed three quivers of arrows from the tent, one standard shape of flint, one of standard shape of bronze, and the last of Terrah's square invention. They also grabbed a spare ordinary self-bow taken from the villagers and set out for the next valley a mile away. There a test range waited. Two long poles were standing. Mounted between the poles at the top was a reed shield, while stretched between the two at the bottom was a hardened bull's hide.

Terrah started, "I've sent the men away with the flocks, so it's just the two of us. I don't want word of these special arrows becoming common knowledge before I see the Council. No one has seen them except the two of us and the blacksmith who made the tips."

They removed their quivers and took up station thirty yards away from the poles—point-blank range. Havram strung a standard flint arrow, drew his bow all the way back, and let fly. The arrow traveled so fast they couldn't see it in flight. Its point stuck in the bull-hide. As they watched, the arrow leaned down, then fell to the ground. The two men moved to pick up the arrow and examine the target. The barest tip set in the hide, but hadn't penetrated and couldn't create enough traction to support its weight. It fell.

They tried the villager's bronze arrow. It stuck the hide and immediately fell straight down. It showed no signs of any penetration.

Terrah gave Havram one of the new copper-tipped arrows. Again, Havram fully drew his bow and released. Surrounding an arrow hole was a copper globule remnant stuck to the hide. They found the arrow thirty yards downrange. Only the bronze tip remained.

Taking the spent arrow back, Havram reshot the spent arrow at the bull-hide five more times. Without its copper covering, it rebounded every time.

Using the second arrow, they repeated the exercise on the shield with identical results. The only arrow to penetrate was Terrah's invention with the copper coating. Without the coating, it wouldn't penetrate.

Havram looked at his father, "Well, that's that. Your invention is the answer to infantry's new armament."

Terrah shook his head, "Not so fast, Havram. We're not finished testing."

Terrah gave Havram the villager's standard self-bow. Using the normal bow, Havram pulled the bow as far back as his arm allowed, and let fly one of Terrah's new arrows at the shield. It bounced. He recovered the arrow and tried four more times. Every time the arrow rebounded. The two advanced to twenty yards. The first arrow just barely pierced the shield, protruding through a scant two inches. A second arrow pierced the shield and flew three feet beyond.

Havram picked up the second arrow and just looked at it. After a minute, Terrah announced, "Havram, now we're done testing."

The two were silent returning to camp.

Once back in the tent, Terrah asked, "Okay, Son, did you get the point?"

Havram cocked his head for a second, "Father, that lacked subtlety. Have you lost your edge? Becoming dull? Need bouncing back?"

Smiles crept on both men's faced. They looked at each other and started laughing. The verbal sparring with puns as weapons sharpened both men's wits.

Terrah started, "Remember, a good pun must first make you groan . . ."

Havram picked up the next phrase, "Then it must make you smile . . ."

"And if it doesn't do both . . ."

" . . . and in that order . . ."

Terrah closed, " . . . it isn't a good pun."

"OK, back to business," Havram said. He asked if he could evaluate the test.

Terrah nodded consent.

Havram tentatively summed up the events, "Using Ur bows, copper sheathed arrows penetrated both the shield and chest armor. In both cases the sheathing deformed into globules surrounding the hole. They fixed the arrow to the hide or shield. Both arrows without the copper sheathing and only the bronze tip failed to penetrate. Using normal self-bows, at thirty yards the arrow failed to penetrate. At twenty yards, only one penetrated, though perhaps not with enough force to impale the man holding the shield.

"Now, 'why'? The arrow only penetrates at maximum stretch or flex. To penetrate either target, the material must be at maximum deformation. During deformation, the arrow-tip must stick to the material surface. Only after maximum deformation can the arrow penetrate. The soft copper sticks to the hide or shield surface, holding the bronze tip against the material. When the material starts rebounding, the arrowhead force punches through. The bow must produce enough force for both full material deformation and arrow penetration. The Ur bows give that force, a self-bow doesn't until point-blank range. That won't work for archers. With only a 50 percent chance of success, an archer won't stand. He'll run first. To sum up: only combining an Ur bow *and* your new arrow design will defeat the new infantry armor."

Terrah grinned his approval.

"Wait, Father. There's another problem."

Terrah's eyebrow arched into a question.

"The arrow will penetrate shields. But, if the soldier also wears chest armor, the arrow won't have copper left to penetrate both shield and armor. The infantry wins."

Terrah's grin morphed into a full-blown smile. "Havram, you have just discovered the history of warfare. One side invents a new weapon for which the other side has no defense. Then someone invents a defense. Then the cycle starts again. I suspect this will remain as long as man lives.

"But this equation isn't complete: you need matching tactics to use it. The weapon isn't enough. You have to develop a method to make best use of the weapon. You need both."

Terrah didn't need to say anything else. He put his hand on Havram's shoulder. That approval gesture said everything. Havram was ready for training.

Ur lay before him, and all he had to do was reach for it.

In the next two months training, Terrah pressed one point over and over. "Remember my arrows. Servants must innovate. After six months training, you will divide into two-to-four-member teams. Each team must select a project. Your project must succeed to become a servant. But you don't want to stop there. You want to join the Council. The Council will choose the best man from the best team and invite him back in ten years for council membership. That's your goal. They will also ask a few to become dygsu—teachers. If they select you, and you succeed in preparing your men to present successful projects, you may also earn an invitation. That's how I earned mine; I was a dygsu. That's your real goal."

Havram asked himself: *Do I want Council membership? No. That's Father's own goal for himself. He simply wants to push his desires onto me, assuming I want the same things he does. I don't. All my life I've promised myself that, when I become an adult, I will do what I want and become who I want. I won't need adults telling me.*

But, I'm still too young to know what I should do. So, I'll trust Father to know better than I do. But, why stop at just council membership? Father may be right about membership. But, if I'm going to aim high, why not go for broke? Why not aim for council leadership?

So—that's my goal. At least for now.

Ur, are you ready for me? Here I come.

Chapter 6

Smithsonian, Washington, DC—Present

The first analysis Doctor Scorton received from intrusive testing was the Bragg Refractive Diffusion Scattering. The large stone block had no coating, but both of the two half-cylinders did. Most coating had eroded, but enough residue remained for identification. One had red ocher coating, the other white calcite.

That raised a question: Were the cylinders coated for protection, identification or decoration? Probably not for protection. Why waste time and money to coat them with different substances for protection only? That left identification or decoration—or possibly both.

He reached for his bottle of aspirin; this artifact had caused stress resulting in headaches more than once: every time he got one answer, the artifact asked two more questions.

****

IN THE WILDERNESS APPROACHING BAGDAD

December 1752

The wilderness the three men traversed was exploding with new growth. The November rains awakened grass dormant and brown-baked through the summer. The old grass glowed a deep, mellow forest green. Seeds fallen from last season and missed by the birds were already three to four inches high. The new growth shined a vibrant, florescent light green. The contrast between the two greens on the brown dirt background gave the landscape a marbled appearance with brilliant, iridescent flecks.

Rather than go straight east to the Euphrates and south along the river-road, Terrah had elected to cut southeast cross-country. That cut miles from their travel distance. By traveling thirty miles or more daily, it ensured any potential enemy couldn't react fast enough to set an ambush in front of them or catch them from behind.

It approached noon. Terrah paused, looking up, darkening clouds rolled in from the south. "Havram, Michel, we go straight east and start jogging. Rain starts late afternoon or evening and it's best if we make it to the Euphrates before its starts."

In the end they reached the river with a half hour to spare. Terrah selected a low, gently sloped hill with broad top. Scraggly bushes grew at intermittent spacing. The bushes were mostly bare, intertwined branches, buds having formed, but too soon for them to grow into branches and leaves. Terrah selected two bushes four-feet high, spaced eight feet apart, just off the hilltop on the north slope. With a stick, he scratched a "V" in the dirt, with its point centered on the two bushes and just uphill.

"Michel," he said, "Use your dagger to cut a three-inch wide, one-inch deep gutter where I've marked. It'll be a trench carrying water around the tent so it won't leak in. Save the dirt to weight down the tarpaulin edges. Havram, see if you can find any heavy branches. You won't find stones here."

Terrah began unrolling their tarpaulin. "Michel, you idiot. I told you to bring the new tarpaulin. There were two reasons I wanted the new one. First it's twenty-feet square, not eighteen-feet like this one. The edges of this tarpaulin won't reach the ground. Wind will blow mist underneath. Second, a careless woman set something hot on it. The fat layer melted and it leaks. I've half a mind to center you under the leak. However, I've got my box of tallow; I'll try sealing it for tonight. Next time, you stupid oaf, don't rush and cut corners; there's a reason I needed what I asked for."

They rushed to complete the makeshift tent and, as the rain-front reached the base of the hill, Terrah finished smearing tallow on the bare spot of the tarpaulin. They climbed inside just as the first raindrops fell around them. The impromptu rain patch worked; the tarpaulin didn't leak.

Under the tarpaulin, Terrah turned to Michel, "Do you understand how to make a tarpaulin; why it's waterproof?"

"No, Terrah, I never thought to find out."

"If you don't understand how something works, you'll never use it properly or to its full potential. We herd a Hircus Agagrus goat. It's prized for its long, black hair. We sell its outer, fine hair for weaving into high quality clothing, but keep the inside, rough, coarse hair. We make that into tarpaulins and tents, which we sell. The women weave the hair into long strands, then dip the strands slowly through a pot of melted fat made of the meat's thick white fat caps we can't eat. They hang the strands to dry and the excess drips off. When woven into a tent and the strands pulled tight, the fat coating blends into a waterproof barrier. The fat will not melt in the sun, but if you put a hot pot against the tent, the fat melts and the tent is no longer waterproof. I knew the eighteen-foot square tarpaulin had a damaged section, which was why I directed you to get the twenty-foot one. Do you understand now why I was mad?"

In the dark of the tent, they couldn't see Michel hang his head in shame, but his voice betrayed it. "Yes, Terrah, it won't happen again."

"All right. Let's eat and go to sleep. Perhaps we can get an early start tomorrow. Our first task is to find the ghoofa wharf."

"Ghoofa, Father?" Havram asked.

"Seeing is understanding. It'll make sense later."

They stretched out between the two bushes and dropped off to sleep.

The rain stopped in the early morning while they slept. They awoke and ate a small meal while still dark. They had forty-five minutes of brightness before sunrise. Michel carried the wet tarpaulin as punishment for bringing the wrong one.

Before starting Terrah commanded, "Take off your sandals and hike your garments above the knee."

Michel didn't understand, "Why do that?"

Terrah explained, "Because this is an alluvium plain. There is no hard ground beneath us; everything is mud. When dry, the top crust will bear a man's weight. But the mud has empty pockets. When wet, you drop in up to your knee. If you wear sandals, you'll lose them. We walk to the river in our bare feet."

Their luck held; they ran into no empty pockets. Arriving at the river, they washed the mud from their feet. Putting on their sandals, they retraced their path to the road and turned south. Ten yards wide, the road stretched north and south as far as they could see, a hundred yards inland from the river. Despite the undulating ground, the roadbed kept a level surface. Every twenty yards a shallow drain traversed underneath to allow upland water to drain to the river.

The road fascinated Havram. Nowhere had the road's dirt surface turned to mud from last night's rain. "Father," he asked, "this is a dirt road, but there is no mud. This road can't be normal dirt."

Terrah replied, "It's not just dirt. When you mix regular dirt with ashes from a fire, and compress it, water won't penetrate. All city streets in towns have this mixture. In this realm Hammurabi is king, and he has built roads throughout his kingdom. You can walk from Ur in southern Sumer to northern Mari and never get muddy feet." He pointed to the right. "See the wagon tracks; wagons may not travel on the road. Their great weight would destroy it."

Five miles later, they reached the top of a small hill. They could just see the ghoofa wharf below past the river's morning mist. The mist was thick over the water, obscuring it, but tapered off on shore. One boat rested by the wharf.

Michel asked Terrah, "How did you know to turn south when we reached the river?"

Terrah didn't take his sight from the wharf; he was looking for possible trouble. "Michel, when you go cross-country, never aim directly for your destination. You'll always miss. Head either to the left or the right; I headed left. Therefore, when we reached the river and the wharf was not in sight, I knew I had missed to the north, turned right, and headed downriver."

As they approached the wharf, the sun began evaporating the river mist. River traffic became visible. A ghoofa was upriver paddling across, heading for the wharf. Another had misjudged the river's speed with the extra water from the rain and wouldn't reach land until downriver. A third boats-man had landed downriver and was walking up the river road with the boat over his head.

As the sun evaporated the mist, Babylon appeared on the far-side, its beauty astounding Havram. Everything was a gleaming white, backlit by the rising sun. He commented on the city's beauty to his father. Terrah just smiled, "Havram, I agree; it's a hundred-yards beautiful." That puzzled Havram.

Never having seen a boat, they didn't know ghoofas were the weirdest ever built. It was round: no bow, no stern, no rudder. A novice paddler could easily put the boat into a spin. Controlling direction depending on twisting the paddle during its pull. The scarcity of wood dictated its design. It used the long central stems of marsh reeds. Although any one stem had little individual strength, when lashed together they formed a light but strong, flexible body. The outside was pitch black—literally. Bitumen pitch smeared over the entire outside provided its watertightness. Without pitch, the boat would sink in minutes.

When they arrived at the wharf, only the original boats-man was there; the three others hadn't arrived. Terrah approached him, "How much to ferry three across the river?

"Fare is one-tenth silver shekel a man, but for three I'll only charge a quarter-shekel.

"That's a fair price." Terrah shook out small balls of silver from his money purse onto his hand. He selected a quarter shekel weight and gave it to the boats-man.

"Which gate to the city do you want to use?"

"We want the North Gate."

"The wharf location targets the River Gate with a normal current, but with your North Gate destination and the stronger current, we'll need to start a mile upriver. Please follow me."

The man picked up his ghoofa and slung it over his back, its inner edge onto his head and his paddle in his hand. He started along the road upriver. They followed.

A mile upriver the man set his ghoofa down. Pulling his tunic off his arms, he tied it around his waist, picked up the ghoofa and put it into the water at the bank's edge. Motioning for the three men to enter, he directed them to get into the downriver side. Pushing off, he jumped in.

Terrah had experienced this before and paid no attention, Michel was oblivious, but Havram was spellbound. The boats-man dipped his paddle deep into the water and his back and arm muscles writhed as he pulled on the water. As he pulled he also twisted the paddle back and forth, preventing the boat from spinning and keeping it traveling straight. It was obvious that he had expert knowledge of the river, for despite the added speed of the current, they reached the far bank at the north wall.

Terrah thanked the man and they watched him drift downriver for the wharf at the River Gate and his next fare.

The three men walked the half-mile alongside the North Wall to its gate. Examining the wall up close, Havram understood his father's comment of one-hundred-yard beauty. They were closer than one-hundred yards and the walls were no longer beautiful. A crushed white limestone façade coated the walls. It appeared smoothly white from a distance, but wasn't uniform up close. Mudbrick peeked from beneath its shell. But twenty-foot high walls were still twenty-foot high, even ones of mudbrick, and that appeared formidable.

At first—and until Havram analyzed it. *Babylon is vulnerable. Sun-baked brick remains soft. Only kiln-fired bricks are impervious. But, there's no supply of wood to bake bricks. Sappers can easily dig tunnels through mud-brick. If archers on the walls had ordinary bows, sappers protected by men with shield walls would be impervious to their arrows. Only swords and spears could resist an assault. But, an army of invaders would outnumber the city's*

*defenders. Protection behind these walls is as dangerous as no walls at all. . . .
No. Babylon is going to fall. Not if. When. My future family and I wouldn't be
safe here.*

When they reached the North Gate, their first task was to find the caravan. A hundred donkeys made that obvious. They located the city scribe
sitting at a table off to the side. The caravan leader was standing beside the
table.

First Terrah paid the caravan leader the price for Havram to travel
with the caravan.

Moving to the table, Terrah said, "Money," and put the gold and silver
balls Havram would need at Ur on the table. The scribe weighed the metal
on a balance scale, calling out the final weight as Terrah watched and verified the weight was accurate. The scribe wrote the weights in cuneiform on
a soft clay tablet. Havram put his two bags of belongings on the ground
before the official, saying "Belongings." The official folded the bag tops tight
and placed a soft clay ball against each. Wrapping a string tightly around
each closed top, he pressed the two ends side-by-side into the clay. Both the
caravan leader and Havram pressed their seal rings into the clay, forming
an impression. No one could open the bag without breaking the seal, immediately signaling theft.

The scribe noted everything in cuneiform on two identical wet clay
tablets. He encased each tablet in the halves of a hollow clay ball, and used
wet clay to seal the edges together. Havram and the caravan leader pressed
their seal rings into the wet clay. Each received one ball. When they reached
Ur, both would present their ball to an Ur city official, who would verify the
ball-seals matched their rings. He would break both balls and verify both
tablets were identical. Then the official would oversee the caravan leader
surrendering the weight in gold, silver and belongings on the tablets. It was
foolproof; ensuring neither the caravan leader nor Havram could cheat.

The trio left for the city.

When they reached the city gate, Havram got his first glimpse of wood.
The gates and gateposts were wood with a thin veneer of bronze. Havram
immediately realized: *The bronze prevents setting the gate on fire.*

Once inside the gate, he looked to his right. Stairs led to the wall's ramparts. They were mudbrick with deep grooves from thousands of sandals
over who knew how many years.

Inside the city the buildings were all mudbrick with a white limestone
painted surface. Only doors and windows were wood.

The thought stuck Havram: *Babylon is an ugly woman in makeup.
Painted to look beautiful, underneath she remained an ugly woman.*

Then it hit him. *The whitewash isn't to make the buildings look beautiful. It was to provide a rainproof coating, so the mud walls wouldn't dissolve in the rain and slowly melt away. So, the whitewash wasn't makeup to make the woman beautiful, it was a walking stick so the old woman wouldn't fall down.*

Terrah unerringly navigated the narrow, crowded streets to a small inn catering to travelers. Few businesses could afford the wood for three-story buildings. It was obvious this wasn't his first visit; the innkeeper recognized him on sight, "Terrah, good to see you. I've saved your favorite room for the night."

"Enusat, good to see you also. Yes, I'll take it, plus dinner and breakfast for the three of us. And we want meat with the dinner."

As Terrah was extracting his money pouch, Enusat continued, "I wanted to bet with the cook whether you'd be here today and leave tomorrow or tomorrow and leave the following day. You've done both, you know. I wanted to bet today and offered two to one odds, but the cook wouldn't take the offer." He shook his head remorsefully, "I would have won the wager."

Terrah replied, "You know, when people know me this well, it means that I've been coming here way too often."

He paid for the room and the three men went upstairs. Havram's first task was removing the arrows and hollow bottom from one quiver, placing his ball inside, and replacing the bottom and arrows. No one would steal his ball.

That night, when they'd quenched the lamp and laid down to sleep, Havram realized he'd never looked deeper than something's façade to evaluate its beauty or ugliness.

As he lay, eyes closed but mind racing, thoughts of the dread he had felt in the wadi washed over him. *Does my future contain another wadi?*

He thought of the twenty-foot-high walls of Babylon: *If I led archers defending these walls with Ur bows and Terrah's arrows, sappers would be unable to break through. My family would be safe.*

The idea began to take hold of him: *I need a city to live in.* An obsession began growing.

The following morning they rose and ate before daybreak. Breakfast was a warm barley porridge—accumulated salinity from irrigation no longer allowed wheat to grow locally. The caravan was leaving Babylon an hour after sunrise and they needed to join before departure.

At the caravan, the three exchanged well-wishes. All realized two years would pass before meeting again.

The caravan began with fourteen candidates. At the first evening meal, they were all seated together, getting acquainted. Havram had a thought, "I have a suggestion. We need to ensure no one else steals anything while we sleep. First, let's all sleep in a group. We could stand three nightly watches in pairs. That would prevent anyone stealing our belongings while we're asleep. It'll be a bit tiring for a few nights, but as more candidates join us on the trip, it'll get easier."

The rest of the young men agreed.

Standing watch probably wasn't necessary, since the caravan leader organized roving watchmen, but the candidates all agreed they wanted to control their own fate.

More candidates joined before reaching Ur. When boarding ship for their second voyage, the group would number seventy-six. Some candidates would use other routes, swelling the year's total to a hundred forty-eight. Adding those going straight to Ur accounted for a hundred eighty-nine prospective candidates.

They usually traveled twenty-five miles a day, sleeping in the open unless it rained. Most days they ate breakfast and dinner at caravan-inns dotting the road every five to ten miles. Having the inn do the cooking enabled an extra hour's travel on each end of the day. They traveled the road on the east bank of the Euphrates; it lessened the risk of attack from the open lands to the west.

The caravan made this journey routinely: five months north, two weeks stopover, five months south, six weeks at home. The leader knew what to provide for and had his own guard of ten professional soldiers.

A day and a half's travel past Mari, they were nearing the city of Tuttul when clear signs of danger lay ahead. As they crested the top of a small hill, two men stood in the road a half-mile ahead. They faced the approaching caravan, drawn swords in their right hands and shields on their left arms.

The caravan stopped. The caravan leader called his soldiers to the front. The boys noticed the change in tension, left the road, and approached the caravan-front from the side of the road. The caravan resumed its advance, moving slower, wary and watchful.

As they slowly advanced, other men appeared from behind shrubbery, joining the two in the road until thirty men stood, waiting. Finally, at a quarter-mile separation, the caravan stopped and the thirty advanced to just over a hundred yards distance—just past effective range for a normal bow. Their leader called out, "I have imposed a tax on travel through the kingdom of Tuttul. Surrender half of all gold, silver, and copper you carry."

The caravan leader called back, "We travel with the candidates for Servants of the Light. We are immune from all tax. Leave at once. Yashub-Dagoo will not allow you to defy his authority."

"Yashub-Dagoo is dead; Yakbar-lim rules in Tuttul."

"Then leave at once or I shall appeal to Yakbar-lim."

"Yakbar-lim is weak. He has no authority outside the city. Tuttul's Servant of the Light has no authority." To drive home his contempt, their leader spat on the ground. "Thus to Yakbar-lim. Thus to The Divine. Surrender the tax or we will seize it by force."

Havram thought quickly. *Can we believe this bandit leader? After surrendering half, would he not want all? Once he's inside our caravan, would he kill us? Even if he allows us to leave, how would we pay for the journey's remaining miles?*

His mind made up, Havram advanced to ten yards in front of the caravan, and pointed at the bandit leader. "Your insolence is offensive. I don't care about Yakbar-lim, but when you insult The Divine and his Servants, you have gone too far. You have no honor. I am a candidate for Servant of the Light. If you wish to regain your honor, I demand you kneel and give homage to The Divine and surrender to your city Servant. If you refuse, I offer a test of your honor: chose nine other men, any nine, and fight me. If you refuse, then this is all that's left of your honor," and Havram spat on the ground.

Havram had put the bandit leader into an untenable position. The leader thought: *My men heard his challenge. If I refuse to fight one man at ten to one odds, I will lose honor and respect in my men's eyes. On the other hand, if I attack the caravan, yes, we will win, but they still have ten soldiers, even if they have no shields. I will probably lose two or three men. On the other hand, if I crush this stupid fool, the caravan will undoubtedly surrender. Doesn't this boy realize that we carry shields and his puny arrows are worthless against men with shields? No matter, this boy will be dead in five minutes. Killing one will convince the rest to surrender.*

His decision made, the bandit leader shouted, "Your death be your choice and on your own head." He called his men with shields to form a line abreast and they started forward, swords drawn, raised and ready.

Havram had two quivers on his back, one with ordinary flint arrows and the second with Terrah's. He strung a Terrah arrow. He allowed the advancing line to get to one hundred yards range. They spread to allow good sword-wielding distance. Aiming at the man on the left at a height of the center of the lungs, at one-hundred yards he loosed the first arrow. Too far for a heart-shot, an arrow in the lung would still be fatal; dying just took longer.

The man fell.

He fitted another arrow in the bow.

The line advanced five yards.

Havram aimed at the man on the right.

Another fell.

Five yards; another arrow.

First the left; then the right, side-to-side.

The bandit leader in the middle.

The leader didn't realize he'd lost any men until only half remained.

The line was eighty yards away.

The leader yelled for a charge.

The five remaining ran pell-mell at Havram, screaming and brandishing their swords.

Havram calmly dropped one man every ten yards, until only the leader remained.

The bandit leader was thirty-five yards away.

Havram took careful aim.

The arrow hit center-chest, breaking the breast-bone, severing his esophagus.

Havram switched to the quiver with flint arrows.

The remaining twenty men huddled tight,

In shock at their leader's death and the loss of all shield-bearers.

Havram aimed at the huddle's midpoint.

He no longer concerned himself with aiming at any particular man.

Six more arrows flew in rapid succession.

Six men dropped.

The remaining fourteen turned and fled as fast as they could run.

Havram let them go.

Havram approached the bandit leader. The leader gazed up at Havram, only half-conscious and gasping for breath that wouldn't come, because air won't displace blood in the lungs. Havram spat in his face.

He turned and collected his spent arrows from the bodies, executing the three still living.

The caravan leader approached Havram. "If I'm not mistaken, you're Terrah's son?"

Havram nodded agreement.

"Terrah asked me to look after you. Looks like I need to ask you to look after us. Thank you."

News of this invincible archer rocketed through the caravan. Havram became the instant leader of the candidates.

News reached Ur before they arrived. The Council wanted to meet and thank the man who'd rescued the honor of The Divine.

Chapter 7

INTERLUDE

Smithsonian, Washington, DC—Present

His telephone rang. Reaching for the handle, he said, "Doctor Scortun, may I help you?"

"Doctor Scortun, Tom Fletcher at Boston University Pollen Lab. I just emailed your lab report. The results conflict with your expectations, so developing a pattern that makes sense means talking it through; that's why the call. Got a few minutes?"

"Yes, please give me a second." Davis put his hand over the receiver and spoke loudly through the open office door, "Nancy, could you please call John and tell him to postpone the start of our meeting by fifteen minutes?"

"Yes, Doctor."

"Thanks."

Removing his hand from the receiver, he continued, "Tom. What did you find?"

"I found confusing lines of evidence. You said the person giving the specimen was from El Paso. Well, we found one tumbleweed pollen, so El Paso fits a present-day location. You said he had Scottish ancestry. However, we only found two thistle grains. If the owner wore the garment outside for any extended time period, it would be flooded with thistledown. But it isn't. It likely remained in an indoor container.

"Let's examine the location you expected, the Middle East. We found various plant species characteristic of the general region, however, these don't pinpoint any specific location. We did find a few grains of river reeds. That variety grows only along the Tigris-Euphrates river. The small number of grains suggest it wasn't worn long, perhaps passing through on a short trip.

"The best provenance evidence for the Middle East is a particular variety of grape only grown on the southern Levant hillsides. We're talking about a stretch between Hebron and Bethlehem in modern-day Israel. Hebron is famous for the grape. That restricts the possible location, but the problem is the owner hardly wore the garment outside. I'd give it a few months total.

"Where did the garment spend the most time outdoors? We're talking at least 90 percent of the time it spent outside being in southwest England."

"What?" David asked in astonishment.

"Yes, southwest England: possibilities are the counties of Cornwall, Devon, Somerset, Dorset, Wiltshire, Hampshire, Berkshire, and Gloucestershire. England is the garment's provenance. The garment spent most of its outside life there. How do I know, you should be asking? First, the variety of mustard grass seeds found in the garment are only found in England. Second, the largest number of grain pollens are spelt, with a fair amount of emmer and a little einkorn. No wheat. That means that its *terminus ad quem*—the latest possible date, is 1400 BCE, when wheat arrived. There is no wheat in the garment. Its *terminus a quo*—the earliest possible date—around 2,000–1800 BCE is when spelt arrived. Before then there was only emmer and einkorn. The measured mixture of the three suggests a time frame of 1750 plus or minus 50 years."

"What is Havram doing in southern England?"

"Doctor Scortun, I only give you facts. I can't explain them."

David thought, *And neither can I.*

****

O'UR OF THE CHALL DIA

June 1751

The final day's journey to Ur was an easy fifteen-mile walk from the Solent harbor landing. Gentle rolling grassland hills, none taller than fifty yards. Small hamlets of a half-dozen homes dotted the countryside, spelt and emmer fields surrounding them. The spelt planted at the end of winter was ready for harvest. The emmer was in a tall-grass stage. Some fields, planted last September, were a brilliant yellow from the flowers of mustard grass. Women were gathering the seeds for mustard oil. Within two more weeks, they would return to harvest the leaves. Enormous trees, mostly cold-weather species he'd never seen, sprinkled the countryside.

The temperatures were moderate: hovering around 75 during the day, 50 to 55 at night, rain averaging every three days. For Havram, used to summer temperatures in the hundreds, this was a cool but enjoyable range. The moderate temperatures made the daytime sky exceptionally blue.

Cresting the final hill, their guide waved an arm, saying "*Avon O'ur yn.*" In the valley lay a river. Deep blue, calm, slow-flowing water. A town on the far side. Verdant, emerald-green grass growing to the water's edge.

Several Ur translators accompanied candidates from the harbor. Havram asked the one who spoke Eastern Semitic, "What was it the guide said?"

The man replied, "The River Avon on Ur."

Havram asked, "So the *yn* at the end is the word for river?"

"No, that's the word for 'at'."

"I thought you said, 'The River Avon on Ur'. Where's the 'at'?"

"I did say it, but the local language uses 'at' when Semitic uses 'on'."

"Then what's the word for river?"

"Avon."

"Wait a minute. If avon is the word for river, what's the river's name?"

"Avon O'ur yn."

"So that's literally 'river at Ur'?"

"Yes. Avon is the word for river. In the local language, you can't give the river a name. To say it was the 'River Avon' would be saying it's the 'river river'. Instead, a river's name is the land location for this section of the river. This is the River at Ur."

"If no river has a name, how do you tell one river from another?"

"You don't. This language has no way. You have to know if this river connects. And by the way, the proper name to pronounce Ur is O'ur."

"I can't hear the difference."

"There is a difference. The locals immediately identify you as country bumpkins by how you pronounce it."

Havram felt a bad foreboding. *This will be harder than I thought. These people don't even think the same way I do. I may be able to learn the local words, but how do I communicate with them when we can't use the same way of thinking?*

Havram decided it was best to keep his mouth shut. *Let someone else play the part of the dunce. Best not to say anything and let them wonder if you are an idiot, rather than open your mouth and confirm their suspicions.*

The contrast with Havram's homeland was startling. The river reeds so native to his country were absent, unable to survive cold winters. The fields were a vibrant deep jade; at home the land had already turned a waterless brown.

The dirt road they followed led to a rope ferry, simple boards glued on lashed-together logs, able to hold two cows or eight people, and no railing. There was no charge; the ferry operator was on Ur's staff. It would take hours for the operator to pull a hundred forty young men to the far side and return, but the men solved that problem—they did the pulling both ways. They wanted to arrive at Ur as fast as possible. The operator didn't complain—his pay was the same.

Ur was a significantly sized town, several hundred people, not counting the candidates. Its sole reason for existence was "The Place" and its training college. "The Place" was "O'ur of the Chall Dia," the "Quietly Pray to the Wise God," or "Pray in silence to the Wise God." Candidates quartered in huts to the right of the road to The Place, or northeast; the townsfolk lived on the left. The living quarters were unlike any he'd ever seen. Candidates had round huts, over twenty feet in diameter, with five-feet-high stone outer walls and steeply pitched, thatched roofs rising to fifteen feet or more in the center. There were no windows. Inside was a center fire pit for warmth and open, communal sleeping on a raised wooden platform around the outer wall. They slept, ate, and studied in their communal hut. Between each candidate hut pair was a smaller hut, where two housemaids lived and cooked their meals. The Council had separate huts.

Havram could understand the need for specialists in the town like a blacksmith, tailor, tanner and cooper. Candidates couldn't "make a living," so Ur subsidized their needs. But, he had no idea what a cobbler did. Four fishers caught the river's plenty, four hunters killed game, four gardeners farmed the vegetable plots, six grazers gathered wild vegetables, and shepherds kept sheep, goats, and cattle.

But they weren't going direct into the huts. There were fourteen tents set up for the incoming "class" of candidates. Their spoken language determined their tent. Half of Havram's tent spoke Eastern Akkadian Semitic, his native tongue. He already knew most of them from sharing their long journey.

The Council was giving the outgoing class its candidacy examinations, and until these graduated on the summer solstice and left a few days later, the new candidates couldn't move into their emptied huts. The new candidates didn't mind: they were finally here, and they had belongings to unpack, needs to attend, and new horizons to explore.

Tomorrow morning they would go up The Road to The Place. Excitement hung in the air.

That night at dinner, Havram experienced what Terrah had warned him about. He could hear his father's words in his ear, *Whatever they serve you, don't ask what it is, don't complain, just eat it. If you complain, you'll make your housemaid angry. And you have to eat her cooking for two more years.*

What was supposed to be familiar wasn't. The biggest difference was bread. The variety of wheat Havram liked wouldn't grow this far north, so the breads used cousins of wheat such as smelt, emmer, and einkorn. Breads made from these didn't taste the same and they had a different texture. They also served rye and oats occasionally, but the shepherds usually fed these to the herd animals during the winter. And, of course, barley was barley.

Only one variety of bean grew this far north, the broad bean, in some languages called green beans. He yearned for lentil stew.

He missed his homeland's vegetables, such as kale, leeks, Brussel sprouts, cauliflower, artichokes, asparagus, broccoli, eggplant, peas, tulips, lilies, and hyacinth. Many spices like turmeric weren't available.

Other vegetables served here were new to him since they wouldn't grow as far south as his homeland. He'd never tasted vegetables such as cabbage, chard, celery, beets, turnips, rutabagas, parsnips, radishes, narcissus, amaryllis, gladiolus, crocus, and daffodils. They also ate something called mushrooms.

Foods like carrots looked similar, but weren't. They were white, not orange, and had a different taste.

The only ones he readily recognized were onions and garlic.

They only cultivated a few vegetables, so you often ate whatever the Gatherers could find.

Tree fruits and nuts were also different. Gone were dates, figs, pomegranates, almonds and pistachios. In were cherries, apples, walnuts, and hazelnuts.

The changes were a bewildering conglomeration. The few constants were leaf vegetables in spring and summer, berries in the fall, and bulbs and nuts in winter. He let his housemaid worry about the vegetables. He was thankful for whatever she put on his plate.

The biggest difference was what *was* on his dinner plate. The cook butchered the food. Even recipes he recognized were universally bad. The mix was bad. There was too much or too little olive oil. When ingredients were correct, technique was lacking. The cook undercooked or overcooked everything. However horrible the food was, it was consistently bad.

When the candles went out and it was time for sleep, Havram suffered from an apprehension the other candidates didn't feel. There were no city walls; there were no guards; there was no defense against an enemy. There was no safety. His stomach refused to loosen enough for sleep until the small night hours when he eventually succumbed to exhaustion.

Most of the candidates were young men aged seventeen to twenty-one. At that age young men are prone to being full of vim and vigor. Adding a five-month trip, as Havram had done, made vim and vigor magnified. Many couldn't sleep, and the rest woke before dawn. They didn't eat breakfast; they inhaled it.

As they were finishing the last giblets and engaging in small talk, two young men in servant robes lifted the tent door and entered. They just stood there until the talk died down. Once there was relative quiet, both started talking, but Havram only understood the one speaking Eastern Akkadian Semitic. "Candidates, my name is Dygsu, and I will be your guide for today. Anyone not in white robes needs to change. I'll give you five minutes."

Most were already wearing them, but the rest hurried.

Dygsu continued, "I remember when I had just arrived. I'm sure you are as excited as I was. However, you need to remember, no matter how excited, you are entering the presence of The Divine. So you need to keep a reverent attitude. We are going to The Place. We will make a circuit so you can see everything, but we must remain outside the outer ditch. You may only enter at your consecration. The stone arrangement will be difficult to understand from outside the ring; however, when we return, I'll do my best to explain. Once we are at The Place, if you need to speak, please do so in whispers. Our tent group is number nine, and we will remain together throughout. When we return, I'll be glad to answer your questions."

After the assigned five minutes elapsed, they went outside and turned toward The Road to The Place. Group-by-group the tents started, keeping thirty yards between groups. The first mile was a gentle uphill climb from the river valley. Shortly after reaching the plain at the top of the hill, the road took a gentle left turn. Standing at the end of the turn there were two wooden pillars, a red one on the left and a white one on the right, six feet tall. Each was one-half of a tree trunk, cut vertically. The flat side faced towards the town, the curved side towards The Place. The pillars were signposts. The Divine Road began here. From the pillars The Road ran straight as a sunbeam to The Place.

When each group rounded the bend and approached the pillars, each paused for their guides to explain what they saw, causing the groups behind them to wait in heightening expectation. Then they left The Road, walking beside it just outside the ditch.

The Road surprised Havram; he'd never seen a thirty-five-foot-wide road. Each side had a large ditch. Thousands of feet had trodden its dirt into hard-packed clay. Rain immediately ran off into the ditches at the roadside.

Dygsu began, "Candidates, human beings did not make The Road or its ditches. We built The Place. The Divine Himself built The Road. The Road, not The Place, is the Holy of Holies. This Road is the original gift of The Divine to us. The pillars and The Place mark each end of The Road. This Road goes straight, never wavering. If someone stands in the far-side middle of The Road when the midwinter sun rises, the sun will rise at the middle of this end. This Road, not The Place at The Road's end, is the original Ur. Arwain conducts all ceremonies standing behind an Altar Stone facing the Holy of Holies. You aren't full candidates yet, so we must travel beside The Road and outside its ditch."

The candidates were awestruck.

Dygsu stopped speaking. Further words would detract from the experience.

At a half-mile's distance The Place disappeared behind the backs of the groups ahead. But as they approached, it grew to dwarf them. The outer ditch surrounding The Place stretched three-hundred feet across. The outer ring of standing stones were six times a man's height. These formed almost a circle, open only with a gap pointing toward The Road, and capped by a solid line of stone lintels. The lintel thickness was half a man's height.

Inside were trilithons forming pairs of standing stones, each pair with its lintel. Between these two standing stone circles were smaller standing stones of a different color and with no lintels.

Havram couldn't imagine how anyone could erect these massive stones and then fit lintels aligned on top. Each stone must weigh forty tons.

The experience delivered its intent: only awe-filled silence was a fit response.

Chapter 8

Smithsonian, Washington, DC—Present

The following day David received the isotope analysis on the stone block. The analysis identified the specific stone type and quarry: bluestone from the Preseli Hills quarry in Wales.

But this contradicted the pollen analysis. The pollen matched England, but not Wales.

What did that mean?

Doctor Scortun's mind kept coming back to the stone holes. Fifty-seven holes. Fifty-seven holes. What pattern does fifty-seven holes fit? Then he thought: fifty-six holes were in the large circle with the last to the side. On a whim he entered "56 holes" into Google. The second answer in the list stopped his mind in its tracks and dropped his jaw to the floor. The screen read, "56 Aubry holes Stonehenge." That would make the 57th hole the heel stone.

The second shock followed immediately. Stonehenge consisted of two types of stones. The large standing holes with lintels were sarsen stone. But the smaller uncapped stones were: bluestone.

He typed "Stonehenge bluestone quarry" into Google. The first entry was: "Stonehenge bluestone quarries confirmed 140 miles away." He opened the link and his mind stopped: the quarry was Preseli Hills quarry in Wales. The double-whammy blew his mind.

Now all data fit into a pattern, but the pattern made no sense.

What possible connection could there be between Havram and Abraham in the Middle East and Stonehenge in England?

****

O'UR OF THE CHALL DIA

June 1751

The candidate's most significant shock was the language. The afternoon of the day they went to The Place, Dygsu began teaching them the local language. They were learning to be a Servant of the Light, and for learning, they needed a common language. Theoretically, any language the instructors wanted would work for the candidates. But, to communicate with their housemaid or the townspeople, there were no alternatives; they needed to speak the local language. So, Dygsu devoted the first thirty days to learning it. For the following two months, they gradually reduced the time spent in each daily lesson. From breakfast to supper, they only spoke the local language—a practice later known as immersion learning.

That's when most of the candidates faced something unexpected. The language spoken by over 40 percent of the candidates, including Havram, was a subject-verb-object (SVO) word order. This sounds like "Tom gave flowers." Forty percent more spoke a subject-object-verb (SOV)—"Tom flowers gave." Only 15 percent spoke the local language order: verb-subject-object (VSO)—"Gave Tom flowers." That wouldn't have posed a major problem for Havram if he had spoken Western Semitic—Canaanite, a proto-Hebrew language which also used a VSO word order. But, he spoke Eastern Semitic—Akkadian. It had SVO order.

If that wasn't bad enough, the other language differences gave him fits. For example, the language didn't use prepositions (pre-position) where phrase objects came after the preposition word, but postpositions (post-position) with phrase objects coming before the postposition word.

What did these two different word orders sound like? A sentence in SVO word order was "Tall Tom gave fresh flowers to pretty Sally." In the local language the VSO word order was: "Gave Tom tall flowers fresh Sally pretty to." It drove Havram crazy trying to figure out which word had what meaning in the sentence. It was almost two months before he could adapt to the point where the language automatically made sense.

The numbering method of Ur was radically different. Havram used the Sumerian scheme. The numbers went:

Lift one finger—one

Lift second finger—two

Lift third finger—three

Lift fourth finger—four

Lift thumb—five

Ball fingers into a fist—six

Six and its multiples were "complete" numbers. Ten fingers of six were sixty. Sixty seconds made a minute. Sixty minutes made an hour. Morning, afternoon, evening, and night were four cycles of six or twenty-four hours in a day.

The Sumerian scheme incorporated the magic of people's lifecycles. Each stage had a natural meaning. Women were children until twelve—two hands. When they had completed childhood, they were eligible for engagement. They married at two hands plus one—thirteen. Boys continued as young men until three hands and married at three hands plus one—nineteen. A full life was ten fistfuls of hands—sixty, ten times six. Until you had reached a fistful of hands—thirty, five times six, or half a lifetime—you were not eligible for priestly leadership.

The Ur scheme kept the Sumerian lifecycle, but lost all its meaning. The boys could not graduate to be servants until nineteen—three hands plus one. Examination for council membership was ten years later when they were "about" thirty. A full life was still sixty. Everything lost its significance. It was just numbers.

The Sumerian numbering scheme revealed its natural "why." There was no "why" in Ur's base ten scheme.

The following day they issued clothes—pants and shirts. Havram's first thought: *Were they crazy? His people wore robes. Pants were for sissy foreigners.* Like Elamites in the mountains east of Sumer. And, Ur required all candidates to attend their appointment with the cobbler for boots.

He approached Dygsu, holding the pants and shirt, "Dygsu, do I have to wear these? These are foreigner's clothes. People from my culture don't wear them."

"No, Havram, except formal occasions in your robe, you can wear any clothes you like. And, you can always wear any clothes under your robe. But, I would suggest you keep them for now. After a year, if you still don't want them, you can give them to a new candidate."

"Thanks, Dygsu."

He steadfastly refused to wear pants. Until the first cold night in the fall, when the temperature at night dipped below forty. He spend a sleepless night shivering, even under his sheepskin blanket. Then, he discovered why everyone in cold countries wore pants.

And now he understood why Dygsu was a teacher. Dygsu didn't force anything. If you weren't ready to learn something, he waited until you were. He would encourage, but that's as far as he went. And, if he suggested you might want to do something, there was invariably a valid reason. You needed to pay attention.

So, Havram continued to wear robes until the cold weather led him to discover why everyone in hot countries wore robes, and cold countries wore pants. It all revolved around regulating body temperature.

In hot environments, it's about the sun's heat. The key is reducing heat to the body. Without clothing, sunlight torches the skin, since the skin will directly absorb all the sun's radiant energy. If the sun hits the skin directly, it forces the body to sweat. The hot surrounding air immediately absorbs all the sweat, resulting in a loss of body fluid. Robes protect the skin from radiant heating. When you do sweat, the moisture stays inside the robe, raising the percent moisture of the inside air. Adding water to hot air immediately lowers its temperature, so the body sweat lowers the temperature inside the robe. The lower temperature also further reduces sweating. The greater the air mass inside the robe, the greater the cooling effect, so loose fitting robes hold more air than pants.

A cold environment's issue is lack of the sun's heat. Because of less sun energy, the body must produce heat, raising the temperature inside the clothes. By reducing the volume of air between the body and its clothing, the energy needed to heat the air lowers, reducing the body's energy loss. By reducing total clothing surface, heat loss through clothing also lowers. The thicker and tighter the garment fit, the less the energy loss.

So, after his sleepless night shivering, Havram overcame his inherent disgust for pants and surrendered to the unavoidable. But, he steadfastly refused to wear boots. He had worn sandals his whole life regardless of the temperature. He wasn't about to change.

Then it snowed. Simply standing in line for breakfast at the housemaid's hut, the snow against his feet melted, sucking the heat from his feet. Snow seeped between his toes. Havram lost all feeling below the ankle. They weren't feet, they were blocks of inert wood. It took an hour after returning to the hut for his feet to regain their normal temperature. Before he went out the next time, Havram put on his boots.

It was three weeks in the tents before the graduating class of servants left and the huts were ready to move into. By that time, Havram had developed a passing ability with the local language. But, he could understand it better than speak it.

The last night in the tents the housemaids served everyone a dish made from cow's milk and cheese. All the other candidates in his group developed stomach cramps. Only he showed tolerance. He discovered most people from Mediterranean regions couldn't tolerate anything made from cow's milk. The result was the Council separated him from the classmates he had grown used to and moved him into a hut serving cow's milk products.

This hut had a different housemaid and a different Dygsu. His new housemaid Coth was from Ur while the Dygsu was northern European. Coth was the first woman he had ever seen with red hair and freckles. She had a caring heart, a listening ear, a ready laugh and was a wonderful cook. She also had two children, a girl, Sarrai, about eleven, and her younger brother, Nahor, about ten. Sarrai had her mother's red hair and freckles. She also didn't act like a young girl from his culture. On his first day in the hut, she waltzed in, looked around at the candidates, pointed her finger at him, and demanded, "Are you the hero?"

So much for expecting women to act demure.

Two other young men also moved to Havram's hut as lactose tolerant transfers: Klymenos from Pylos in Mycenae in southwest Greece, and Kikkuli from Washukkari in the Hurrian Empire on the southeast plains of Turkey. All three young men had multi-generations of stewardship and their ancestors had married local Ur women. This resulted in their offspring inheriting the genes to digest cow's milk. The three men became fast friends.

Each week the prospective candidates got one day off with no scheduled work. They were free to do whatever they wanted. For the first few months Havram usually walked the countryside. On a good day, he would trek for twenty or thirty miles, out and back, taking slightly different routes each way. Occasionally either Klymenos or Kikkuli went with him, but usually Havram was alone. He needed the time alone to think through all he was learning.

Green predominated the land. Many fields had brilliant butter-yellow flowers they called mustard. It wasn't the mustard bushes he knew from home. A field of mustard grass would almost hide its green.

There was little brown. Even trees often showed no brown trunks because their leaves stretched almost to the ground. And, unless the hand of man had altered the landscape for farming or other use, vibrant green grass coated the countryside.

Temperatures were universally moderate with few baking hot days and few sub-freezing nights. Daytime highs ranged from the mid-forties in winter to the seventies and eighties in the summer. Nighttime averages ranged from just above freezing in the winter to the mid-fifties in the summer.

And it rained. In the Middle East you routinely went five months or more without rain between summer and fall. In Ur's summer, rain averaged every third day. No wonder rivers, streams and brooks abounded. In the Middle East, you worried about getting enough water. In Ur, you worried about getting too much.

People were sparse. Forty to fifty thousand people spread over ninety thousand square miles. If he kept to the back hill country, it wasn't unusual for him to not see another person for the whole day.

That made him understand something else. There were no city walls, no hill forts, no defensive fortifications. Why fight for someplace when you could move a few miles and have more land than you needed without fighting?

His nighttime anxieties about finding a home within strong city walls subsided.

But, his concerns about what he wanted to do and who he wanted to become remained. Yes, he had decided the next two years. His first goal was to earn stewardship. Then, earning a council seat. But, he kept wondering. *Yes, becoming a servant fits who I am. But, does this bring happiness? Will my life be fulfilling?*

After being in his new hut for a few days, Havram sought out his housemaid, "Coth, do you mind if I ask you a question?"

"No, dearie, I'd be glad to help you any way I can."

"Do you know why they separated me from all my friends?"

"By friends, I gather you mean from everyone else who speaks your native language?"

"Yes."

"That I can answer. You can digest cow's milk products; the rest of your friends can't."

"What difference does that make?"

"Dearie, it doesn't make *a* difference; it is *all* the difference. You see, I have to feed anywhere from a dozen to almost twenty hungry young men. I don't have the time, cooking pots, or fire to make twenty individual meals, or even two. So I need to make dishes like a stew where I can serve individual portions from a large pot or cauldron. To make a stew, you start with a sauce and then add ingredients to cook. To start and thicken the sauce, you use a fat and flour, and stir them together. In Ur we use cow's butter for the fat. In Mediterranean countries, they use olive oil. Olives won't grow this far north, so we have to import it in large amphorae jars to feed those candidates who can't tolerate cow's milk. And that's expensive.

She winked at him, "But Dearie, that's not why you want to stay here. Our housemaids didn't grow up cooking with olive oil, so they don't know how to prepare it correctly. They butcher most of the meals. You should hear the comments those women have to endure. Tell you what, this fire can go unattended for fifteen or twenty minutes. First, taste a spoonful of tonight's dinner. It's almost done, so you can see what it tastes like."

She gave Havram a spoonful of the stew. "See what it tastes like? Now, we go visit another hut and see what they're having for dinner."

Coth led him out of her hut and down two sets of huts. They stopped at the outside pantry cupboard containing their amphorae. There were several full and one partially used jar, each five to six feet high, pointed on the end, and sticking into the ground using their pointed end. Coth said, "See all this oil? It only lasts a few months, then she'll need a new supply. We'll get a new shipment of oil from this year's olive crop a month or so before she runs out of last year's oil."

They stopped just before they got to the hut's door. "Now, no matter what you think, don't say anything negative about her cooking." They ducked into the hut. The lady beamed in pleasure, "Coth, it's good to see you. What brings you today?"

"Aderyn, I'd like to you to meet Havram." The two nodded in greeting. "He's a candidate. I was explaining sauces and the difference between oil-based and butter-based. Could you please let him have a spoonful of an oil-based sauce; I've already given him a sample of the butter-based."

"Surely, Havram, be glad to help. Here . . ." She dipped a spoon into her stew and gave it to Havram. He tasted it, "Thank you, Aderyn, that was delicious."

Aderyn's smile split her face in two, it was so wide. "No problem, Havram, anytime, anytime."

The two took their leave.

Once back to Coth's hut, Havram told the truth, "Coth, that was terrible. That dish isn't close to how it should taste."

Coth interjected, "Havram . . ."

"Yes."

"Aderyn is one of the better cooks using olive oil."

Havram vividly remembered his first few week's meals before moving to Coth's hut. The thought crossed His mind about what it would be like eating Aderyn's cooking for two years. He shuddered.

Coth read the shudder for its meaning. "Havram. Do you want to join your old friends in an olive oil hut?"

"Coth, I prefer your cooking—any day. Thank you for helping me understand." He gave her a hug, and left.

He didn't see her appreciative response. Her grin was as wide as Aderyn's.

On his way back to his hut, Havram decided he wouldn't complain and try to rejoin his old group. Like many young men, his stomach ruled a good portion of his life.

Over time, Coth became Havram's surrogate mother. Havram had never known his own mother; she had died giving him birth. Terrah talked many times about her, telling him of her golden hair.

Chapter 9

Smithsonian, Washington, DC—Present

Doctor Scortun spread report documents on his desk. The reports provided all the factual evidence to the questions he could think to ask. Had he missed something? He took a blank sheet of paper and wrote down his questions, evidence, and answers.

When—Time Frame:

Clay tablet: based on number of names: 1700–1800 BCE

Garment: Radiocarbon dating: 1750 BCE

Box: Radiocarbon dating: 1725 BCE

Answer: 1750–1725 BCE

Confidence level: high

Where—Location in World:

Garment: Tigris-Euphrates river valley: short period of time

Garment: Palestinian Levant: either a short period of time or longer if only worn occasionally

Garment: Stonehenge, England: extensive period of time

Answer: all three places, but time spent in each unknown

Confidence level: high

Who—Likely Connected to Time Frame of 1750–1725 BCE

Havram (evidence indirect): most likely, based on being first name and lack of evidence to independently date otherwise

Abraham (evidence indirect): Possibility, based on being second name—date agrees with other evidence

Isaac (evidence indirect): Unlikely since Bible suggests he was so trau-
matized by almost being sacrificed that he rarely left his tent, let alone make
a trip to Stonehenge

Jacob-Israel: Unlikely. Bible records Joseph (Jacob's son) was sold into
slavery during time of Hyksos. This places Jacob and Joseph later in history
than artifacts allow. (Jacob would have had to be roughly 120–30 years old
at beginning of Joseph's slavery)

Why—What was the Context of the Artifact?

Religious Context:

Tablet referred to as ephod, which had known Biblical ties only to Jewish high priest

Confidence level: high

Secular Context: no supporting evidence

Organizing all the evidence helped. Instead of a myriad of individual
facts chasing in circles in his head, now he had everything in front of him.

He shook his head. He still didn't have a clear pattern, so he had to be
missing something.

Stonehenge was the pattern's key.

What was Stonehenge's purpose?

1. Stonehenge was a summer and winter solstice predictor. But that
   wasn't unique; other standing stone circles throughout Europe and the
   Middle East predicted the sun's movements.

2. Stonehenge predicted the movements of the moon. But other stone
   circles tracked the moon's movements.

Havram got bluestone from the Stonehenge quarry in Wales and modeled his 57-hole stone after Stonehenge. Therefore, he had almost certainly
visited Stonehenge—the pollen analysis almost certainly confirmed that.
That meant Stonehenge provided something he couldn't get elsewhere.

What made Stonehenge unique?

A memory of a book he read years ago and buried in his memory suddenly popped to the front of his mind. Eclipses. Only a stone circle built at
the latitude of Stonehenge could predict an eclipse.

He knew he was close to solving the pattern. He needed that book.

****

O'UR OF THE CHALL DIA

July 1751

The first six weeks dragged on forever. The candidates did nothing but learn the local language. When he moved to Coth's hut after his first few weeks, Havram had no one else speaking his language to help him. At first, he could go to his old hut and ask his native speakers to help, but soon his former hut solidified their friendship bonds and effectively excluded him from comradeship.

His new Dygsu taught the language as he had learned it. Learn twenty-five lexicon words a day. Learn the grammar step-by-step. Learn constructions and declensions. Slow, tedious, boring—and ineffectual. You do learn it—step by painful step—eventually. About as helpful as drinking castor oil when you're not sick.

His best language instructor turned out to be Sarrai, his housemaid Coth's daughter. Sarrai was always underfoot. She had inherited a keen mind and was an adept and rapid learner. From repeated exposure to candidates from early youth, she was essentially a candidate in all but name. She'd overheard the same teaching multiple times, and her mind, although still a pre-adult's, had every bit the same reasoning ability.

Through watching candidates struggling to master her language, she had discovered the most effective methods the candidates could use to learn rapidly and effectively.

Sarrai adopted Havram , and actually taught him more than their Dygsu. He presented it as a static, uninteresting chore. She taught him whole phrases he could use in day-to-day living. By incorporating everything using whole thoughts at a time, the language soon came alive.

Good morning . . . my name is Havram . . . How are you? . . . did you enjoy dinner? . . . how can I get to . . . can you tell me . . . would you please pass the . . . .

The two spent many afternoons together. Both enjoyed the time and company. Most of Havram's hut-mates ignored the children, but Havram was considerate. He'd grown up without a mother, so he empathized with her life without a father.

Gradually he began to think that, if Sarrai could grow up to be like her mother, a great mind, a kind heart and a listening ear, she might make someone a good wife. She already had a sharp mind, as good perhaps as his own. He remembered the women in his father's band. You could only talk *at* them, you couldn't talk *with* them. Sarrai could think and use complex and abstract reasoning. Half the men in his hut couldn't do that.

And she was cute. Someday she might mature to become beautiful. But, it would be her mind that would make her a fit companion, not her beauty.

Then he rethought his priorities. *No*, he thought, *I don't want her to grow to be beautiful.* Every beautiful woman he'd known was haughty. They thought their beauty made them better than all other women. Like beauty conferred on them a special status. Beauty and brains never seemed to go together. *No*, he decided, *I want her to be good-looking, but not beautiful.*

After their first month with the new candidates, Sarrai told her mother, "I have made up my mind. When I become of age, I'm going to marry Havram."

Coth answered, "Honey, you can't decide who you will marry. The man decides."

"I know, but I have decided that he will decide to marry me." Sarrai examined the incredulous look on her mother's face, and smiled, "Just watch me. I will give him no choice. I think I already know the answer, but let me ask anyway. Think of women's traditional skills: cooking, spinning, sewing, weaving, basket making, and so on. Which ones would a man notice and appreciate?"

"Honey, men notice women for sex and food. They appreciate good looks, and many think that good looks means good sex." Coth winked at her daughter, "They only find out later that's not true. Most men ask the father to marry their daughter based only on looks. And, you have little control over how you look. And, no one will notice good looks until you are old enough to grow breasts. The best children can look is cute.

"The problem is different men like different looks. For example, some like large breasts and others small, high held ones. Some like brown hair, some blonde, and some red. You have red hair. Red is the most divisive color for men. They will either love or hate your hair—there are no half measures. And, you can't control the color of hair you have.

"What can you do? Notice the women they look at the most. This gives you clues on what they like. If they look at you, give them encouraging signs that you like them also. But that's no guarantee. Always remember: you can influence a man, but you can never control him.

"Now, to answer your question: only women will notice or care because you can spin, sew, or weave. But men *will* notice how you *cook*. There is a saying at least as old as my grandmother: the best way to a man's heart is through his stomach. The companion saying is that your good looks gets him to nibble the worm on the hook, and your good food catches him."

"Then," said Sarrai, "my first task is to learn to cook, and I'll start by learning how you cook. If I'm going to catch Havram, I need to become the best cook in Ur. I have two years to learn."

Coth went on, "I can give you one other word of advice. Some men tell jokes, especially improvised puns. Your father is a prime example. Laughing at a man's jokes is important to them. If you don't like their style of humor, you won't make a good wife for him. You can't fake laughter. Eventually he'll learn it's fake, and that will dissatisfy him. And, after a while, his endless puns will make you unhappy. So if his jokes don't make you laugh, look somewhere else."

Sarrai thought for a minute, "But Mother, Havram doesn't tell puns."

"No, Honey, it's more accurate to say that Havram doesn't tell puns yet. He doesn't know our language well enough to make up puns. Wait six months. If he is an itinerant punster, you'll know it, because he'll start thinking of them. For example, that's what happened with your father. He had my cousin and I rolling on the floor in laughter.

"Mother, when is Father coming back?"

"Honey, I don't know for sure. I expect in two or three years. When he left I was so pregnant I couldn't travel with him. And, a lone woman with small children doesn't travel on her own—it's too dangerous. When he was a candidate, he married my cousin. They left. When she died in childbirth, the Council asked him to return as a Dygsu. That's when I married him. But, after his Dygsu duties were over, they assigned him as a servant and he hasn't been able to return. His last letter said the Council wants him to return, and we'll be together again. At least the Council recognized our problem and gave me this housemaid job until he returns. Believe me, Honey, he's worth the wait."

Coth began teaching Sarrai what she knew about cooking. Coth was a good cook, just unimaginative. She prepared the same set of meals on a two-week cycle. She never altered her recipe; nor did she ever trade recipes with other women of the community, so she was never a serious contestant for the annual cooking competitions.

On the other hand, Sarrai had absorbed the innovative thinking techniques taught to the candidates. If the Council had admitted females, she would have been a candidate. For the first six months, she studied and learned all her mother could teach her. Different cuts of meat, fish and fowl. Different methods of preparing and cooking meats: roasting, stewing, broiling, and boiling. Different methods of preparing vegetables: braising, and sautéing. Different methods of preparing and baking grains. How different herbs and spices affect taste. She absorbed hundreds of little details.

Although individually innocuous, when combined they separated the bland from the tasty, the ordinary from the magnificent.

Coth was happy to teach Sarrai. It was her loving duty to prepare her daughter for marriage. It also gave her pleasure to pass on what she knew. And, a bonus came attached. Cooking and preparing three meals a day for ravenous, still-growing young men was tedious. She welcomed the extra hands to share to load.

Starting with their second month, Dygsu began training how to solve problems. For the next four months, they reviewed already solved problems.

Dygsu taught them the four-step method. First, break down the problem into parts. Second, find the the weak link or an improvement which, if implemented, would most improve the solution. Third, devise a solution to the weak link. Fourth, test the new method to corroborate improvement.

It turned out Dygsu taught little that Terrah hadn't already covered with him. However, the first time Terrah gave the lessons, they were hurrying so much Havram missed many details and nuances. He hadn't yet built up a working mental model of how to think through problems, so he wasn't able to incorporate many subtleties. Now he grasped them, and this enriched both his knowledge base and his discriminating ability.

As the instructors presented these problem-solving techniques, some prospective candidates proved unable to understand and use the ideas. These disappeared, returning to their homelands with no explanation. One day they were there, the next they were gone. In the first six months, almost half left. The huts, once crowded, had plenty of room.

But even going through solved problems occasionally resulted in innovations.

One day Dygsu was discussing the solution of irrigation.

Dygsu advised them that far to the south were two lands that, unlike Ur, did not receive much annual rain, and had a much hotter climate. Their rivers were much wider, longer and carried more water. The two best examples were a country called Egypt with its Nile River, and Babylonia with the Tigris and Euphrates. In both countries, the rivers fed the land next to the river with plentiful water. But as populations grew, they needed more land under cultivation to feed the people. So, the Servants invented a method of lifting water out of the river into ditches, allowing water to flow into fields far from the river. By using dirt dams to open and close these water channels, food production increased.

Ur had kept a working model of the original invention two miles upriver. The hut went to examine how it worked. Havram was the only man in his hut who had been to a land where people used irrigation, and added further details where Dygsu lacked experience and knowledge.

Returning, Havram considered the problem.

When they had gathered around the warming fire in their hut's center, Havram asked to speak. "Dygsu, candidates, I believe the solution of irrigation may mask another problem. By solving one problem, we may have unknowingly introduced another. I am thinking of four different lands. Everyone in the Tigris-Euphrates river valley uses irrigation, and it does multiply the food supply. However, they used to grow wheat, but in places wheat will no longer grow. Only barley grows. Why?

"To answer that question, we have to examine the other three lands. In Syria there is a large lake called Sabkhat al-Jabbu. There is no lake in summer when the water has evaporated. When the early rains come, the rainwater washes down the mountain and fills the lake. The water is sweet to drink and shepherds take their flocks to drink. I have watered our flocks there. But there is no river to carry water downstream. The rainwater carries mud from the mountains into the lake, refreshing the soil so water reeds grow profusely every year. But the water also carries salt. When the water evaporates, the salt leaves a white haze. As the water begins evaporating, the lake water grows so salty that, if you water your flock in the late spring, the sheep will die. Only reeds can tolerate the salt. The salt layer is so thick people come to cut out blocks of salt to sell.

"The Tigris-Euphrates experiences salt buildup. Increased salt in the irrigated fields kills all grains except barley. At some future time, if we do nothing, even barley won't grow."

Dygsu asked, "How do we solve the problem?"

"I am not sure, but you remember I said we needed to compare four lands? Two others are Ur and Egypt. Ur has plentiful rainfall. There is no salt buildup because rain is pure water. If there are salts in the soil, the pure water absorbs them and carries them away downriver to the ocean. In Ur there is no salt problem.

"The last land is Egypt. I haven't visited Egypt, but the land floods as much as twenty feet deep every year. Dygsu, do we have any Egyptian candidates we can ask?"

"No, Egypt is the one land that refuses to allow any candidates. They only recognize their own gods."

"Then I can only tell you what little I know. Their annual flood carries silt that deposits and fertilizes the soil. The plentiful water dissolves and carries away last year's salts. Because salt doesn't build up, the ground stays fertile.

"Along the Tigris-Euphrates people report great floods only every twenty to fifty years. Occasional flooding can only delay the salt problem; it cannot solve it.

"We need another solution. The key is salt doesn't get enough pure water to carry it downstream. What if we replaced the top six inches of soil with soil from further inland? That soil would have no salt buildup, so fertility should return to the fields. The replacement soil will begin having salt problems in fifty or a hundred years, but by then the soil moved inland would have fifty years of pure rain to leach out its salt. Alternating the soil in the fields with the soil inland every fifty years should allow the field to stay fertile forever.

"However, you must understand, Dygsu, I am only a beginning candidate and only starting to learn problem-solving. Experienced thinkers would improve my idea."

"No, Havram. I think you have masterfully summarized the problem. Your solution is an answer, if not the best answer. But, we weren't aware there was a problem. I will seek a Council meeting so you may present your idea."

The following day the Council met to hear Havram's ideas. They never told him, but the Council decided Havram passed the standard to become a servant. After a few days' discussion, the Council sent a letter to Hammurabi, the King of Babylonia, recommending he test the solution. It worked. The following year the king ate wheat from his own lands. Unfortunately, when the first fifty-year renewal cycle was due, the king and his son had died, Babylonia had fallen, and no one remembered the idea.

As the calendar closed in on the day of the Winter Solstice, the candidate's excitement increased exponentially. They wanted to know what it was like. What would happen? Asking Dygsu was like talking to a brick wall. All he did was smile, then say, "Just wait."

But, they wouldn't wait. A couple of hut-members had older family or cousins in the second year of study. They sought them out and pumped them for answers. They got no further. One gave another smile like Dygsu. "Wait, and grow," said a second. The last merely said, "There are no words to describe it." Nothing further. No clarification. Nothing.

This was worse than saying nothing. What did the second mean, "Wait, and grow?" What did he think we've been doing the past six months? We're tired of waiting!

What did the last mean, "There are no words to describe it?" There are always words describing it!

It was hard deciding which was greater: expectation or frustration. But, finally, tomorrow was The Day. The day of the winter solstice. Tomorrow at dawn they would face the mystery. Tomorrow morning they would make the journey. Tomorrow morning they would know.

The Day finally arrived. The day of the winter solstice. The day of their initiation as official candidates. They would go to the The Place *beside* the divine Ur-Road for the last time. They would return *on* The Road.

Dygsu entered the hut. "Candidates," he began, "we'll go over this one last time"—as if they didn't already know. However, over the last few weeks, the emotional intensity had exploded, so some needed a last-minute reminder. "Once we make the left turn beside the Ur-Road, no talking. Remember, visitors may whisper, but this is your last trip beside The Road and you must begin the formal transition from potential to full candidate status. We will go around The Place to the moon-side before the sun rises. We enter The Place from the darkness of this world's ignorance into the light of The Divine's countenance. We are Hut Six, so our place is under lintel six. The ritual is in complete silence; even crying out in pain from stubbing your toe will result in banishment for three months while you cleanse yourself from ritual defilement. At sunrise, The Divine will join us over the Altar Stone. We become "One." The Arwain will conduct the Welcoming Ceremony for The Divine and ask him to begin the cycle for a new year by causing the sun to rise earlier and shine longer each day.

"After the Council leaves and rounds the bend we will begin the Candidacy Ritual. Each of you will receive your cup of elixir. It is a broth made from a combination of three different psilocybe mushrooms. Each helps you on your journey in different but complementary ways. They help loosen the bonds chaining your soul into your body so your soul can travel where your body cannot go. No two candidates will share the same experience, and no later journey will be the same. A few, perhaps one in five, will experience direct union with The Divine, the majority will bask in His presence, and there are all sorts of in-betweens.

"We want your body to remain under the shade of the lintels. If your physical eyes look at the sun while your soul is on its journey, you will become physically blind. Therefore, we may need to move your body out of the sun. When your soul returns, you will have completed your transition to candidacy. Any questions?"

There weren't.

The trip to The Place was uneventful. Even though Havram's perch was slightly to the side of the Altar Stone, it still allowed him an excellent view.

The sun rose above the Altar Stone's exact center. Arwain, standing behind the Altar Stone, raised his arms in welcome, then bowed in reverence.

Arwain's heart silently spoke all words. Words spoken aloud interfere with words spoken by the heart. Words spoken aloud benefit humanity. The Divine was spirit. He heard words spoken by the heart. And The Divine, who hears the heart, blessed it. Only Council members knew the ceremonial words. They committed no words to writing. The words remained a mystery. Therefore, the secular could not blaspheme the sacred. This was a living religion; handed down person to person for a thousand years. Only dead religions committed the sacred to writing.

After the Arwain had bowed, the Council rounded the Altar Stone, formed in pairs, and slowly recessed down the Ur Road, past the pillars, and turned right towards town.

Havram found a comfortable spot on the grass, sat and leaned against the upright stone, Klymenos and Kikkuli sitting to his left. Dygsu carried a flat wooden holding tray. There were sixteen holes in a four-by-four grid cut through the board. Nine holes held one cup for each candidate. One by one they took a cup from the tray. When each candidate received their cup, they drank the elixir and returned their cup to the tray.

At first Havram did not experience any change; everything was normal. After a while—two minutes, five, fifteen, thirty—Havram couldn't tell, he began to feel strange. His whole body felt as if he was dissolving into an invisible pillow. Just before the pillow engulfed him, Havram tried to lift his arm to look at his hand. His body failed to respond. This world dissolved: sight, sound, and feeling slowly melted into a uniform gray mist of gray dots. The dots remained gray, but they also constantly morphed from color to color. Both gray and colorful. He could not say changing in front of his eyes because he no longer had eyes. He wasn't seeing; he was perceiving, observing, understanding without physical eyes and physical brain. His body moved in his normal world, but this body had no limbs. Instead it flowed effortlessly. Havram willed and the body moved. But did his body move or the world around him move? Was this world flowing past him? Havram could not tell; there was no reference to know the difference. He had no ears to hear, but this world was both silent and filled with a choir harmoniously singing all notes simultaneously. Over and surrounding him was a feeling of warmth, comfort, and peace permeating and suffusing him. Accepting him as he was, affirming him. Was this The Divine he was experiencing? He didn't know. He surrendered to the experience, basking in its warmth. It couldn't be The Divine because he felt no "presence." He had no words to describe it. How long was his spirit-world journey? There is no "how long" where there is no time.

After a while—a minute, an hour, just short of forever—the other-world began dissolving. The familiar slowly reformed around him. He knew he was on his side. He felt mildly disoriented. His world wasn't stationary. He waited until it stopped moving. Then he opened his eyes, suddenly realizing that Dygsu must have closed his eyelids while he was on his journey.

He had returned.

One by one candidates regained control of their bodies. Dygsu gave the "rise" hand signal and they all stood and followed him: past the Altar Stone, and down the Ur Road. No one spoke until they were back in their hut.

They separated into the usual cliques. Havram, Klymenos, and Kikkuli began sharing their experience. Each described their experience using different words.

But did they? When they were using different words, were they in fact describing the same experience? Also, when they were using the same words, were they describing a different experience? They couldn't tell. Only "feeling" words formed any common meaning for them. Only Kikkuli felt a "presence." But, he couldn't describe it. Was that "presence" The Divine? He didn't know. Every time they opened their mouth to try to explain what happened, they ran full-speed into a solid wall. They stopped even before they started. They couldn't get anywhere trying to suggest what had happened. Their feelings wouldn't translate. They kept going around in circles, going nowhere.

That day Havram learned that people use words to carry meaning from one person to another. Any particular set of sounds we call a word has no intrinsic meaning—in and of itself. Its meaning is an arbitrary convention, accepted by all members of people speaking that language. An example is the word "goat." Other languages call the same animal gafr, ahuntz, bizin, ozka, or echkilar. Each word is different, but each follows its unique language conventions. If we need something more specific, we could say this variety of goat is hircus agagrus, while others are saanen, togenburg or oberhasli. If we need to identify one particular goat, we give it a name like Fred, Sally, or Nanos. Many animals, like Nanos the sheep, learn when you use their name; they know you are calling them and not another animal.

The key in this common convention is, with every concrete example, you can see, hear, feel, smell, or taste what it means. It's tangible—of this world. You can say this specific noun you are using refers to this class of examples (goat), and not that class of examples (sheep), and everyone will agree.

But, other problems remain. Different languages use different categories. For example, in Europe and the Middle East, the language convention uses frequency of light as a category. "Color" is their descriptive word. Other languages don't have the word "color" in their language. Instead, something is "bright" or "dull." The colors rose, fuchsia, and turquoise are all "bright." whereas maroon and navy-blue are "dull." You can't translate "red" into their language because they don't use a category for color. Without a word for the category, they can't even think "red."

Words referring to something nonphysical are especially hard to define. Some languages use one word for all "love" categories. Others use different words for the love of man and woman, siblings, friends, and eroticism.

At least these language problems happen in this world. We can see them or their affects. However, the candidates had experienced the otherworldly. How do you give meaning to something you can't see, hear, feel, taste, or smell? If someone's experience was or wasn't exactly alike, no words could describe it, so no one could tell if it were the same or different.

Simply, there was no describing their experience. They had journeyed to another existence. Words only have meaning when they have equivalent definitions. When experiencing the otherworldly, rational description fails. Some words retain meaning. Others lose it. But neither speaker nor listener knows which.

Now they understood what the older candidates meant by saying, "There are no words describing it." And there was no way to transfer their experience to someone who hadn't made the journey. Next year some prospective candidates would try to pump them to describe what the journey was like. Their response must be, "Words can't describe it." Meaning is meaningless unless it can be shared.

Chapter 10

Smithsonian, Washington, DC—Present

The Smithsonian has an excellent library with scholarly and reference material on all manner of scientific disciplines, including archaeology. They also have excellent reference librarians. It took Debra twenty minutes to identify and locate the book he was trying to remember: "Stonehenge Decoded" by Gerald S. Hawkins, an astronomer (that made sense), copyright 1965, published by Delta Books and first released about fifty years ago.

Much of the book didn't tackle the eclipse issue. The beginning chapters talked about the history and builders of Stonehenge; he skipped them. The author had limited archaeological knowledge; he skipped those sections. His carbon fourteen dates were inaccurate because scientists hadn't yet determined how to adjust radiocarbon dates for the changing carbon dioxide levels throughout the centuries. He put little faith in these sections.

But he did know his astronomy.

As Doctor Scortun reread the book, passages flooded back into his memory. He found the section he needed, beginning at page 138. The moon has a repeating cycle of moonrise, moonset, northwards and southwards movement, and eclipses every 18.61 years. The moon's movements were well-known even in prehistoric times. Diodorus mentioned the metonic cycle of nineteen years, and both Jewish and Chinese calendars have nineteen-year cycles.

But calendars don't track eclipses. And two nineteen-year cycles—without correction—would only have been accurate for two nineteen-year cycles. The third cycle would be wrong. But by switching to a 19-19-18 cycle, it averages almost exactly 18.61. Stonehenge did exactly that: "19 + 19 + 18 = 56," the number of Aubrey holes.

Eclipses don't happen every year. They only happen when the sun and moon align at solstices or equinoxes. That happens roughly every five years, and can sometimes happen twice within a single year. The Aubrey holes predicted this with posts moving yearly. Roughly, every five years would be a "danger year." During "danger" times, the sun rises at the same time the moon sets, or vice versa. One will predict a moon eclipse, the other a sun eclipse. The priests at Stonehenge could see the danger approaching because they could track the changes in the daily rises and sets and see them starting to approach one another. Thus, they could give several days' warning of the approaching "danger." Hawkins used a model of six stones, three white, three black, aligned at intervals of "9-9-10-9-9-10." He also admits he could adjust his model to work with as few as one signal stone by adjusting the number and position of danger holes to match.

As Hawkins stated on page 138, "eclipses would clearly be among the most impressive and frightening natural phenomena that primitive men could encounter. What terror would strike the people as the god, or goddess, was swallowed up."

David put the book down. That explained the unique purpose of Stonehenge. If Stonehenge were sixty miles either north or south, a square wouldn't produce the Aubrey holes. A parallelogram could do it, but the Windmill Hill culture built the first generation of Stonehenge in 3,000 BCE, and they didn't have that sophisticated a knowledge of geometry.

David still didn't have an exact fit, so he hadn't fully solved the puzzle. There weren't six half-cylinders encased in the clay tablet; there were two. He'd discovered the purpose of Stonehenge, but he hadn't discovered it's intent. How were they using the Stonehenge eclipse information? He reached for his bottle of aspirin; he could feel another headache approaching.

****

O'UR OF THE CHALL DIA

December 1751 BC

The day after their ceremony, Dygsu entered the hut. "Gentlemen, the time has arrived for the next stage in your servant candidacy. The first task is to assign your new names."

"New names?" one candidate asked. "What's wrong with our old names?"

Dygsu smiled, "Nothing is *wrong*—exactly. It isn't what's wrong; it's what is no longer right. You are no longer prospective candidates. The person you are today is not the person you were yesterday. You aren't a servant yet, but your character has already changed. Names reflect your character. That's why names have magical ability. Your name needs to match your character. Your character has changed; therefore, you need a new name. Questions? Does that make sense?

There were questions galore, but no one wanted to ask them. By now everyone in the hut knew the old mantra: it is better to keep your mouth closed and make people wonder if you are a fool, rather than open your mouth and confirm it.

Dygsu picked up where he had left off. "Okay. You are welcome to use your old names when you are not wearing your servant robe. However, when you have your robe on, you may only use your candidate name." And he began to read them off, finishing with "Kikkuli: your name is Glyfar; Havram, yours is Gliocas; and Klymenos, you will be Morthwyl. Any questions?"

No one said anything. Most were thinking, "Yes, that name matches his character." Havram thought, *Glyfar means clever. Yes, Kikkuli has a sharp mind; his name fits. And Morthwyl means hammer. For Klymenos, I would have used "battering ram," but hammer isn't bad. He's two hundred pounds of muscle; all action. He has an above-average mind; it's just that he doesn't always use it. He has a tendency to brute-force problems, forcing solutions. But me? Wisdom? That's going too far. I don't think so.*

Kikkuli and Klymenos were both thinking, *Gliocus, wisdom, spot on. His knowledge and reasoning ability exceed everyone else's.*

Dygsu continued, "Let me repeat project rules again. Teams must be two to four members. Projects must fix a problem needing innovation or improvement. The Council must approve each project. They will not approve easy projects. You have one and a half years, eighteen months, to solve it. Only successful projects result in becoming servants.

"The Council will give everyone a grant of twelve bunnoedd of gold to spend. Your project must fall within that budget or it's out of your own purse."

Dygsu paused, studying the hut, then continued, "It's time to select team partners and your project. Please let me know tomorrow who the teams will be. You have two weeks to decide on a project. If you are struggling, let me know and I'll help."

The candidates knew this was coming. Klymenos, Kikkuli, and Havram had already decided they would comprise a three-member team. Their project must succeed.

Havram suggested, "Let's go outside. If we're going to beat the other teams, I don't want someone stealing our ideas."

It was an early winter day with a warm afternoon; Klymenos and Kikkuli agreed. They headed uphill for the Scots Pine tree grove. It had a grotto where Havram often went to ponder tough problems. The surrounding trees were so dense, disturbed branches would warn them of anyone approaching. They settled in, the overhead sun shining its warmth, the trees deflecting the cool breeze. They looked down, avoiding eye contact. No one wanted to speak first. Their ideas might prompt laughter.

Havram thought: *Should we select an ordinary project, or should we try a harder one, which will get us an invitation for Council membership? What do I want? Do I want to become Arwain? . . . Why not?*

Finally, Havram broke the silence: "I've told you of the two battles I've been in, where I believed the key to winning was power. With our bows, my father and I could apply power. The villagers couldn't. But I've changed my mind. I've think it's more complicated than power alone.

"Imagine two different groups of men. The first is six feet tall while the second is five feet. The two groups each walk at ninety paces a minute. Even though both groups walk at the same pace, because the six-foot-tall group has longer legs, they move at a faster speed. If the five-foot-tall group is following the tall one, they will never overtake them. Conversely, if the six-foot group follows, they have to slow down. In other words, speed is important. The six-foot group can maneuver to engage or avoid at their choice. The meaning: speed trumps power. The side having greater speed dictates the choice of the battlefield. And with the ability to choose the battlefield goes selecting the best conditions for your side and the worst conditions for the enemy."

Both Kikkuli and Klymenos agreed. "Yes," Klymenos went on, "I agree with your logic, but the last time I checked, no one had an army of six-foot tall men."

Havram answered, "I'm only using this as a thought experiment to make a point. Allow me to continue. Are power and speed enough to explain warfare? No. To understand, I need to put warfare in perspective. How does one kingdom fight another? Let's call them Kingdom A and B. Each uses trained sword-fighters as their army's core. Each arm peasants with spears. Both kingdoms form a line of men perhaps three or five deep against the other kingdoms, and the two lines advance to fight. It's one semi-organized mob against another. Each force can only move in one direction: straight ahead. Now, assume a different group from Kingdom A joins the battle. They attack Kingdom B's line from the side or rear. Kingdom B can't swing their line to face the new attackers. I will use the term 'balance.' They can't rebalance to face the attackers. Therefore, they lose whatever balance they have. The result: they panic, break ranks, and run. The next section of line becomes unbalanced and runs. The result: the side losing its balance loses the battle. The lesson? Balance is more important than speed. Speed is more important than power. Maneuver your forces faster than the enemy can adjust. Use superior speed to disrupt the opposite side's balance. This results in your side using your full force and denying the enemy his use of force. Am I making sense? Can you see any flaw in the logic?"

Both of the two men nodded agreement, but Kikkuli chimed in, "In theory, that's all well and good"—meaning it wasn't well and good at all. "But, how?"

Havram smiled, "Imagine carts carrying five hundred foot soldiers or archers to attack the enemy from their flank."

Klymenos smirked, "Carts? That's not speed; don't you know that a man could outwalk a cart pulled by oxen?"

Havram parried the smirk, "I'm not talking about oxen—I agree, they don't have speed." He shifted his gaze, "Kikkuli, what is the fastest large animal?"

"That's easy," Kikkuli answered, "a horse. It can run four times as fast as a man. But it can't pull a cart. You put a rope around a horse's neck pulling that much weight and it will strangle the horse."

"Imagine if you could shift the load from the horse's neck to his chest." Havram asked.

Kikkuli thought for a minute, "Yes, that would solve the problem."

"But," pointed out Klymenos, "Even moderate speed tears the cart apart."

Kikkuli looked puzzled, "How can you know that?"

Klymenos answered, "That's what my family does: we make and sell carts. Carts have two problems. The first is no one knows how to make a round axle. The second is no one knows how to make balanced wheels. One complete wheel has two layers of boards—two different wheels—glued together. One side's boards align vertically and the other horizontally. The problem is getting consistent thickness on both horizontal and vertical boards. Inconsistent thickness means inconsistent weight distribution, and that means the wheel doesn't spin smoothly. No one knows how to solve the problem."

Havram smiled, "Don't you see what you are both doing? The two of you keep saying, 'Yeah, that might work, but . . .' and on that I agree. However, I suggest that instead of thinking why it will *never* work, let's switch our mindset. Ask what a working solution *would* look like. Then ask what needs improvement for that image to happen. Last, ask if we can devise each needed improvement. Here's a starting suggestion for the final goal: a cart carrying a driver and an archer pulled at high-speed by one or two horses. Our first problem is finding a way to shift the load from the horse's neck to its chest. The second is inventing a new axle and wheel that balanced at high-speed."

From the nods of approval, Kikkuli and Klymenos agreed.

Havram continued, "What else needs solving?"

Klymenos added, "We need an improved bow. A longbow is too large for carts. You're going to be bouncing and can't hit the bow on the cart's floor. Short bows are weak."

Kikkuli pointed out another severe issue, "Can we use one horse, or must we use two? Using one, the pulling bar is on its side. That's unbalanced. Using two horses, we need coordinated movements so they're a team. Disjoint movement at high speed will cause the cart to overturn."

They continued brainstorming ideas for several hours, but all other problems were trivial. Only these could seriously risk project success.

Then they divided the problems to solve: Klymenos with his family knowledge of cart-making got the issues of a new axle and wheel design. The Kikkuli family culture of working with horses assigned him the design of the horse chest collar and the control of one or two horses. By default, the improved bow went to Havram.

"You know, friends," Havram closed, "We need to give this invention a name. Something we can talk openly about, and if someone overhears us, they won't understand what we're talking about."

The other two agreed. Klymenos recommended "chariot," and that became its name.

They agreed to think on the project separately for a week, and meet next week to compare thoughts.

That satisfied Havram. *It's go for broke; shoot for the moon. Arwain, get ready, here I come.*

When the three men left, the observer crept out of the adjoining grotto's shallow dirt tunnel under its branch and pine needle covering. *Chariot,* the observer thought. *I knew Havram would devise a novel idea. What can I do? I will probably need to contact Hirben, but not yet.*

By their next weekly meeting in the Scots Pine grove, the three young men learned why Ur candidacy training lasts two years. It's easy to have brilliant ideas. The problem is implementing those ideas. There is usually a good reason the implementation doesn't exist. When you start trying, you discover why. The three young men were embracing a daunting series of tasks. Each task was almost impossible for ordinary teams. They needed to complete all three.

Kikkuli had rented two horses until the plowing season began. He discovered the local people bred horses for work. They were strong, but slow. He had to send back to his family in Washukkari to have them send three Hurrian horses bred for speed. And, his first trial with the local horses was nearly the last.

At their first weekly design progress meeting, Kikkuli reported, "I'm not sure having a horse pull a chariot by rope will work. I tried putting the rope across the horse's chest, and the horse didn't choke, but he developed abrasions so severe he has a large welt across his chest."

Havram countered, "Let's go look."

Kikkuli was correct. The welt across the chest was at least a hand-width wide, raised and blistered. The horse shied at the slightest touch.

But on closer examination, Havram noticed the rope and wound didn't match. The rope was one inch wide, but the chest wound was four. He thought about that for a minute and mentally reviewed how they had planned the test. "Kikkuli," he pointed out, "I'm not sure you've identified the real problem."

At Kikkuli's questioning stare, Havram continued, "It appears the rope didn't stay fixed in one position. It moved back and forth, up and down. It looks as if, when the cart hit a bump or rut, the rope moved, and when the horse pulled the rope tight, it slid, producing a rope burn on his chest. The issue wasn't pulling the cart; the problem was the rope not remaining stable. What do you think?"

Kikkuli knew horses, and he looked at the evidence with fresh eyes, "Havram, I think you're right. But, how do we hold the rope in place unless we use another rope? A third holds the second. This looks like an unending chain of ropes."

Havram thought for a minute. "To me it looks like two problems. First problem: having one rope carry the entire cart's pull force. A solution might be using multiple ropes to spread the force, reducing pressure in any one spot on the horse. Spreading the force lessens the problem's severity. Second problem: stabilize the rope. Suppose we could insert a padding between the rope and the horse, say by sewing three ropes side-by-side to a long leather strip. That would prevent rope movement and therefore stop rope burns. What do you think?"

"Havram, that's a great idea. Let me find a leather-smith and we can fit a custom chest pad for the horse. Making the pad will probably take two weeks. Since it will take two weeks for the horse to heal, we won't lose time."

On returning to the grove, Klymenos reported on his cart progress, "We haven't started the work.

"But I can tell you one piece of promising news. It's the axle. If the axle isn't round, the cart won't survive at high speed. As part of my curiosity and my family business, I visited a local cartwright. There I saw the most magnificent invention I've ever seen. You know the turn-bows we used as kids to start fires? The ones shaped like a bow with a string between the two ends. Wrapping the string around a twig and pushing the bow back and forth forces the twig to spin and create friction. Friction causes the twig to heat up and start a fire. They had a monster bow eight feet long and three feet high. It wraps around a whole axle. Two strong men push and pull on the bow, causing the axle to spin back and forth so a cutter can shave off thin layers of wood. They can make an axle precisely round. It's magnificent. That's the hardest problem in building a cart and they've already solved it for us.

"The local wheelwrights and I started discussions on how we can make a consistent wheel thickness. They have some ideas for improvements, but we won't know how much improved stability we'll get until we build the cart. We are going to try using the existing double-wheel technology if we can. The last piece of information they need is at what height the tongue needs to transfer the load to the horses, since that affects how we build the tongue. They haven't started cutting wood yet, so I don't know if we've made progress."

Kikkuli asked, "Havram, how are you progressing on your composite bow?"

Havram gave a soft sigh, "I'm about ready to start in earnest. I've spent the last week with the bow makers learning the craft of making longbows. They have little knowledge of compound bows, of course, but there's more to making a bow than I suspected.

"Are you ready for this? It's complicated. The archer pulls the front of the bow—the side facing him—into compression, making it smaller. The front's compression pulls the back into tension. When the archer releases the string, the front pushes back to its original shape. Simultaneously, the back's tension pulls back. The front of the bow is middle-tree heartwood. It resists compression. The back is sapwood. Sapwood resists the wind blowing on the tree. It resists tension. This snap back must transition smoothly.

Compression and tension must blend. Therefore, the bow needs to be exactly balanced with the midline centered between these two woods or the bow will break.

"Next, each wood variety has different amounts of resistive force for compression and tension. So, yew is best for longbows, but not short bows. Pine can't store the same energy as yew, so pine bows won't shoot an arrow as far. And even with yew, we can only use the main branches, and even then two out of three bows will break. Who knows, if the bowsmiths can ever solve the issues to be able to use trunk wood, maybe they can increase the maximum range from today's three hundred feet or so to over four hundred. Anyway, that's the theory behind self-bow archery."

Klymenos chimed in, "I never thought archery and complicated belonged in the same sentence."

Havram continued, "You think that's bad? The problems multiply in a compound bow. I found a candidate who brought his compound bow with him to Ur. I bought a new longbow and traded with him to learn how they work. I've spent several days examining and firing it. That's given me ideas.

"Compound bow theory doesn't change. The face must go into compression; the back tension. A compound bow's face uses bone. But, the bone is carved and shaped, so you can't tell what animal's bone they used. Also, the back uses animal tendon, but you can't tell the animal. And whatever wood they used, it's not from Britain. There are no clues which materials to use.

"What are the best starting materials? The bow face is bone, but which animal bone is best? I expect cow will be too strong and deer too flimsy. The center backbone is wood. I expect oak will be too tough and pine too weak. The back side is animal leg tendon. Cow should be too tough. Deer too weak. I suspect the tendon strength must match the animal bone's density. I need to discover which are the best materials for the final bow.

"To test all combinations would need 280 bows. We don't have that money or time. Each bow takes two weeks to produce and six months to dry before testing. Even if we could afford it, we don't have the time to make 280 bows. Last, the final bow needs made nine months before the project presentation to dry and test. We only have time for two rounds of bows. I will start with six bows. I'm betting medium strength will be the final answer, so I'll test maximum, medium and minimum strength of bone, wood and tendon. I'm betting birch wood with ibex bone and tendon will be the winner, so one bow will use these.

The three men stared at one another. The full weight of the task they had undertaken suddenly became apparent. They felt its full weight dropping onto their shoulders. They began wondering if their shoulders could carry the weight.

As the three men rose and left the grotto, the observer smiled. The three men had looked around to make sure that they were alone, but they were looking aboveground. They failed to examine the terrain for suspect hiding places. Observant ears heard every word spoken. The ears connected to a brilliant mind. The observer stayed in the tunnel until the three men left.

Interesting, the Observer thought, *ibex bone strength. Time to begin work.*

Lying in bed that night, Havram thought, *I was overconfident and convinced my friends to go for broke. We may have bitten off more than we can chew and this project may fail. If so, we don't become servants, let alone me joining the council. Has my ambition caused failure for all of us? What have I done?*

The following day the observer visited Hirben. "I need you to perform a task. You need to convince the hunters to kill an ibex for a candidate's meal.

"Ibex? The ibex mountains lie over thirty miles away from Ur. Why do you need an ibex?"

"For an ibex breastbone and sinew. When the hunters give the carcass to the butchers, I need them to save the collarbones and leg sinew."

Hirben shook his head. The observer was as daffy as Ur's servants. But, the observer couldn't do it. And, the observer was family. And family was family.

The next week the huts ate ibex meat. They had only eaten ibex one other time since Havram had arrived at Ur. After the meal, he went to the butchers, but they had already closed for the night. He was there when they opened the following day.

He asked for the breast bones and leg sinew from their waste pile.

"Funny you should ask," the butcher told him. "A blond-haired man came in last week. Said his name was Hirben and he was looking to buy ibex breast bones and leg sinew. Promised him we'd save them if we got an animal to butcher. Sorry, I can't give them to you, but tell you what. He said that, if he was still interested, he'd be back within ten days. Give this man a week. If he doesn't come back, they're yours."

Havram asked, "Do you know if he's from Ur?"

"Don't know where he comes from, but not from Ur. Maybe a candidate. Never seen him before. See you in a week. If this Hirben fellow doesn't claim them, they're yours."

After supper Havram sought out the hunters' hut and asked if anyone had shot an ibex lately. They pointed to the man. Havram asked him, "Did a blond-haired man not from Ur named Hirben ask you to hunt ibex?"

The man's eyebrows went up. "How'd you know that?" He asked. "Yeah, never seen him before. Gave me a suckling lamb. Said to give the ibex to the butchers; they'd know what to do."

Havram's mind went into overdrive. *Ibex bones. Either someone had already invented the compound bow and was making a new one, or . . . someone had overheard Kikkuli, Klymenos, or himself talking. If he already knew how to build a composite bow and was just making a new one, then it confirmed Havram was on the right track. However, if Hirben was a candidate. . . . Was this Hirben trying to steal his invention?*

After six months learning what Coth could teach her, Sarrai began visiting other housemaids. Ur conducted an annual cooking competition, and she began with the last few year's contest winners. Yes, she wanted to know the recipes they used, the "what" they had done. But, she went beyond that. She wanted to know "why" that recipe worked. What knowledge and skills enabled using the ingredients to bring out the best taste?

Over time, she assembled this mosaic of myriad individual details into a mental pattern. From this pattern she developed a theory for how these women became contest winners.

Sarrai learned the two techniques for superior cooking: augmenting the taste inherent in the main ingredient, or supplementing its taste with complementary ingredients. That's all. However, individual techniques doing these simple steps were endless.

She learned to balance the herbs and spices. For any recipe, choose one of the four taste pairs of sweet-salty and sour-bitter to dominate. The primary taste got 40 percent taste intensity. Its complementary taste got 25 percent. Divide the last 35 percent between the other taste pair.

Herbs dissolve in water but not in oils. Spices dissolve in oils but not in water. To get a rich tasting sauce, combine water and oil ingredients with an emulsifier, like eggs or butter. To get a smooth, thickened sauce, start with a roux—a mixture of half fat and half flour.

There was one essential ingredient that was plentiful: sea salt. The ocean at Solent Bay was only fifteen miles distant, so carts carrying sea salt made regular deliveries. Salt enabled the use of brines or rubs to give meat more juiciness. It muted sour or bitter in vegetables and balanced sweetness in fruits.

Havram had some heavy thinking to do on who The Divine was, so he hunkered down in the Scots Pine grove. *Okay. Project number two. I need to add to our knowledge of The Divine. How am I going to do that?*

Let's start with what we know.

Fact. There is tangible evidence The Divine exists. The Road is a fact. Something like this exists nowhere else on earth. It just happens to be located where a square-sided rope layout predicts eclipses. Located anywhere else on earth, the Ancients couldn't build The Place. Man couldn't have created this set of circumstances. That is so odd it must be by design. That suggests a superior Being.

First conclusion. The Divine is real.

Okay. That proves existence. That's old hat. No one questions that. What I need is the next step—determining The Divine's character.

What can we know about The Divine? He created The Road. The only reason to do that is to initiate interaction with the world He created. In effect, The Road is a sign pointing to Himself. Humans are the only creatures with the capacity to understand The Road.

Second conclusion. The Divine wants to interact with us. Reworded, in His eyes, and in some way, we are important to Him. Reworded, He cares about us enough to initiate interaction with Himself.

Next fact. The Ancients built the original The Place and began the worship of The Divine. So, The Divine blessed them. Then, when the Ancients began making the world a better place, The Divine further blessed them. When they stopped inventing, The Divine called the Servants to The Road and allowed the Ancients to die of sickness.

Third conclusion. As long as the Ancients continued to make the world better, The Divine blessed them. When they stopped, He withdrew His blessing and called the Servants. Since then the Servants have continually improved the world and He has blessed them. In effect, what were the Ancients doing during the time The Divine blessed them? They were improving the world. Reworded, they were acting as the brains and hands for The Divine. What are stewards? Someone who substitutes for their lord.

Fourth conclusion: we are called to be The Divine's stewards in His World.

What meaning results from these conclusions? The Divine gives His blessing when mankind acts as His stewards. If mankind stops, He withdraws his blessing. That means The Divine cares about His world. And . . . that means The Divine's stewards must care for the world like The Divine does. I will substitute the word love for care, because the evidence points to it.

Sanity check. Does everything make sense? Does everything hang together?

Yes.

Okay. That's my starting position.

Now, what can I learn from this? If there is one world and one The Divine . . . and The Divine cares for us and wants us to be His stewards . . . would he not care for all of humanity? After all, we're all in His World. Would He not try to guide everyone to Himself? Perhaps in some other way . . . and, if in some other way, can other peoples help us learn about some aspect or character of The Divine that The Road can't help us see? Reworded, are there other signs pointing to Him that other peoples and religions have experienced? What can they tell us about The Divine's character?

I need to find out.

Therefore, what can I learn from other religions? What do they believe? Can their beliefs and experiences help us learn about The Divine? That's my next step.

At their next meeting in the Scots Pine grove, Kikkuli's face was beaming, so Havram and Klymenos knew he was bursting at the seams with his news.

No sooner had they settled in than Kikkuli began. "I have great news. We tested the horse padding and it worked like a charm. The horse was understandably skittish at first, but I walked him for a half hour with my hand on the bridle and that calmed him down. When we hooked up the cart, the padding strap didn't move and the horse carried a full load of two men with no problem. No chafing, no welts."

"That is great news," chimed Klymenos. "We're one-third done."

"Wait a minute. Yes, I proved the idea worked. The load spreads across the chest horizontally. But I need to stabilize the load straps using a girth strap vertically. We also need some way of attaching the chariot to the horse. Until we design the chariot tongue, I won't know what we need to adjust. I'll go to build a harness for our existing cart, hoping that trial saves time later. So, I'm on hold. I can do extra testing, but can't advance. Oh, and remember, I rented these horses, so I'll lose them for the spring plowing season mid-April through mid-June."

"That's okay," put in Havram. "At this point we'll take a partial win. It's still progress."

The following week, Havram brought up an issue. "I've been thinking over the chariot issues, and I realized we missed an important requirement when we first did our planning."

"What," Kikkuli responded, "I thought we had the bow nailed down."

"So did I. What was lacking wasn't the bow. We didn't define the tactics that have to match the weapon. That's what was missing."

Kikkuli thought for a minute. "OK, you're our battle-man. What tactic do we need? Can the bow do it?"

"OK, the current self-bows fire an accuracy range of seventy-five yards. The current compound bow accurately fires sixty-five yards. So, the chariot must get within the defender's self-bow range. But, defending archers will shoot the horses before the chariot gets within compound bow range. That's a losing condition."

"I believe our new compound bow must accurately fire one hundred twenty-five yards. Why? Range is power. If your side's bow fires a greater range than their side's bow, you can hit them when they can't hit you. With a one-hundred twenty-five yard range, the defenders can't hit the horses. That's what I'm facing. I think we can do it, but it's a harder problem than I thought it was. What it means is we also need a stronger glue."

Klymenos shook his head, "Wow, my head is spinning. And I thought the chariot was a hard problem."

Havram added, "There's one last consideration with these new bows. When we made our test bows, we used the same thickness and bone length as the sample bow I bought. But, we're using different animals. What is the best thickness and length for the animal we're using? It's bound to be different. It means I'm going to need another round of bows made. That makes the second bow version ready a scant three months before the presentation. We have no time for anything to go wrong. The problem is the bow's compression and tension lengths aren't equal. The bone isn't as long as the wood. The imbalance creates a jerk when transitioning from compression to tension. This knocks the arrow off target. How much imbalance will we experience? We won't know until we build it."

"Havram," injected Kikkuli, "you're our only archer. Don't get sick."

"Kikkuli, it's not about me. It's about the bow."

That night, after the hut was snoring, the bow strength problem wouldn't let Havram sleep.

It's too late for the first bows. They're made. Even if I get a stronger glue, should I make another bow immediately, or wait for the second set? I don't have another ibex. Should I pay for another ibex or use different materials? If I guess wrong, there's no time for more bows. What should I do? Have I screwed up the whole project?

Wait! I already know what I have to do. It's a go-for-broke project. I have to hire the hunters and make another bow.

The next morning Havram hired one of the hunters to bring back an ibex.

Later that day the observer visited Hirben. "I need you for another task. Contact the Ur glue makers. You need them to make two batches of glue. The first batch is the standard animal hide blend, the other uses oxen or horse hooves. Call the new mixture an 'improved strength blend.' Instead of an eight-hour standard boil, they are to boil it for three days."

"Why do that?"

"It's a test ingredient. Hooves are harder and stronger than hide. I've learned about chemistry, and I predict hoof glue should be stronger. Stronger should also mean harder to extract, so it needs a longer boil."

The next day Havram sought out the glue master. "First, I need a quart of your latest batch of glue. Then, I need to talk about any ideas you might have to make a stronger glue."

"Lucky you asked. Had a chap yesterday with an idea for improving strength. Paid in advance handsomely: a suckling lamb. We're making it, but it won't be ready for two days. How much will you need?"

"A quart. If it works, we'll put in another order."

"After he picks up his order, we should have plenty. Come back day after tomorrow in the afternoon."

Havram asked, "By the way, who ordered the glue?"

"Never seen him before. He's not from Ur. Blond-haired chap, said his name was Hirben. Your glue will be ready. Just know this is a test run. We don't know how it will work."

"I understand. I'll let you know how it performs."

Havram wondered, *Who was Hirben? He can't be building a replacement bow or he would have ordered stronger glue a month ago. That means he's a spy. Is he stealing our ideas? Is he also trying to build a chariot?*

Two days later, he got his glue sample. It proved almost twice as strong as hide glue.

Havram set the bowmakers to making an ibex bow using the ibex the hunters would bring. Even knowing that the optimum bone length would probably have to change, he needed a known length for the first bow. He ordered the same length as the original compound bow he had bought.

"Ysgrifennydd, I want to thank you again for agreeing to be my scribe."

As Ysgrifennydd started to raise his hand as a prelude to saying something, Havram continued, "I know, I know. I'm paying you for your time. But I'm still thankful. To go on, as I told you, my father may have taught me to read cuneiform, but I can't write it," Havram began. "After talking with a dozen different candidates about their country's religious beliefs, I've discovered their creation myths should give us the best basis for comparison. So, I'm making a second round just for creation stories. Ready?"

Ysgrifennydd nodded agreement.

"OK. The most comprehensive mythology is Babylonian. That's where we'll start." As Havram dictated, Ysgrifennydd wrote the words in cuneiform on a velum scroll.

Before anything existed, Apsu (freshwater) and Tiamat (saltwater) comingled. No other gods existed, nor were any future destinies foretold.

From the mixture of Apsu and Tiamat, they made other gods: Lahmu, Lahamu, Anshar, Kishar, Anu, and Ea. These disturbed Tiamat so Apsu proposed to destroy them; however, Tiamat was reluctant to destroy what they had made.

Ea crafted a spell to put Apsu to sleep, after which he slew Apsu and took his halo to wear.

Ea and his wife Damika lived inside Apsu's corpse, and the two created Marduk. Marduk exceeded Ea and all the other gods in godliness, so Ea called him "My son, the sun."

The other gods said to Tiamat, "When Ea killed Apsu, you did nothing." Tiamat proposed to make monsters to do battle with the other gods. She created eleven chimeric creatures armed with weapons and the god Kingu to be their general. She gave the "Tablet of Destiny" to Kingu, making his command unchallengeable.

Ea heard of Tiamat's plan to avenge Apsu and spoke to Anshar, telling him that many gods backed Tiamat's cause. Anshar became worried that no god would oppose Tiamat, and proposed Marduk as their champion. Marduk agreed, but only on condition they make him the supreme god if he succeeded. The other gods agreed and gave him a throne.

Marduk fought Tiamat in single combat and succeeded in killing her and splitting her body in half. Half became earth. Half the heavens. He created night and day, the moon and clouds, causing them to water the earth, which made the Tigris and Euphrates. He captured the other opposing gods and monsters and broke their weapons. He took Kingu to the Angel of Death, Uggae, and the Igigi (heavenly gods) suggested Marduk sacrifice Kingu. Marduk took the "Tablet of Destiny" and killed him.

Then Marduk made humanity by mixing Kingu's blood with dirt from Tiamat's corpse. Man's task is to serve the gods.

Marduk placed three hundred gods in the heavens and six hundred on earth.

What can we infer? Let me summarize.

1. Claim. Before the world's creation, there were one male and one female god. Both were in water form. Conclusion. Gods existed before the world.

2. The original two gods made other gods. Conclusion. Some gods weren't original.

3. Gods irritated one another. Conclusion. Gods aren't perfect.

4. Marduk is the supreme god. Conclusion. All gods are not equal. There are greater and lesser gods.

5. Marduk slew Tiamat. Conclusion. Gods can die.

6. Apsu had a halo. Marduk had weapons before creating earth. Conclusion. There is some form of matter outside this world.

7. Marduk made earth from Tiamat's rotting corpse. Conclusion. The world is not "good."

8. Marduk caused clouds to rain, forming the Tigris and Euphrates. Conclusion. Earth existed before rain and flowing water.

9. Marduk made humanity from Tiamat's corpse and Kingu's blood, Conclusion. Humanity is not "good."

10. Ea put Apsu to sleep by a spell. Conclusion. Magic is real.

11. Marduk made man to serve the gods. Conclusion. Humanity's reason for existence is to be a servant or slave. Conclusion. That implies gods need something that man supplies.

Conclusion. This story is self-contradicting. Marduk could not "capture" a Tablet of Destiny from someone who could command what he wanted and it not be denied.

At the next meeting, Kikkuli wore his characteristic conceited smirk, advertising he'd pulled off something special. Havram challenged him, "Okay, Kikkuli, what's the coup you've performed?

"Been working with the harness masters. Got a solution hooking horses to the chariot. Want to see?"

Klymenos tilted his head, "Does water run downhill? Is grass green? Don't ask stupid questions. Lead on."

Klymenos and Havram followed him to the edge of the grove, where Kikkuli had tied up his horse team. He'd hitched them to the harness master's cart. Kikkuli explained each part of the rigging. He put his hand on each rigging piece and explained its purpose, "The horse has a chest strap with five encased ropes in a leather cover. That spreads the force of the load he's pulling. The chest strap connects on both sides to a girth wrapping vertically behind the front legs. The girth performs several roles. First, it stabilizes the chest strap so it won't move. That prevents the rope burn from our original tests. The girth has three leather-encased ropes. These braid together so only one protrudes. Like the chest strap, this spreads the load."

Kikkuli stepped beside the girth strap, "One end of the girth rope exits above the chest strap and holds a bronze ring. The bottom end encircles from underneath. Run the rope's end through the ring and tighten. Tie a cow hitch knot, holding the girth in place."

Kikkuli put his hand on a wooden collar fitting over the top of the girth. It had an upside-down "U" shape. "The collar's flat inside rests against the horse. The horse collar goes on after tying the girth. The collar ties with clove hitches to the girth using three small ropes on each side. That transfers the cart's load. Note the bronze post on top.

"Pointing to the top of the collar, the yoke joining the horses has a hole fitting over the collar post. Bronze pins join the yoke to the collar. Now let's go round the horse and look at the how the cart's tongue hooks to the yoke."

The three walked between the horses. The yoke went from the girth post horizontally until no longer over the horse. Then, it curved down level with the horse's chest straps midway between the horses. The cart tongue rested on the yoke by the same bronze post and pin attachment as the horse collar. "By lowering the yoke, we put the cart's load force at the same height as the horse's chest strap."

He stepped back and the same smirk reappeared on his face. "Well, what do you think?" Without waiting for an answer, he continued, "Want a ride?"

"Is the sky blue? You keep asking stupid questions," Klymenos said. The three men climbed in and Kikkuli took them for a fifteen-minute tour around the upper plain.

The horses had no problem pulling the weight, but occasionally they fought each other for control. Kikkuli explained, "The horses have learned to feel each other pulling the yoke, but they haven't had enough time to learn to work together. That comes with time. Give me two months and they'll act as a team. Reworded, I can handle this. Yes, the Hurrian horses are smaller. I'll need to fit them with their own rigging. And yes, I'll need three months to train the team. But, ensuring we have a working solution is complete. This works. There's just one caution. I'll need the chariot at least three months before we have to perform. We don't have a working chariot.

Finally, the cartwrights completed the chariot. But, two more months passed before testing. They'd lost one of the horses when good weather allowed its owner to plow earlier than normal.

They led the horses out of town and hooked them up to the chariot. Kikkuli and Havram climbed aboard. Kikkuli slowly walked the horses up the road to the Ur plain, but instead of turning left toward The Place, they turned right into the open grasslands used to pasture Ur's animals. Klymenos followed them on foot.

At a slow walk, they could feel the unevenness in wheel balance in the cart floor under them. It rocked gently up and down, side to side. But, it was bearable.

Havram pointed out the straw manikin target he had stationed in the open field. "Kikkuli, can you slow-walk the cart parallel to the target and fifty yards away?"

"You got it, Havram."

The first six bows Havram had contracted were drying. He carried the compound bow he had bought. Kikkuli made three passes, Havram shooting three arrows each one. Havram consistently hit the target, but cart rocking threw off the aim. Precision shooting was impossible. The arrows were all over the target.

After the third pass, Havram collected the arrows and climbed aboard again. He didn't want to confuse hits and misses from a second pass with the first. "Kikkuli, I've got a bad feeling about this. Let's try a fast walk at fifty yards."

Again, they made three passes. The rocking cart started vibrating and shaking. Havram had no stable platform as a base for him to stand. He only hit the target once.

Collecting the arrows again, they tried a third pass at a trot. The cart wiggled, wobbled, and shook. They had to hold onto the handrails to stay on the cart. Kikkuli brought the horses to a slow walk and stopped the cart at Klymenos. "Klymenos, the wheels are useless. At a trot, I can hardly hold the cart steady, let alone allow Havram to shoot. This won't work."

They were silent on the return to Ur. They had used four months. They had seven left before the Hurrian horses arrived and needed to begin training. For the chariot, they were at square one with no solution in sight.

Chapter 11

George Washington University, Washington, DC—Present

George Washington University occupies multiple city blocks off 23rd and Virginia. It was a nontrivial task to explore the labyrinthine professors' offices, but finally the name on the door matched the name on the card in his hand. Since the door was already open, Doctor Scortun knocked softly on the door jam. The man inside had an opened book in his lap and sandaled feet on his desk; slovenly appearance in disheveled clothes, about fifty with gray streaks and his hair in a ponytail. His office was in complete disarray, the wall bookcase overflowing, stacks of books on the floor and chairs, piled on his desk, many still opened. David had to remind himself he came for this man's knowledge and wisdom, not appearances.

The man put his book on top of an already overflowing pile and came around to meet him, hand extended, "Yes, yes, you must be Doctor Scortun, I presume?"

"Please call me David." David detected a hint of a British Isles accent lingering under the American English veneer.

"Mine's Miles, Doctor. Please have a seat." Looking around the room for an unoccupied chair to point to, he discovered there weren't any. He removed the stack from the nearest chair and unceremoniously dropped it on the floor. Moving the chair beside the desk, he motioned for David to sit down and resumed his desk chair. "Yes, yes, David, what can I help you with?"

"I've got several questions I don't have the experience to resolve. Let me explain: a donor has given us an artifact, a rectangular sun-hardened clay tablet fourteen by sixteen inches by one and a half thick. The tablet contains a hundred eighty-seven seal imprints spanning the history of the donor's family. The clay tablet rests on a linen garment bed, encased in a wooden container. That garment matches the Biblical description of the Hebrew and Jewish high priest's ephod. The garment has an inner breast pocket fitting the tablet. The donor insists the tablet, not the garment, is the ephod. What he didn't know was that, contained within the clay, was a bluestone tablet replica of the Aubrey holes of the first construction phase of Stonehenge."

Miles' eyebrows went up. "Stonehenge?"

"Yes, Stonehenge. The donor did not know where the specimen originated. However, we've carbon-dated the garment and box. They date to 1750 BCE +/-45 years. Pollen analysis corroborates the garment has been in the upper Tigris-Euphrates river valley, the Palestinian Levant, and southwest England. The first five seal imprints as recorded in cuneiform are Havram, Abraham, Isaac, Jacob, and Israel."

Miles' eyebrows stayed up and his eyes got bigger.

David let the information sink in, then continued. "We thought Havram was Abraham's father or grandfather, but the Bible states his father is Terah and grandfather Nahor.

"My first question: The Bible states that Abraham's original name was Abram. Could the cuneiform written name pronounced Havram be identical with the Hebrew Abram?"

Miles calmed down and began thinking. He rummaged through his bookcase for a Hebrew Bible. "As I understand your question, we need to resolve two separate issues.

"The first difference is the 'H' at the name's beginning. I'm looking at Genesis 12:1, where Abram begins with an aleph. Aleph is an unvoiced letter—a placeholder with no sound. The 'A' sound comes from the vowel symbol in small dots and lines below the consonant. It's a philologist mantra that unvoiced letters were originally voiced, but the language changed. The original sound is unknown. An example: in old English the 'K' in knight used to sound 'ka-nikt'. To think the unvoiced aleph's original voicing was an 'H' is reasonable. 'H' is a glottal sound—like a puff of air. Another example: Biblical Koine Greek had no 'H'. You had to memorize whether a word beginning with a vowel had a voiced or unvoiced 'H' sound at the beginning. Later scribes added a comma above a word beginning with a vowel. If there was a no 'voiced-sound' before the first letter, the comma pointed to the word's beginning. If there was a 'voiced-sound', the comma pointed into the word and was voiced as an 'H'. So dropping the 'H' glottal sound makes perfect sense in this case.

"Now for the proposed 'V' to 'B' change. A 'B' in English is a bi-labial, meaning it is voiced using both lips, whereas the 'V' is a fricative labio-dental, meaning it uses the lower lip against the upper teeth. These are closely related even in English. In some languages such as Spanish, the difference is only a voiced or unvoiced bi-labial fricative. Don't let the technical words confuse you; it simply means that in some languages they are essentially interchangeable. For example, in Hebrew one letter represents both 'B' and 'V.' In six hundred CE, Jewish scribes added a dot within the 'B' to tell them apart. Only after 600 can we be sure which sound to use. So a 1750 BCE cuneiform Havram and Hebrew Abram are likely the same man."

David nodded. "Thank you. I was hoping I wasn't completely crazy. The second question is more speculative. The Stonehenge of Abraham's time was settled by a proto-Celtic people. It is a reasonable assumption that they spoke a pre-Welsh language. The Bible records that Abraham left Ur of the Chaldeans to go to the Palestinian Levant. The only Ur in the Bible and that archaeologists have been able to locate is Ur of the Sumerians in the south. The very fact that the Bible doesn't record him simply leaving Ur, but specifies Ur of the Chaldeans, means that Abraham left from somewhere else than the Sumerian Ur.

"The Chaldeans may mean further up the Tigris to the area later ruled by the Assyrians. That land was also known earlier as the land of the Chaldeans. The problem is that we have very good records throughout history and there has never been a city or area named Ur in this region.

"What if the Ur of the Chaldeans was actually at Stonehenge? We would have to assume there would be at least a loose connection between modern Welsh and Gaelic and the proto-Celtic language. We couldn't be assured the pronunciation and spelling would be precisely consistent. But, what if it resembled an "O'ur Chall Dia" translated loosely as 'Pray silently to the wise God.' O'ur is to pray silently, chall is wise, and dia is God. If passed down by word of mouth for a thousand years until the Bible was recorded in the form we have it today in the exile in Babylon, would the recorders have presented it in the only form that made sense to them at the time: Ur of the Chaldeans?"

Miles thought for a minute. "That's is a good proposal. All the tonal shifts that would be necessary for that to happen follow the standard patterns of language change. There are no exceptions. The only problem is that we have no known proto-Celtic writings to verify it, so it will have to remain a conjecture."

"Thank you," David sighed. "That confirmed what I suspected, but couldn't be certain. The last question is more difficult. The English word ephod is a transliteration of the Hebrew letters 'aleph'-'pe'-'dalet'. When the 'pe' has an inside dot it has the pronunciation 'pe,' but when it doesn't, it is 'fe.' We're into that 'which is the original one' question? I will offer a premise based on three assumptions:

"1. Assume the present record reflects the original no-dotted 'f.'

"2. Assume Hebrew absorbed the word 'ephod' almost unchanged from another language.

"3. Assume the original language was spoken at Stonehenge.

"We know Abraham lived in the 1700s BCE. That is the time frame of the Beaker culture, who had a Proto-Indo-European language. The Celtic peoples absorbed the Beaker culture peacefully when they arrived around 800 BCE. A peaceful merging likely means the two peoples and their languages were similar.

"This set of assumptions might indicate what conclusion? The original language might have two words which combined when absorbed into Hebrew. So ephod might originally have been 'ef fod.' In modern Welsh ef means 'he/him,' and fod means '(to) be.' These are both root words in languages and therefore resist change. Could the sentence in English mean 'he is'?"

"No, no," broke in Miles. "You don't understand. Welsh doesn't work that way. Welsh and all the other Celtic-Gaelic languages have VSO (verb-subject-object) word structure, not SVO (subject-verb-object) like English. The verb comes first in Welsh. So *ef-fod* would have to be *fod-ef* in Welsh, and that wouldn't make ephod. The only way you could get ephod is if some country bumpkin from another language went to Stonehenge, stayed just long enough to learn the language basics, and then reversed the individual Welsh words."

David smiled, "That's exactly what I'm saying. Abram was a country bumpkin."

Miles caught on fast. His trying to challenge the possibility of ephod's meaning had just showed it to be the most likely explanation.

The two men were silent for a minute, then Miles had a thought. He searched his Hebrew Bible for a minute, "Yes, yes, here it is: Exodus 3:14. The passage is the 'burning bush in the wilderness.' God says, 'I am who I am.' Transliterated, the letters are 'aleph-he-vav-he.' In English that's 'a-h-w-h.' The 'he-vav-he' is the verb 'to be,' and the aleph means first person singular 'I.' In the next verse it says, 'this is my name for ever.' But what happened? In the following verse, and for the rest of the Bible, the first letter of God's name changes from 'aleph' to 'yod,' third-person singular—'y.' That's how we get YHWH (Yahweh): 'yod-he-vav-he,' not 'I am,' but 'he is.' In other words, in Exodus God originally said, 'My name is 'I am.' But the Hebrew immediately reverts to the name of God they had used since the time of Abraham four hundred fifty years earlier: 'he is,' not 'I am.' The only difference is that *fod-ef* (ephod) is a Proto-Indo-European Welsh and 'yhwh' is a Hebrew word. In both languages the meaning translates 'he is.'"

Both men sat in silence; both were flabbergasted.

****

O'UR OF THE CHALL DIA

April 1750 BC

Klymenos' wheel proved a difficult problem. The Ur wheelwrights were no more capable than Mycenae's. Every double-layer wheel proved unstable. After three months, the unavoidable forced the three men to surrender. Their present technology wouldn't work. They had to conjure an invention.

At their weekly review in the Scots Pine grotto, the three men sat in silence for five minutes. Finally, Havram spoke. "I haven't got solutions, but can we think through the problem? Let's start with the basic idea: what is a wheel?"

"Are you crazy?" asked Klymenos. "What is a wheel? A wheel is a wheel!"

"That's not what I'm saying," answered Havram. "Look, see if you can follow my logic. A wheel has three parts. One: to spin on an axle, the hub's inner diameter must match the axle's outer diameter. Two: the wheel's outside rim must hold the riding platform above rocks. Three: the hub must connect to the rim. Nothing says the wheel must be solid or one piece. Have I made sense?"

"You are crazy," repeated Klymenos.

"Hold on, Klymenos," Kikkuli said, "maybe Havram has something. Maybe he's crazy smart rather than crazy dumb." He turned to Havram, "If we split the wheel into three separate parts, can we solve each part's problems individually? If we can, when we reconnect the pieces, will the result have separate problems?"

Havram replied, "I don't know, but we're getting nowhere solving the wheel as a whole. If we solve each part's problems, the whole may work. It's worth a try."

Klymenos was skeptical. "Look, there's an old saying: don't try to reinvent the wheel."

Kikkuli handled that one, "But, that's what we have to do. If we want to invent a chariot, we have to invent a new wheel first."

Klymenos hung his head, "My family is going to disown me."

Havram spoke up, "You'll be the black sheep of your family?"

Kikkuli chimed in, "No, he'll be the goat of the family. The black goat."

Havram added, "The hircus agagrus goat."

Klymenos looked back and forth, trying to follow the conversation's logic. And couldn't. Now both Klymenos and Kikkuli looked at Havram, puzzled looks on their faces. Havram apologized, "Sorry, it's a shepherd's joke. You have to know the context. Let's move on. You know the lost wax method molders use making one-of-a-kind jewelry? What if we used it to make a hub? Shape the wax on the axle. The wax melts when melted bronze hits it. The resulting hub will match the axle."

Kikkuli asked, "That only makes the hub's inside round. How can we get the outside balanced so it won't spin lopsided?"

Havram continued, "Spin the hub. The heavier side settles down. Shave off wax until it doesn't stop in any particular place. Now it's balanced. The problem is that I've never seen the lost wax method scaled up for the size of a hub. Has anyone? Do you think we can do it?"

Klymenos thought for a minute, "I've never watched a caster plying his trade. But I've seen god statues having more bronze than our hub. So, someone should know how. We can scour the village for someone willing to try."

Kikkuli asked, "But if the wax has the same inner diameter as the axle's outside, won't the wheel bind?"

Havram answered, "No. After we make the hub, we put the axle back on the lathe. Shaving off another thin layer provides a gap for melted tallow grease. That solves the hub. But, I'm stumped on the wheel rim."

It was Klymenos' turn, "I know that solution. In my country's mountains, we have tall trees growing straight and round for thirty feet. They're two or two-and-a-half feet thick. Since it's a cold climate tree, the tree probably grows here. The locals would know. Two side-by-side cuts through the trunk would produce matching outside diameters. I had worried about cutting them to an identical thickness, but it isn't necessary. Neither individual wheel affects the other. We can cut them to identical outside diameter, then shaving them creates balance."

No one said anything. They hadn't tackled the last piece: the connector between the hub and the rim. They postponed that discussion until the following week.

No sooner had the three left than the observer exited the tunnel. *They're right, the wheel is a tough problem.*

That afternoon the observer visited the Ur jewelers. Yes, they did small-piece lost wax jewelry. They'd never tried something large. Could they try? If they could get wax.

Two days later a blond-haired gentleman left a sheep as payment. He stipulated it was for chariot wheel-hubs, and another man would teach them how to build it.

The man also went to the carpenters to order a tree-trunk section one foot thick and two feet in diameter. He paid for it with a suckling lamb. He stated it was for chariot wheels. Another man would tell them how to build them.

No one had seen the man before. This time he left no name.

The following week the three friends met in the Scots Pine grove for their design progress review. The first agenda item was the wheel. Havram could tell from the way his two friends didn't make eye contact that they hadn't thought of a solution. *That's too bad*, he thought. *If anyone would have an insight, it would be Klymenos with his family's background in cart-making. Oh well, I can at least propose something to keep the project going.*

Havram spoke. "This is going to sound crazy; it even sounds crazy to me. I have a working idea."

At these words, his companions looked up and paid attention.

"Start with the rim. Drill four one-inch diameter holes through the rim from the outside in. We space these equidistant around the rim. To get that, measure using four right-angle triangles butted together. We want our wheel to be two inches in width. That will finish the rim portion.

"Next, the hub. Drill four one-inch deep holes into the hub wax casting equidistant around the hub and one inch deep.

"Finally: the connector between hub and rim. Suppose we use the bow-lathe to turn a one-inch diameter straight branch. We make it the same diameter for four feet. Once that's done, cut it into four roughly one-foot lengths, then put all four in a line and cut them to the same length. These one-foot-long rods we'll call 'spokes.' They'll fit through the rim holes into the hub holes. They'll all be exactly alike, so the wheel should balance.

"Now comes the unbelievable part. How do we keep the spokes from coming back out? First, wrap the wheel twice around with something whose thickness is constant. I recommend trying birch bark. We can pound on it until it's flat. There are two problems. How do we keep the birch attached to the wheel? Glue will help, but glue alone isn't strong enough. And bark is weak. So we reinforce the birch with two windings of soaked leather so it shrinks onto the wheel as it dries. We then wrap each strip's edges around the wheel's edge and sew the two sides together on the rim's inside. When fully dry, it will shrink and conform to the wheel's diameter, making the leather tight and fitting exactly to the rim. The longest leather strip a cow or horse will yield from rear end around the chest to the other rear end is about twelve feet. That's also the length we need to wrap around the wheel two times. I'll call the leather wrapping a 'tire'. This tire will wear overtime, but it should last fifty miles before it needs replacement. That should demonstrate a working invention. Now, am I still crazy?"

"Yeah, my friend," Kikkuli said, "like I intimated earlier, you're crazy all right—crazy smart. What do you think, Klymenos, you think it's worth trying?"

"I agree. It won't even delay the project." he answered, "Remember, we've lost the horses during plowing season until mid-June anyway."

No sooner had the three left than the observer exited the tunnel. *They're right, Havram was crazy smart.*

The following day a blond-haired man visited the tanner. He ordered a pair of two-foot-wide fourteen-foot-long strips of leather. He stated someone would specify how to craft it.

The following day Klymenos and Havram visited the tanner, discovering the material needed was available for someone building a chariot.

Klymenos was unsuspecting. He stated they were building the chariot, and described how to craft the material.

Havram read the clues for their meaning. There were five people who knew the word chariot. Three of them coined the word. The fourth was a spy. The fifth was the spy's accomplice, Hirben.

How did Havram know? Because the first two times Hirben had mentioned his name, but not since. That meant the spy told Hirben he made a mistake leaving his name. And the only way the spy could know was overhearing that they knew Hirben's name.

It confirmed a spy was stealing their ideas.

When the three inventors took their ideas to the jewelers and wheelwrights, it immediately caused a confrontation.

There was a donnybrook impasse with the wheelwrights. The owner of the business, Bricriu, steadfastly refused to build anything but traditional two-layer wheels, "I refuse to be a laughingstock and suffer loss of my reputation by indulging some fly-by-night candidates' unrealistic fantasies."

The other casus belli was between the two professions. First was the wheelwrights claiming that only they could build wheels. Likewise, the jewelers claimed that only they could build the hub. Both factions stood on their high ground. No amount of persuasion. reasoning, or cajolery by Klymenos, Kikkuli, and Havram would make either budge.

Finally, out of options, the trio reported to the council that, not due to any effort on their part, they would not be able to complete their project. They asked for guidance. They were told to wait a week or two and the council would get back with them.

A few days later, Coth announced her hut companion, the housemaid for the next candidate's hut, would be preparing their meals for the next three days. She and her children were going to visit her sister Rhosin and her husband Hirben.

At the word Hirben, Havram almost gasped in surprise. He asked, "Hirben's the blond shepherd, right?"

The information surprised Coth, "Why, yes. I didn't know you'd met him."

Havram replied smoothly, "Oh, I haven't met him, someone told me about him."

Havram had connected the dots, but Coth couldn't. She never realized she disclosed the clue solving the spy problem.

Havram mulled what he'd learned about the spy. *The puzzling reasons Hirben never came to collect the goods now made sense. There was a spy. But the spy was an ally, not competitor.* That quelled his harbored doubts.

Havram had all the clues needed to identify the observer. He went to his team's Scots Pine grotto, methodically searching the bordering grottos. Finally, in the grotto directly opposite how they always entered, he found the observer's tunnel. Dug into the ground, branches with leaves strewn over the top covered it.

As he thought, it was obvious why they missed seeing it. They only looked into the bordering grottoes; they didn't go in. The only way to see the observer's hiding place was from the far side.

He ducked down, peering inside. *It's small. I couldn't fit. It's too small for me. If I tried, I'd disturb the tunnel.*

I need to decide how to use this knowledge.

Four days later, the three friends were in the Scots Pine grotto, ready to start another review session. Just before they were to start, Havram held up his hand for silence from his companions.

He spoke loudly, "Oh no, it's starting to rain. Let's open the tarpaulin and climb under until the rain stops." He turned and faced the hidden tunnel, calling out, "Sarrai, before it gets too muddy in there, do you want to join us under the tarpaulin?"

A loud gasp sounded from the tunnel and a small red-haired form rapidly backed out, turned, and disappeared as fast as she could run.

Havram smiled. *Now we can work in peace.*

The following week, Dygsu asked the three inventors to remain after breakfast. A half-hour later, he returned with a man he introduced as Ansgar. They recognized him as the man making the axels. He announced that he was the new owner of the carpenter shop and had already made an agreement with the jewelers for the hubs.

Morthwyl asked, "But what of Bricriu?"

"Arwain, Deallus, and Brysur met with him. He refused to budge. They reminded him that the agreement allowing him to work in O'ur was that he would support whatever inventions the candidates required, successful or not. Bricriu still refused. Whereupon they reminded him that he might own the business, but the college owned the building and every invention made by the candidates, such as the turn-bow. They revoked their orders for wagons—over 80 percent of his orders. Last, they ordered him to vacate the building and his house, which was also the property of the college. Bricriu has left O'ur.

"First, they asked me to manage the carpenter shop. I accepted. Then they showed me a letter from the King of Washukkari. If the chariot proves successful, he wants to order ten more. I would be honored to make your chariot wheels. When can I start?"

"Ysgrifennydd, the oldest story is Sumerian. Here goes."

Time existed before god's pantheon. Only the earth and heaven existed. With no sunlight or moonlight, all was dark. The earth was green and water was in the ground. Because there was no light, there was no vegetation. At first Anunna and Anunnaki were the two most powerful gods and lived with Anu in heaven. But Anunna came to be the god of the underworld, heading the seven judges.

In the beginning, gods had to work to live. Anunna made a category of inferior gods to work for the superior gods, but they rebelled and refused to work. So, Enki made humans so they could continue making the food needed by gods.

Okay. What conclusions can we draw?

1. The world and heaven existed before time, before light, and before the gods. Conclusion. Gods did not create heaven and earth.

2. Question. There is no story how light began. Conclusion. Although there was green (vegetation) before light, it couldn't grow.

3. Anunna changed from a heavenly to an underworld god. Conclusion. Gods do not have set duties. Superior gods can become inferior gods.

4. At first gods had to work to grow food to eat. Conclusion. Gods are not self-sufficient. They depend on food from the earth.

5. The superior gods created inferior gods to do the work for them. Conclusion. Gods can be of unequal status.

6. Enki created humans to provide food for the gods. Conclusion. Humanity's task is to provide food for the gods.

7. This story is self-contradictory. The gods Anu, Anunna, and Anunnaki existed before light. What did they eat?

Sarrai benefited from a fortunate event. Every year, three days after the summer solstice, the graduating class of new Servants left for their homeland throughout Europe and the Middle East. Many of the children and young adults of Ur routinely accompanied them to Solent Bay. By chance Sarrai was with the group this year, and the day they traveled happened to be the June day the mackerel returned to the bay. This day marked an annual festival for the bay fishermen.

When the Ur party reached Solent around noon, they found flowers decorating windows, music, dancing, fresh mackerel cooking on the coals, and a freshly slaughtered cow and pig on spits, slowly roasting over their fires. The mayor came to greet them, "Welcome, welcome to the Solent Mackerel Festival. We would like to invite you to stay for the feast as our guests. Your ships won't leave until late afternoon."

A new servant asked, "What's a mackerel?"

"A mackerel is a small fish. Once a year they come to spawn in the bay. They almost jump into the nets. We celebrate with a feast by opening last year's barrels."

"Last year's barrels? What's in the barrels?"

"Please stay and find out."

The combination of free alcohol, free feasting, and their ships not leaving convinced everyone to accept. They started serving soon afterwards.

When the mayor asked if anyone would like to see the barrels opened, Sarrai jumped at the chance to see something new. When the bakers removed the first lid, she was underwhelmed, "It's just fish."

"No," the Mayor said, "it only looks like 'just fish'. Let me show you something. Dip your finger into the brine and taste it."

She put her finger in halfway and put it to her mouth, "It doesn't taste like fish, it only tastes salty."

The Mayor asked for a small slice of cow-meat. He tore it in half, giving one-half to Sarrai, "Taste this."

Sarrai put it into her mouth, "It tastes like ordinary cow-meat, good, but nothing special."

The Mayor smiled and gave her the other half, "Now dip this in the fish broth."

The beefiness of the meat exploded in her mouth, three times as intense as the first morsel she'd just tasted. She closed her eyes, the better to savor the sensation in her mouth. "That's magic," she said when her taste buds came back to normal.

The Mayor bore a broad smile, "Now you know why we celebrate the return of the mackerel for another year. Would you like a half-gallon jar to take back with you?"

"Oh, could I? Of course I would."

"We'd be glad to. Promise me that, when you get back, you'll let Arwain and Deallus know we'll be sending them their jars on tomorrow's salt wagon."

On the walk home, the jar carefully cradled in her arms, she pondered this jar and her new knowledge. How could she use it? This find was exactly what she needed to lure her future husband with his estimation of her cooking skills, and the husband she was angling to catch was Havram.

Sarrai began drizzling a thin coating of fish sauce on every meat serving she gave Havram. The adage of the best way to a man's heart is through his stomach proved correct, and Havram was an unsuspecting victim. Sarrai knew her cooking would lure Havram's stomach onto her hook. Then she must figure out a way to maneuver him into her net.

Sarrai began trading off the evening meals with her mother: one day Coth, the next Sarrai. As Sarrai's expertise grew, the candidates she cooked for noticed the change. They began expecting evening meals for the days Sarrai cooked. No one wanted to be tardy for her dinners; only scraps would remain.

The long-awaited day arrived—the first six bows were ready. A five-member progression—Havram, Kikkuli, Klymenos, and the bowmakers—walked up the hill to the targets. The bowmakers also couldn't contain their enthusiasm.

The range had two firing lanes. The first had a target at seventy-five yards—the maximum self-bow accuracy range. The second had firing distance markers every five yards from eighty to two hundred yards. Havram went to the second.

Turning to the bowmakers, Havram asked them to open the package of bows. "May I please have the oak bow."

Giving it some tentative pulls, Havram warned, "This feels stiff. Don't be surprised if this doesn't work."

It didn't. The arrow only flew eighty-five yards.

Walnut did better, going ninety-five. Aspen matched the hundred twenty range of the compound bow Havram had brought. Birch with deer bone performed the best, going a hundred thirty.

Havram asked for the two other birch bows. The birch with cow bone and tendon flew a hundred yards. Havram took two deep breaths, and pulled on the birch with ibex bone and tendon. The arrow flew downrange one-hundred forty yards.

Havram went to the target range. He fired five arrows in quick succession, discovering how high above the target he needed to aim to give the arrow the right trajectory. He noticed a jerk before the arrow left the string.

Oh-oh, he thought. *That's what I was afraid of. The bone thickness and length don't match what ibex needs.*

Taking aim, he launched ten arrows. He got nine hits at seventy-five yards, but all over the target. The jerking was random.

Not noticing the jerkiness, his companions were ecstatic, "Havram, it works."

"Don't get your hopes up. Remember, this bow doesn't have the range we need. Wait until we get the improved strength bow. Remember, the different glue may have other issues."

I've got to hope, don't I, thought Havram.

Ur's entire population fixated on innovation. The town's population competed at being the best at their profession. That included housemaids. Ur had an annual cooking competition with two contests. The first was a compulsory dish, such as a beef roast stew. Apart from the meat, they could alter any remaining ingredients. The second was open; the cook could prepare any dish.

Finally, the improved-strength glue bow was ready. The five men lined up at the distance range. Taking some test pulls, Havram felt the improved resilience. He let fly three arrows at a forty-five-degree angle. Two flew a hundred fifty-five yards and the third a hundred sixty.

Smiles graced four faces as they moved to the accuracy range. Havram was the lone dissenter; the others couldn't see the jerkiness that Havram could feel.

His worst fear happened. The imbalanced load transfer from compression to tension resulted in erratic arrow release. One shot in ten hit.

Havram was thinking as they trudged back. *Thank The Divine that last week I hired the hunters to bag two more ibex. That will give us four shoulder bones—enough for four bows. Bow length, bone length and bone thickness must balance. I need to spend time talking over one last round of bows with the bowmakers. One of the four bows must work. Or . . . we don't become servants.*

I also need to ask the fletcher for thirty arrows made to fit the compound bow. The length and weight need adjustments.

Havram didn't sleep well that night.

"Ysgrifennydd, if you thought the Babylonian and Sumerian stories were weird, you haven't heard anything yet. The Etruscan is in a different category."

There is no creation story.

Matter doesn't exist."

Everything is an expression of the gods.

Mortal man cannot persuade or dissuade the gods.

Where our neighbors believe lightning is a result of the collision of two clouds, we believe the clouds collide so they can release lightning.

Nothing has meaning in itself. It happens so it can have a meaning.

"This is so different, I'm not sure how to summarize it. However, let's commit it to writing and I'll think on it. Ready?"

1. There is no matter, everything is an expression of one or more gods.

2. A reworded account of the clouds. Clouds do not cause lightning and thunder. That is a beginning-cause to aftereffect. What happens is the gods desire thunder—the effect. So, they create the cause—the clouds colliding. The thunder is primary, the clouds are incidental. Only the thunder has meaning.

3. Question. Mankind cannot influence the gods by what they do or fail to do. So why offer sacrifices?

4. Question. If man has no meaning, why is there man at all?

It seemed an eternity, but was only three months. Not unexpectedly, because they'd never attempted anything with the hub's mass, the jewelers didn't succeed at first. But they honed their techniques. The second hub produced a smoothly spinning wheel. And the wheelwrights had time to rebuild the chariot.

When the three friends performed their test, there was no imbalance. The acid test was holding a jar of water with the British horses at sprint speed. There were no waves on the water's surface—their design worked. They had a functioning chariot.

Their remaining problem was the bow, where there was no discernable progress. They had nine months left.

A breathless candidate rushed through the door, "The horses are here. The horses are here." That emptied the hut. Kikkuli was the first to the dock. Most candidates had seen their chariot testing and there was significant interest throughout the candidates. A good portion of the townspeople also gathered at the dock.

One horse had already crossed the river, another was on the raft, and a third on the far bank with their handler, waiting its turn. The handler was an old friend of Kikkuli, hired to look after the horses.

Few had seen this horse-breed before. They didn't have the heavy British workhorse musculature. Smaller by several hands, they were more lean. But they also pranced. Even to the uninitiated, it was obvious that these were bred to run.

When the last had crossed the river, Kikkuli made an announcement to the gathered onlookers, "May I have your attention, please. We'll take the horses to the stable for tonight. They need to rest from the rigors of the trip the same as we would. Anyone interested meet us in the upland pasture plain tomorrow morning an hour after breakfast. We'll need to see if any of the horses have suffered any ill-effect during the trip, and a part of that will be a speed demonstration. Everyone is welcome. I thank you all."

The excited murmuring from the crown suggested many would attend.

Kikkuli and the handler led the horses to their stable, fed them, and put them in their stalls for the night. The handler had brought a letter, which he gave to Kikkuli, who took it to Ysgrifennydd.

"Yes, Kikkuli, it is written in cuneiform, so I can read the letter for you. However, you need to understand the advantages and disadvantages of cuneiform. Each cuneiform symbol records the sound of a single syllable, so the same symbol is used for the same syllable sound, no matter what the language. I can read the syllables in the order in which they're written. That's the good news. The bad news is that I don't know Hurrian, the language this letter records. So I can read the syllables in the correct order, but cuneiform does not record which syllables belong to which words so I won't know where the word breaks are supposed to be. Likewise, I won't know where the sentence breaks are. You'll have to interpret these as I read the syllables. There are also just over nine hundred symbols, so I may not remember some symbols that your language uses and will have to look them up." With that introduction, he began reading:

"Dear son.

First, your mother and I want you to know how proud we are of you.

In case one of the horses is injured in the trip, we have sent Tushtrata, your old friend, with three horses. In addition, we have sent money to care and feed them and for the return trip. We look forward to seeing you with a fod-ef in your tunic.

Mom and Dad

It was all Kikkuli could do to avoid letting a tear of joy fall down his face.

In the morning, instead of the seventy-five or so Kikkuli expected, the news of the demonstration had spread and over two hundred spectators gathered to watch.

Kikkuli didn't disappoint them. His father and mother had sent horses already superlatively trained. Two of the three were ones Kikkuli already knew, and who knew and trusted him, so they enabled Kikkuli to put on a show. With a guide stick, he first walked the horses, then trotted, pranced, and danced them. Oohs and aahs sounded from the audience. Last he had Tushtrata lead them a quarter-mile away and line them up. With a drop of the stick, the horses took off in a full gallop, thundering at top speed to the stick's prompting of a finish line. No one in the audience had even seen horses run like the wind in a full gale. The audience first gawked, then gasped, and finally tried to put their eyes back in their sockets. The applause continued a full five minutes. Kikkuli announced that was the end of the demonstration and thanked them for coming.

He led the horses down the hill to Ur where the fitters already had everything necessary to construct their harnesses. They only needed to get the measurements for each animal.

In two weeks, the wagonmakers would fabricate a new tongue sized for the lower height of the horses. Now, full chariot training could begin in earnest.

Three months before the competition, the judges announced the compulsory dish: an adult goose. The panel would judge on five categories: 1) taste of breast meat, 2) taste of thigh meat, 3) juiciness, 4) tenderness, and 5) crispness of skin. Every three weeks for three months the panel would provide a thirteen-pound practice bird, five in all. The panel would judge using a thirteen-pound bird.

Sarrai checked with the most experienced cooks. They were glad to help because they didn't expect competition from a twelve-year-old girl. But Sarrai was no ordinary twelve-year-old. A goose, like a duck, is all dark meat, but the breasts and legs are different dark meats. They don't cook at the same speed, and they aren't properly cooked at the same temperature. The thighs need a higher temperature and longer time to cook, and, because they contain so much more collagen, when overcooked, they melt their collagen to form a smooth, silky, melt-in-your-mouth texture on the tongue.

True to most first tries, Sarrai's first bird was an unmitigated disaster. She'd removed the bird from the brine too soon. It wasn't juicy. She'd overcooked the breast meat. It dried tough. She'd undercooked the thighs. They were tough. The skin was soggy. The next three experimental birds grew progressively better until, on the fourth practice bird, she'd perfected her techniques. The fifth test bird she served to Havram's hut. The men went wild over the meat, devouring every last morsel.

She developed a simple technique, but she had to perform each step properly.

1. Brine the bird for six hours. Remove and pat dry.

2. Mince four cloves of garlic and four button mushrooms.

3. Melt one tablespoon of butter and cook the garlic for one minute to soften the garlic bite, then stir in the mushrooms until they lost their water and softened.

4. Remove from the heat and allow to cool.

5. Mash the garlic and mushrooms together into a smooth paste.

6. Melt three pounds of butter in the saucepan, then pour in the garlic-mushroom paste and mix thoroughly.

7. Remove from the heat.

8. Allow the mixture to cool until just warm, then pour in three teaspoons of fish sauce and mix until thoroughly blended.

9. Allow mixture to finish cooling and harden.

10. Using a sharpened one-eighth-inch diameter stiff oak twig, poke deep holes all over the bird.

11. Using a blunt-ended one-eighth-inch diameter stiff oak twig, push a small dollop of the butter-garlic-mushroom mixture as far into each hole as possible until the entire mixture is in the bird.

12. Using birch bark, cover the breast meat to shield it from the heat.

13. Cook the bird over medium-high indirect heat for two and a half hours. Every half-hour, turn the bird, heating both sides equally.

14. After two and a half hours, remove the birch bark from the breasts and lightly salt the skin.

15. Return the bird to the medium-high heat for two more hours, rotating every half hour.

16. Cover bird under a heavy garment for thirty minutes to allow the natural bird juices to redistribute evenly. Serve immediately.

"Ysgrifennydd, this is the Mycenaean account."

First came Chawos, but next wide-bosomed Gaia (earth), the ever-sure foundations of Olympus, and dim Tartarus and Eros, fairest among the deathless gods. From Chawos came forth Erebus and black night, but night gave birth to Aether and Day. And Earth brought forth Heaven to cover herself.

"OK. Let's try to summarize the important points."

1. Chawos. It's primary meaning is a gap. But, gaps have two sides. Conclusion. This cosmos is our side. Question. What's on the other? The story doesn't say. Question. Chawos can also mean undifferentiated, but undifferentiated what? Again, the story doesn't say.

2. In some unexplained way three gods first come to be.

3. From the Chawos and black night came the fourth god, Erebus.

4. Black night gave birth to the fifth and sixth gods without copulation.

5. The three first gods are deathless. The story doesn't say what other gods are deathless. This implies some gods can die. That also implies a hierarchy among gods. Some are greater than others.

Let's stop here. I don't need the Hurrians with their Baal and Tessub. It doesn't matter if they make their offerings to the chthonic powers by placing them in offering pits dug into the ground, or believe Baal separated the earth from the sky using a copper sickle.

The various Celtic stories are worse—they form no consistent pattern.

My first problem is discovering an underlying theme. My second is discovering how The Divine fits into this scheme.

"Thank you, Ysgrifennydd; I believe that's it for today."

When the day of the first judging arrived, the judges wouldn't allow Sarrai to put in a separate entry. For the compulsory category, she and her mother stood behind her goose as a pair of contestants. The judges had tasted Coth's cooking for years and unsuspectingly progressed to their entry. As they tasted the samples cut from the breast and thigh, their eyes opened wide, then they reached for a second sample to confirm they weren't hallucinating. The vote was unanimous: Coth and Sarrai were the undisputed winners of the compulsory dish competition. Both meats were juicy and tender, cooked perfectly, and the skin was crisp. The head judge asked Coth how she managed to get everything right at the same time. She didn't answer; she just smiled and advised him to ask Sarrai. He refused to compromise his exalted status by asking a child, so Sarrai never divulged her secrets.

Several weeks went by, during which Havram let these different datum points stew in his subconscious.

One question cleared up his first confusion: Were these stories literal or figurative? If they were literally true, they should agree. The first claimed matter existed before gods. The second said gods existed before matter. The last claimed matter was nonexistent. If literal truth was the criteria, there was no solution to resolving the difference. If only one could be literally true, it was likely none were. Their truth must be figurative. What did that mean?

One of the tales he had heard popped into his mind. It wasn't about creation, so he didn't record it and now he couldn't remember which culture it belonged to. The image was a cupid firing love arrows. Cupid shooting you resulted in instant love with whoever you were with. The cupid wasn't literally real, but sometimes falling in love can be as rapid as a love arrow. In other words, although the literal cupid and love arrow were made up, sometimes falling in love quickly was true. So this story was an example of a myth using physical means to tell a spiritual truth. The physical story was invented; but the spiritual point of the story was true.

Assume they were all trying to tell a spiritual truth. Then the issue wasn't whether these different creation myths were trying to tell *a* spiritual truth. The real problem was: were they trying to tell the *same* spiritual truth. Reworded: was The Divine leading different cultures to understand the same spiritual truth?

He reviewed the various creation myths. Each tried to highlight different spiritual truths. That explained why they didn't align. They weren't trying to be literally true; they were trying to be spiritually true! But, each story had different details because each emphasized different truths.

Every creation myth used the same medium to carry their truth. Stories. People are endless storytellers. We wrap our lives around story. That explained the myths. The creation myths were:

1. Trying to tell a spiritual truth.

2. Using physical events.

3. Wrapped in a story.

4. The facts and story were spiritually, not literally, true.

Suddenly all the creation stories, all their myriad details, fell into place like a jigsaw puzzle. It was 1,000 pieces intricately arranged.

However, he had 1,001 pieces, and only 1,000 fit into the puzzle. The extra piece was the first phrase of the Mycenaean creation story: in the beginning chawos—the gap. This didn't belong to the story. It was disjoint. What story role did it play?

Suddenly it made sense! It didn't belong to the story. It was a literal truth attached before the story began. This piece wasn't a part of the myth puzzle. It wasn't a myth at all.

The only religion founded on literal truth was the religion of The Divine, The Place, and The Road. The religion of The Divine had no myths; it had no stories. The Road was a tangible place. The Divine asked His followers to figure out who He was and what He wanted by logic and revelation.

Was this "in the beginning chawos" The Divine's new revelation? What did that mean?

What should he tell the Council at his interview? He had many questions, and no answers.

Chapter 12

Smithsonian, Washington, DC—Present

David was sitting in his office, both feet on his desk, leaning back, eyes closed, hands joined under his jaw and head propped up with his two index fingers. He was thinking; lost to this world.

Patterns, always follow the patterns. They reveal the "why" behind the specific instance you see before you.

"Ephod" was the confirming link between Stonehenge and the Middle East. It connected the beaker culture language with Hebrew. The stone tablet and garment were crucial archaeological evidence of a previously unknown connection between them. And the context was religious.

The puzzle pieces were starting to fall together in his mind. In the original Stonehenge, the Windmill Hill peoples used the Aubrey Holes. There was no Sarcen Circle or Bluestone ring. These peoples didn't have six pillars like Stonehenge Decoded suggested; they had two. The sequence didn't begin with the pillars in the solstice direction. When they were looking at the rising sun, the pillars were on the right and the left, halfway around, at ninety degrees to the solstice. That explained the Old Testament predilection for "right and left." David's ears could almost hear an old Windmill Hill priest chanting Isaiah 30:21, "And whether you turn to the right, or whether you turn to the left, your ears shall hear a word behind you saying, 'This is the way, walk in it.'" Meaning straight ahead, down the road at the solstice. Or Job 23:9, when it says, "On the left hand I seek him, but I cannot behold him; I turn to the right, but I cannot see him," meaning God had already gone before them down the road, calling for them to follow.

There were at least a dozen references throughout the Bible to "the right and the left," suggesting a deep and enduring collective memory. For twelve hundred fifty years before Abraham, Stonehenge peoples had worshiped here. For another twelve hundred fifty years after Abraham, Hebrew inheritance and language of "right and left" endured in oral memory until codified in the Babylonian exile into the Bible we have today. David could imagine heated arguments between two camps arguing whether to preserve the northern kingdom's version of "Horeb," or the southern one's "Sinai" for the Holy Mountain—and in the end preserved both.

And when the Windmill People died out and the Beaker People assumed control, they built the sarcen stone structure we see today. Did the original fifty-six hole monument die out? No, they preserved it in the ephod tablets each priest carried over their heart.

But what happened to the two original pillars? Once something assumes religious importance, it is never just discarded. They moved the pillars where the straight road curved down the hill to the town. That explained the two post holes on either side of the road: it marked the change from the sacred original straight road to the secular road made by man.

But that happened seven hundred fifty years before Abraham. What meaning did Abraham understand those two rods to have? The clue was the rods didn't rest with the ephod stone in the large pocket—they had their own pocket. That suggested that after the Breaker people built the sarcen circle, they repurposed the pillars for a separate use, apart from the ephod itself. What could that be?

****

O'UR OF THE CHALL DIA

December 1750

Round two of the cooking competition was held a week after the first.

This contest was both easier and harder for Sarrai. It was easier because she believed she had a killer recipe. It was harder because she didn't know what killer recipes other women might have, and she didn't know the judge's preferences. What if they didn't like bread or sweet deserts?

Her sweetener had taken months of learning to prepare. The housemaids used leaves of wild white beets for salads, but discarded the faintly sweet roots. Sarrai collected these leftover roots, thinking to make a root mash as a vegetable. Perhaps the men might like the slightly sweet taste. That proved a bad idea; they didn't like the rough grainy texture, refusing to eat it. By accident she discovered the mash's sweetness leached into water. To get more sweetness from the root, she tried using hot water. As the water cooled, milky white crystals of pure concentrated sweetness solidified. Instead of the crystals depositing onto the mash, she removed the mash before the water cooled. She also used thin, soft horse's mane hairs hung from a stick in the water and discovered the crystals of concentrated sweetness formed on the hairs.

Breaking the coated hairs into small pieces allowed her to mix the sweetener with butter in a hot skillet and whisk it into a brown caramel sauce.

She had her sweetening ingredient, but she needed a recipe. She found a housemaid with a technique for a light, airy bread containing holes for breakfast muffins. Sarrai got a small unbaked sample with its yeast still active. Over several days she mixed in small bits of fresh flour into the sample to allow the yeast to spread into a starter batch large enough to test.

Then she had to find out how to bake the bread in small clay cups three inches deep and three across. When the bread had baked, she used her one-eighth-inch skewer to poke twenty-five holes down into each bread cup. Each hole went near, but didn't hit, the cup's bottom. Next she poured her sweetener mixture over the bread, allowing a half hour for the caramel syrup to seep down into the holes and air pockets in the bread. Warming the bread for serving was the last step.

The men in the hut raved over the new desert creation. If allowed, they would eat rolls for appetizer, supper and desert.

The judges couldn't rave outright, that would have broached proper decorum. But their first bite sealed the victory. Their eyes first opened in surprised delight, then closed to exclude all sensation except caramel cookie-candy sweet roll. Disputes among the judges were particularly contentious deciding who would win second place.

To the wounding of their self-esteem, the housemaids realized a twelve-year-old youth had beaten them all. This waif of a woman had invented tastes and techniques they'd never experienced.

Did the men of her hut take note and congratulate her on her success? They were men; of course they noticed. But, they were men: cooking contests were beneath their dignity, so of course they didn't congratulate her. But did her hut's men brag to the other huts about which hut had the best cook? They were men.

There was, however, one man in Coth's hut who did take note of Sarrai's culinary competence. He allowed himself a week after her victory, and finally decided. He was afraid that his wild attraction for red hair and freck-les would overcome his reason. He enjoyed her company. She was the only woman he had met to match him mentally. Now he'd discovered she had skills and strengths as a woman to mimic his as a man. And he wasn't going to let any other man get a chance at her.

Havram asked Coth for Sarrai's hand in marriage when she turned the age of two hands plus one in another six months.

Coth dropped her ladle into the pot and one balled hand went to her mouth as she gasped. She hugged him and said yes.

Coth yelled for Sarrai.

Thinking her mother needed help, she rushed into the hut, "What's wrong?"

"Nothing is wrong, Honey. It's what's right. Havram has asked for your hand in marriage when you become of age. I told him yes."

Her head slewed around to look at him. "Havram," she gasped, and flew into his arms.

He was ready for her. Since they were engaged, it was now proper to kiss her, and he swept her into his arms and did so.

A long time later they untangled. "Darling," he said, "I want to ask something of you."

A quizzical look came across her face, "Yes?"

"After we're married, what I desire is plain salad."

Her quizzical look intensified into puzzlement. "What?"

"Yes, plain salad. Let-tuce alone—with no dressing."

It took a half-second for her to realize what he'd actually said, and in quick half-second increments, her puzzlement turned to shock, then em-barrassment, then a smile.

Coth had to brace herself against the wall with her arm to keep from collapsing on the floor from laughter.

Sarrai's gentle smile turned into a half-chiding, "Havram!" was the only word she said. But her tone carried more mirth than scold.

"I love you, Darling," he said as he turned to the door. He left almost as happy a man as the newly engaged young woman.

Coth turned to her daughter, "Honey, that's exactly the double-enten-dre pun your father would have said. You marry that man."

The long-awaited day arrived. The last round of bows was cleared as the glue being fully cured and delivered by the bow-wrights. It was seven weeks until the start of candidate demonstrations, and no one knew where they would appear in the sequence.

All the bows from this round were made of birch wood, ibex bone, and sinew. All were four feet in length. All used the new, higher-strength glue. The only difference was the bone length, maximum thickness, and thin-down rate. The candidates and bowyers had done the best they could, but no one could tell ahead of time whether their efforts would prove successful.

The first task was to attach the cat-gut bowstring. (Not the wives' tale of a feline sacrificed under a full moon, but cat as short for cattle—a cow or sheep.) The bow needed to acclimate to its new life of living under tension, and settle overnight before firing.

The following morning the nervous tension among the three inventors was so palpable it could be cut with a meat cleaver. Their very servant-ship rode on the results of this test.

They erected the straw target and backed up to the seventy-five-yard firing line. Havram first dry-shot all four bows. Two exhibited obvious jerks, and Havram set these aside as unusable—no sense in even attempting arrow shots. The other two seems to jitter rather than jerk, but the difference between them was so indistinguishable that Havram couldn't tell which might be better.

To get a feel for the two bows, Havram shot a consecutive five arrows from one bow, then five from the second. Then, to compare them, he shot five more from each, but altering each shot from one to the other. The first bow tended to have a left-right erratic pull, the second seemed to softly push the arrow into a trajectory a foot higher than expected, but no sideways motion. Havram put the first bow down.

Taking the second bow in his hand, he announced, "This is the best bow of the lot. It has some issues, like wanting to make the arrow flutter rather than fly straight, but with a couple of weeks getting used to it, I may be able to make it work. The real test will be from a moving chariot. I'll need to estimate how much to lead the target for each different chariot speed, and also how much arc to give the arrow for each distance. I think I can compensate enough for the arrow's wobble, but I won't know for sure for a while."

Now the really hard work began: integrating the different skillsets of chariot driving, horsemanship, and archery into a seamless, coherent system. And the practice time per day was limited to the horse's stamina.

It was time to push all the chips on the table, bet the ranch, go for broke. The next few weeks would earn them a tablet in their tunic or send them home with an empty pocket.

Chapter 13

Smithsonian, Washington, DC—Present

David thought, *If the original two pillars were repurposed and used for something else, what could that be?*

Ironically, it was a doughnut that answered David's question. Someone brought a dozen doughnuts and David opened the box to get one. In the box rested a bear claw. That triggered a cascade of lightning thoughts. Bear claw—talisman—Daoist fortune sticks—Urim and Thummim.

Daoist divination sticks are both red, so it isn't possible to distinguish between them. One side flat, the other curved. If a worshiper needs a fortune, they ask for divine guidance, then toss the sticks. If both curved sides land up, the answer is yes. If both curved sides land down, the answer is no. If one lands up and the other down, there is no answer.

The Daoist origin is so old it's lost to memory. However, one leading theory is that these were originally real bear claws, cut in half lengthwise.

The Bible makes reference to either or both the Urim and Thummim at least a dozen times. The Hebrews believed God directed the Urim and Thummim to answer the priest's question. If the priest needed a simple yes or no answer, he threw Urim, as in Numbers 27:21, where the question was "should the people go out today?" If the priest asked to distinguish between two parties, such as 1 Samuel 14:31 in deciding "which of two parties has sinned: Saul or Jonathan," he assigned Urim to one and Thummim to the other. Whichever, or both, had a "yes" answer was guilty of sin. It was also necessary to have the fourth answer: neither one has sinned. The last example is from 1 Samuel 14:36–37. To a question like "should we go to battle today," God obviously had to be able to answer yes and no, but he also needed to be able to say "no answer." That implied throwing both Urim and Thummin.

The need to distinguish Urim from Thummin meant they couldn't be identical. Having one coated white and the other red fulfilled that requirement.

David nodded his head. Yes, the evidence of the semicircular rods fit Bible requirements. These could be the Biblical Urim and Thummmim, but there wasn't enough evidence to be certain. It had to remain a tantalizing conjecture.

****

O'UR OF THE CHALL DIA

June 1749 BC

"Terrah," shrieked Coth's voice. The hut's men ran to the housemaid's hut to discover the scream's reason. Coth was in a man's arms with her feet six inches off the floor, and both were doing their best ecstatic kiss demonstration. After another minute, he lowered her to the floor.

The sight startled Havram when he realized the man was Terrah. "Father, what are you doing here?"

"Havram, I told you I was coming."

"Yes, and I have been expecting you. Why are you kissing Coth?"

"Son, I'd like to introduce you to your mother."

"My what?"

"Actually your stepmother. After your mother, Melyn, passed away, I married her cousin, Coth."

"So you know Coth?"

"Know her? I married her."

"Coth's been my housemaid for two years. In two days I'm marrying her daughter Sarrai."

"You're marrying my daughter?"

"Father, wait, let's stop and take a breath. This is too much, too fast."

Havram noticed another man leaning against the wall, and recognition kicked in. "Harran, what are you doing here?"

"Do you think I would miss the ceremony when my little snot-nosed brother earns his ephod? What kind of brother do you take me for?"

Havram stepped over to embrace him. As Harran pushed off from the wall to accept the embrace, he staggered, then caught himself. As Havram had him in his arms, he realized Harran wasn't standing; Harran was leaning on him to keep upright. "Harran, what's wrong?"

"Nothing. Caught some sickness during the trip." He smiled, "They told me to stick with the wine and not drink the water, but I didn't listen. I'll recover."

Havram held his brother at arm's length, "You're skin and bones."

Havram noticed the six-year-old boy standing beside his brother, "You must be Lot. Your granddad's told me about you. It's a long way to Uruk where your dad is servant. I'm glad to meet you." Holding on to Harran with one arm, he hugged his nephew with the other.

Terrah advised, "Let's sit down. We need to trade news." He turned to Coth. "Where are Sarrai and Nahor?"

Coth answered, "There've gone to see what the Gatherers have available for us to prepare dinner. They'll return soon."

Terrah continued, "Then let's sit down on the platform ledge and trade news. Just think; my daughter getting married—I must be getting old."

After sitting, Havram asked, "Father, our family has always called the tunic tablet an ephod, but I've learned the proper name is 'fod-ef'—the verb goes first in this language, not the noun. Why do we always call it an ephod? That's wrong.

Terrah hung his head and sighed. After a few seconds he looked up at Havram, "It's a long story. Your grandfather Nahor was our family's first servant. I'm not sure how well you remember him, for you were only a young boy when he passed away. He was a kind and gentle man, but frankly, he wasn't very smart. I'm not sure how he passed the training to become a servant, but he did. We evidently got our intelligence from his wife. To put it delicately, Nahor was 'linguistically challenged.' In other words, he was a country bumpkin. He butchered Aramean Semitic, so you can image how he murdered the language from Ur. Anyway, he always got it backwards, calling it an ephod rather than 'fod-ef'. By the time I had learned the truth, me, my brothers and sisters, our extended family, all our shepherds and their wives knew it as an ephod. It was too late to change. I suggest you just bow to the unavoidable and continue calling it an ephod.

The following day was Havram's examination before the Council. The Council Elder, Arwain, began. "Gliocas, please have a seat. I want you to relax; this is not an examination. For a thousand years we've asked this question of every candidate, and from their wisdom and insight, we've improved what the Ancients bequeathed to us. We also know that you are still young and have not achieved full wisdom or ability. What we want to know is any insight you may have about The Divine. Who He is. What He wants of us. How we can grow. How we can become better stewards."

Havram took a seat. "Arwain, gentlemen of the Council, thank you. I am still just a young man and, although I have thought about The Divine since I arrived, I do not believe I am wise enough that you should give much credence to my tentative ideas. However, I understand that you need what little I can offer to help the Servants bring this world closer to what The Divine wants.

"To start, I have examined this world. Some claim this world always existed. This can't be true. When the Sumerians built Ur a thousand years ago, it was at the seashore. That shore is now ten miles downriver from Ur. The city hasn't moved; the land has changed. Mud and silt drifted downriver and deposited where the river empties into the sea. That material came from the mountains. There is no way to build new mountains. If this world had always existed, there'd be no mountains left. Therefore, this world hasn't always existed.

"I needed a name for my ideas, so I call this world 'Becoming.' It's 'Becoming' because it's constantly changing. This state of 'Becoming' plus the limited time the world has existed means something happened to create the world at a specific past time.

"I've talked to many companion candidates. Each culture understands the meaning of divine differently. Most believe in gods they call immortal. However, their idea of immortal doesn't mean always-existing. Instead, they believe immortal means ageless and undying. To clarify: first, many gods can be killed. Second, at some undetermined past time most were born or in some way came into being. Gods that 'became' and can be killed means they belong to this 'Becoming' world.

"Next: a 'Becoming' world can't create itself. Claiming a different 'Becoming' world created it only prolongs, not solves, the issue. What created the second world?

"A 'Becoming' world and a creation require a 'Beginning' Agent. I believe this 'Beginning' Agent provides revelations pointing to himself. The Divine-Road is one. Therefore, the 'Beginning' Agent is The Divine.

"I believe The Divine has given us another revelation. My friend Klymenos related the Mycenaean creation story to me. It's unique. The story starts 'First, *Chawos* came into being.' *Chawos* has two meanings in the Mycenaean language: first, it can mean a gap or chasm, and second, it can mean unordered or undifferentiated.

"A gap implies two sides. One side is this 'Becoming' world. I think the other is a 'Being' world. It's always existed. It's the source of our world. Since the two worlds are so different, it's necessary for a gap separating them. They are so different they cannot touch.

"What of the second meaning: unordered? Think of water. It has substance, but no shape. It flows to fill its container. Whatever fills the gap is like water.

"Perhaps the gap is emptiness. Nothingness. I have no words to describe a vacuum. All my words describe something—'some-thing'; I have no words to describe nothing—'no-thing'. It's beyond my understanding. I cannot describe something I cannot understand. I have tried and I cannot think of what 'no-thing' means. My mind is inadequate.

"The Divine is on the gap's 'Being' side. He's unlike anything in our 'Becoming' world. Like understanding 'no-thing', The Divine is incomprehensible. Perhaps we should expect this. The Divine is too great to understand. Nothingness in the gap is too small. Both are 'other'. Both force us to accept what we cannot understand. They force us to be humble.

"I have used the word 'He' to refer to The Divine, but I don't believe that is accurate. Our spoken language has only masculine and feminine genders. This forces us to think of stones as either male or female, when they're neither. The Mycenaean language has a neuter gender used to describe something like stones. I think it likely the Ancient's language had a fourth gender: both male and female. They used this gender to refer to The Divine. The Divine is not solely masculine nor solely feminine. The Divine is both. So referring to The Divine as 'He' is misleading. The Divine is 'other'.

"What do I mean by 'other'? Think about going to the sea and filling a bucket with water. We can say water fills the bucket, but we can't say the sea fills the bucket. We can say the water in the bucket is like the sea. However, it's impossible to understand what it's like in a boat on the open ocean when you've only experienced water in a bucket. Similarly, using 'Becoming' words to describe 'Being' cannot adequately describe 'Being's' entirety.

"What is The Divine like? You need to take anything I say with caution. But, I believe we can say the following:

"First, does The Divine care for us? I believe we can say yes with confidence. The Divine left us The Road and inspired the Mycenaean creation story. If he didn't care for us, this wouldn't have happened. The Divine does care for us. But, is this care for individuals, for tribes, or for the human race? I don't know; I have no information that could lead to a conclusion.

"Second, what does The Divine want of us? At best I can give a tentative answer. First, from the example of The Divine caring for us, I believe that we are to learn to care for each other and for the world as much as The Divine cares. Reworded, we are to learn to love as The Divine loves.

"Last, although the Divine first blessed the Ancients, when the Ancients stopped solving problems, The Divine allowed them to die out. Did The Divine allow this because the Ancients stopped growing in wisdom or because they stopped using their wisdom to make the world better? Reworded, The Divine wants us to be better stewards of this world. Could it be, to become better stewards, we must first grow? Which comes first, our growth or making the world better? Is there a difference? I don't know.

"I am sorry, council, this is as far as I am now able to judge. I know I am still a young man; I expect I have more growing before I mature."

Arwain closed the session, "Gliocas, thank you. You have given us insights no one has before. We need a few days to think and discuss them. We may ask you to return. Thank you."

On the way back to his hut, Havram had a novel thought. There are twelve men on the Council. The council is led by an Arwain—a thirteenth. Why twelve plus one? There are twelve moon cycles in a year, one council member for each month. However, the moon and solar cycle do not align. Every few years the calendar must add an extra moon month to align the different cycles. So, a thirteenth month controls the twelve. The thirteenth man, the Arwain, reflects the heavenly cycles. Twelve plus one to control them.

Chapter 14

Smithsonian, Washington, DC—Present

"Doctor Scortun," started Karen, a lab technician. "I took the linen garment out of the box as you asked. I'm afraid we can't display it in its present condition. It's soiled, stained, and deteriorating from age. I don't think it will survive cleaning. But there's another problem."

"Yes, Karen?"

"You told me there's a large pocket on the inside. There's a second inside pocket."

"Two pockets?"

"Yes, Sir. Under the large pocket is a smaller one. Before I went further, I thought I'd better show you."

David hung his head in exasperation for a moment. *Every time I think I have this specimen figured out, it throws me another curveball.*

He finally lifted his head, "Okay, Karen. Lead on."

They left for the lab. The robe lay on a steel table, front side up. She was right, the robe was in terrible shape. They couldn't display it in its current condition. There were grass and dirt stains on the robe's bottom edge, and the material was decaying. Plant fibers degrade faster than animal.

Karen traced out the large pocket stitch threads. David followed her gestures. Then she showed him the smaller pocket stitch threads centered underneath.

He just shook his head from side to side. *Will this never end?*

"OK, please measure the dimensions of the inside pocket and get back to me."

David went back to his office, put his feet on his desk, leaned back, closed his hands under his jaw and propped his head up with his two index fingers. His eyes assumed an unfocused appearance.

His secretary, Nancy, had seen this too many times. David didn't say anything, but when lost in thought, he might as well be in another world. She checked his schedule for the day and called those scheduled for the next two hours and asked them to put off their meetings. She was a good secretary.

Twenty-five minutes later, Karen knocked on David's door. David looked up, took his index fingers from under his jaw and moved his feet to the floor. "Please come in, Karen."

As she began the trek to his desk, David continued, "I assume you're about to tell me the pocket is sized for a cylinder or square rod three-eighths-inch square and two and three-quarter inches long?"

She stopped in her tracks and her jaw dropped, although she managed to keep her mouth from falling open, "How did you know that?"

"Because that's the size of the semi-circular rods in the ephod tablet."

He thought a minute, then continued, "Karen, I have a critically important task. Get someone to help you; I'd suggest asking George if he can spare Molly. The two of you drop whatever you're doing and spend the next week going over every square millimeter of the inside of the robe with a large magnifying glass. I want you to look for underarm hair stuck in the fabric, blood stains or scabs from small wounds or scrapes, skin flecks from rubbing at the elbows and knees, anything. Wear sterile gloves and breathing masks to ensure you don't contaminate the sample. Find anything yielding DNA of the person wearing that robe."

****

O'UR OF THE CHALL DIA

June 1749 BC

The next day was the last project presentation. The Council had scheduled the chariot last. The three tried guarding the project's secrecy, but there was no hiding horse training. No one had seen a functional horse pair, and it took six months to team-train them. No secrecy was possible with archery practice at thirty miles an hour.

Saying this project drew interest was understatement. The town's curiosity was so excited nearly everyone was watching the event.

For the chariot part of the demonstration, Klymenos stood with the Council to explain the chariot design. Everyone formed a hundred fifty-yard line. Terrah, standing near the Council in the center of the line, propped Harran up so he could witness the event.

For the first pass Kikkuli walked the horses down-the-line. It was little different from an ox-pulled cart. That interested the audience, but didn't excite them.

He moved out ten yards and made the second pass at thirty miles an hour. That dropped jaws. Sounds of mingled gasps and cheers erupted from the audience. They began applause.

The third pass consisted of S-curves at fifteen miles an hour, displaying maneuvering ability, ending in a tight circle in front of the Council. More "ooh"s and "aahs." Many children pointed their fingers at the chariot and asked questions their parents couldn't answer. They hadn't seen anything like this either.

The chariot stopped.

For the archery demonstration, there were two targets, each of cloth-covered straw bundles in roughly the shape and size of a man, positioned a hundred twenty-five yards away from the chariot track. To begin, Havram, standing in front of the council, demonstrated the composite bow's ability. He fired one arrow at each target. The arrows hit the target's center-chest. The arrow had a flattened trajectory, not arched like normal self-bows. That elicited gasps from the audience. Few had ever seen a compound bow. Ur didn't use them. Longbows had much greater range and power.

Kikkuli drove the chariot up and Havram climbed aboard.

Their first pass was ten miles an hour straight down-the-line of on-lookers. Havram loosed three arrows at each target. The second was twenty miles an hour with two at each target. The last three passes were thirty miles an hour with one arrow each.

Kikkuli drove the chariot back to stop in front of the council. The two men got off and Klymenos joined them. Kikkuli announced the demonstration was complete, invited everyone to see the chariot, and the three bowed to the council. The audience erupted in prolonged cheers and applause. They surged forward. Everyone wanted to see and touch this invention.

Kikkuli stayed with the chariot, allowing the children to climb aboard or pet the horses.

The Council first wanted to examine the bow's accuracy. Fifteen of the eighteen arrows fired impaled the targets at a hundred twenty-five yards with a compound bow at up to thirty miles an hour.

Havram surrendered the bow to Arwain. He accepted it, but first wanted to see how they managed to have horses, not oxen, do the pulling, and how they controlled them. The Council fired question after question at the three men.

"Yes, Arwain, we had to invent a harness which transferred the load from the horse's neck to the chest."

"Yes, Arwain, the strap around the horse's girth stabilizes the chest collar so it doesn't move."

"No, Arwain, we couldn't attach the cart's tongue directly to the horses because every bump would transfer force straight to the horse. By suspending a floating shaft between them, it acted as a shock absorber, decoupling the horses from an uneven road's impact."

"No, Arwain, the wooden collar connecting the horse's necks allows each horse to 'feel' what the other is doing. By feeling what the other's doing, they learn to coordinate their actions."

"Yes, Arwain, it's a small wheel, but it's the largest we could make from the cow's leather strips. We need the leather tires to keep the spokes in the wheel. We considered trying to make a tire from bronze, but we didn't know if the blacksmiths could develop the necessary technology in time. A bronze tire would need to have a constant thickness. We also didn't have time to invent a lost-wax retention collar for the spokes. We didn't have time to test the idea. If we could develop a bronze tire, we could make the wheel larger and that would lessen the shock from hitting rocks or bumps."

"Yes, Arwain, we had to test different animal bones, wood, and sinew before we found a combination that had the strength needed. And we had to develop a stronger glue. Instead of using the hide, we boiled hooves for three days. But the glue is still susceptible to rain and high humidity. That's as far as we could improve it in the time available."

"Yes, Arwain, we had to dry the glue for six months before the sinew would properly adhere."

"Yes, Arwain, standard arrows were the wrong length for this size bow, we had to have a fletcher make a special run."

The council was thorough, therefore questioning seemingly took forever. The council finally understood how much thought, time, and effort the team took to result in the chariot. Even the three inventors, reviewing what they'd done, realized how momentous the task had been.

Finally, it was over. Just before allowing them to leave, Arwain spoke to Havram. "Havram, the council would like to hear more about your thoughts on the Mycenaean creation story. Would you please see us at the council hut tomorrow an hour after breakfast?

"Of course, Arwain."

After taking care of the horses, the three companions were ready to drop from exhaustion. They were thankful to escape the crowd and return to their hut.

They found Terrah waiting for them. "You realize what you've done?"

"No," Havram replied.

Terrah made it short. "With twenty thousand men and fifty chariots armed with your bows, I could conquer the world."

With his father's comment, the last year and a half's efforts distilled in Havram's consciousness. Havram had been reluctant to anticipate the future. Like a horse with blinders, he only looked at what was just ahead. He couldn't see down the road to make out if success or failure lay there. He was afraid to feel what might be a false success, and more afraid to feel abject failure. Everything he'd done, all his hopes and dreams, had led here. He'd bet the ranch on success.

It was done. They'd succeeded. The three friends had an invention never before seen—or imagined. They had done the impossible.

Havram finally allowed himself to feel what he had until now sternly suppressed. A euphoric feeling surged through Havram's being. He felt more alive than he had ever been in his life. He was sitting on top of the world.

What did he want in this life? If being a servant resulted in this accomplishment euphoria, he wanted more. This was worth spending your life.

And, this project was so exceptional, the council would certainly invite him for council evaluation. Havram mentally pictured himself in Arwain's chair. With a little luck, it was an attainable goal.

After lunch, Havram excused himself and headed for the Scots Pine grove. Hunkering down, he began thinking. He needed to forget today's success and face tomorrow's hazards.

It was obvious that the council had never heard of the Mycenaean creation story.

Why did they invite him back? Yes, they needed to revisit his insights of The Divine. But why? Would they be objective? Ask information questions? Or clarification? Would they be defensive? Ask attacking questions? How much should he reveal? Should he give additional reasoning? Was his servantship at stake?

For example, the status hierarchy was obvious: The Divine, the Becoming gods, humans, and animals. It must be. It followed from simple reasoning. Becoming gods came into being, ate food, and could be killed. They underwent change, so they must be of this world. But many culture's myths didn't agree with that.

The Divine was from a Being world. Therefore, He must have always been. That implied that He couldn't change. But in some way, The Divine could create change. He created this world, so change was possible , even if He didn't change. Could The Divine move? Havram remembered his body in his psychedelic trance at his ordination ceremony. He had a body without limbs that moved without exerting any effort on his part. He thought and his body moved. Was The Divine like that?

The problem was that every thought Havram had of what The Divine must be like resulted in a contradiction. He had reasoned that, like animals of this world, The Divine had to eat to get energy to perform work. But eating meant that The Divine would be changing. That was a contradiction. He couldn't sleep because that would be a mental change. He couldn't. . . . And the list went on. There was one consistent characteristic of all Havram's thoughts. Every example was from this world—and The Divine was not from this world; He was "other."

What should I do? What should I say? I run a risk if I give a full answer; I run a risk if I fail to give a complete answer. And I have no way to judge which risk is greater.

He didn't know what to do. When that had happened in Assur, he had remained faithful. He fully and truthfully answered the question. It had succeeded there. Because he had remained faithful, so The Divine had remained faithful.

In the end he decided he would trust The Divine. He could do nothing else. He would answer every question as truthfully as possible, and trust for the result that glorified The Divine. Succeed or fail, he would remain faithful.

Arwain started the proceedings, "Gliocas, thank you for returning. We need some added insight into your ideas. Brysur, would you please begin?"

Brysur asked, "You told us the Mycenaean creation story starts: 'First, *Chawos* came into being.' Explain how *Chawos* (chaos) came into being."

"I can't. The story doesn't explain it, and I cannot understand it."

"That's irrational."

"Yes and no. What I am trying to say is that we cannot explain what we do not fully understand. I agree it is irrational in the sense I cannot explain it. But it isn't irrational in the sense that no rational explanation exists. An example is trying to explain adult sexual desire to a six-year-old. Until a man grows a beard or a woman breasts, they cannot fully understand adult sexual desire. That does not mean adult sexual desire is irrational, only that children are incapable of fully understanding it. The Mycenaean story's message isn't its details, but the fact of creation. The details aren't important. I suspect this is why the story doesn't try explaining it's meaning."

Brysur thought for a minute. "A message isn't a message when the message has no meaning."

Gliocas answered, "Brysur, I cannot fully agree. I would reword it with a different emphasis. I would say that a message, even if not understood, is still a message. Just because we do not yet understand its meaning, that doesn't mean there is no meaning. The meaning may be there even if we cannot comprehend it. Therefore, it is still a message. I will explain by giving the example of The Road.

"There's a distinction between the message itself and the meaning of the message. The Road was the message. The Road, simply as The Road, was not what was important. It was only the message. However, The Road pointed to The Divine. The Divine was the ultimate meaning behind the message. As originally understood by the Ancients, The Road's surface message signaled the summer and winter solstice. However, the deeper, latent meaning was that The Divine created an orderly world. The sun's cycle repeats. The Ancients first understood the surface message, then came to discern the latent meaning in numerous stages. From their initial understanding, they deduced The Divine made The Road. This was their first growth stage. The Ancients were like little children becoming teenagers.

"But The Road's message carried a still deeper meaning. Though no one recognized it at the time, it was there at the beginning. The Divine created the moon to also have cycles. The Ancients grew to understand that also. To predict the movements of both the sun and moon, they built the original The Place with the 56-hole circle. What changed? The 56-hole circle became the messenger, taking over the role of The Road. The 56-hole circle also pointed to The Divine. It enabled an even deeper and richer understanding. In other words, the Ancients grew in knowledge and wisdom. But the original meaning remained: there was a The Divine and He created an orderly world. The Divine created the sun and moon to be orderly. The Ancients couldn't fully understand this deeper meaning until they had built the circle. This was their second growth stage. They were now teenagers becoming young adults.

"Building the original 56-hole circle led the Ancients to recognize there was a still deeper meaning behind eclipses. Even though no one fully understands them yet, we can recognize the danger signs and control for them.

"All this meaning was there in the beginning, just not discerned. The original The Road pointed to The Divine and all of its meaning, but it took time and growth to discern. What changed? The Ancients used the 56-hole circle—the new messenger—for a purpose they didn't anticipate. The result? The Ancients again grew in knowledge and wisdom. This was their third growth stage. The young adults became full adults.

"But there is a still deeper meaning within the original message. The Divine was using the Road, The Place and their successive levels of meaning to point to Himself and this world He created. An orderly world points to its source of order, The Divine Himself. We must use the knowledge we have been given to grow in wisdom. The Ancients took three successive steps of discerning order in the world, growing in knowledge and wisdom with each step.

"What was key? The meaning was always there, but not yet understood.

"In summary, the message is still a message even when we don't yet understand its full meaning. The message is only a tool for directing attention to the meaning. The message's meaning is what's important. What is this meaning? The message points to The Divine who gives the message meaning. That's what we need to discern. Note an important fact. The Divine did not ask the Ancients to learn everything at once. He guided them step-by-step. Their early progress satisfied The Divine at first. But the Ancients stopped after the third step. They stopped growing.

"However, even when they were growing, they never fully acted as The Divine's stewards, making this whole world a better place. Yes, they did enable mankind to use the heavenly cycles for mankind's benefit. But, they failed in their steward role of benefitting the whole creation. They only benefitted mankind. The result? The Divine allowed them to die out.

"We must always remember: The Divine only asks us to grow step by step. No single step will get us to His intended destination. We only get closer. I believe that The Divine's message of The Road has still deeper levels of meaning we have not yet detected. The first message only started a long conversation. We cannot understand everything at once—and we progress only in small steps. If we ever think that we have received the final and complete understanding of the meaning of The Divine's message, we are probably wrong.

"This, Brysur, is why I believe you were in error to say, 'A message isn't a message when the message has no meaning.' The meaning in The Road's original message was latent from the beginning, though the Ancients didn't understand it. I believe a better understanding would be, when a message from The Divine doesn't seem to have meaning, it probably signals that we haven't grown enough in knowledge and wisdom to understand it."

"So, what does this mean?" asked Brysur.

"As I said, we must remember to revere The One who sent the message, not the message itself. When the Ancients built the original The Place, they learned something new about the world at each step. They built the original 56-hole The Place to learn something they could not detect using The Road alone. Their emphasis was on growth.

"We built The Place we have today. Has it given us any knowledge beyond the 56-hole circle the Ancients built? No. Does it teach us something enabling us to revere The Divine any more than the Ancients could? No. Have we grown as The Divine defines it? No.

"What does it do? The Place should be the message, not the meaning. Don't misunderstand what I am saying; it is an awesome structure and a grand accomplishment of humankind's technological prowess. But, what draws the observer's attention? Where does the awe point? This awe points towards The Place itself. Not the meaning of The Place. Not The Divine. The result? We have no more knowledge and wisdom from today's The Place than the 56-hole circle the Ancients built.

Remember, the Ancients were supposed to improve the world, but only ended up improving mankind, often at the expense of the world. When they failed at their calling, The Divine allowed them to die out and called us. Have we become the stewards the Ancients were called to be, or have we fallen into the same failure mode as the Ancients?

"This world glorifies The Divine. He has asked us to become better stewards of His world. Are we caring for The Divine's creation as his steward? I will give one example. The brown bear used to roam across this country. They were never a threat. There was plenty of room for both man and bear. But, when our population grew, we encroached on the bear's natural home. That made the bear dangerous, so we killed most of them. In other words, we have killed a portion of The Divine's creation because the bears were inconvenient for mankind. Was killing the bears being respectful of The Divine's creation? Now the brown bear only roams the northern mountains. Have we assigned a melchizadek for the brown bear?

"I will give another specific example of what I believe we have failed to do. Stewards place their master's desires before their own. I have talked with my fellow candidates. Not one candidate has chosen a project which improves the world for The Divine. They have all chosen projects that promote our welfare, sometimes at the expense of the world. That priority places humans first, The Divine second. When we were choosing projects, no one advised us to consider projects for The Divine's glory. Have we become so self-centered we no longer consider The Divine our priority?

"Last. I believe we must remember The Divine designed this world for Becoming, not Arriving. We haven't arrived at what He wishes us to eventually be; we are only Becoming. If we ever think we were to suddenly Become, we would grow proud and haughty. But we can only grow step-by-step, never fully Becoming, so we must remain humble.

"How does the Mycenaean creation story fit into this evaluation? Has The Divine planned our development? Have His promptings been a continuing story? Has The Divine become impatient with His Servants' lack of development as His stewards? If so, has He now given His next message to someone else—the Mycenaeans? Have we refused to listen for His next Message, so He has chosen someone else? If this is His next message and we ignore it, will we become like the Ancients—discarded as time passes us by?"

Brysur grew red-faced, but said nothing.

Arwain noted the change in his colleague and stepped in, "Thank you, Gliocas. You have given us something to think about.

Brysur kept his composure until Gliocas had left, then burst out, "What Gliocas said is pure blasphemy. We built Stonehenge for *our* glory? We have *done nothing* in seven hundred fifty years? Blasphemy!"

Several others in the council mirrored his vehemence.

Brysur summed up, "I call an immediate vote. We need no time for discussion. Should we consider inviting the blasphemer back in ten years?" He didn't wait for an answer, "I vote no."

Arwain had never seen the council in this state of passion before, and agreed to an immediate vote. The passion was an accurate predictor: there were five ayes and eight nays: Gliocas would not return.

With Gliocas voted down, Brysur felt emboldened. "We had selected the Chariot as the winning innovation and clearly Gliocas was its most significant contributor. However, having just voted him down for an invitation to return, I recommend we substitute his friend Glyfar the Hurrian in his place. I believe Glyfar is also a worthy candidate, and choosing him avoids violating a precedent of artificially elevating the number two innovation, the alphabet, into first place. Arwain, would a vote be acceptable?"

Arwain agreed, and asked for discussion. There was none. He then called for a vote. It was a matter of form. The council would invite Glyfar to return for council evaluation in ten years.

Brysur spoke again, "If I could, I would recommend we revoke Gliocas' servant-ship, but it's too late. However, I do not wish to spread his heresy anywhere significant." He turned and faced the scribe, "Where is the most distant, insignificant place in the Middle East that currently has no servant?"

Ysgrifennydd examined the list of available places. "The furthest from major cities is Hebron in the Canaanite Levant. Their servant passed away ten years ago."

"Council, I vote to exile Gliocas there."

Brysur had boxed Arwain into a corner. He allowed the vote and the Council assigned Gliocas to Hebron.

Despite having two other candidates scheduled for interviews, Arwain dismissed the council. They would no longer be dispassionate.

When all had left except the elder statesman and Arwain, Deallus spoke. "Arwain, I am worried. Despite my feelings, I must agree that what Gliocus said has a basis in truth. He was trying to remain objective. I marvel he could have achieved so much at his young age.

"Inspired by what he told us on the first occasion, I reviewed what we've carried out in my lifetime. The common thread in almost all improvement projects is to take advantage of this world for *humanity's* benefit. These projects did not make the world a better place. They did not lead us closer to The Divine. What does The Divine think about our commitment to Him and His creation?

"What has me especially worried is the Mycenaean creation story. Remember what Morthwyl told us? In his language, he described it as a mythos—myth in our language. A mythos is a spiritual truth told in physical form, and always written in the form of poetry. Mythos is the opposite of logos, which is physical truth and always written in prose form. Mythos is heartfelt. Logos is mind-understood. You can use reason to understand logos, but not mythos. Then, what did Morthwyl do? He went straight to the lines about Gaia; he skipped right over the introductory lines about chawos. Chawos is the logos portion of the story. Beginning with Gaia it is mythos.

"First, examine The Divine. His religion is Logos. Now review every other candidate. Without exception, everyone related The Divine within their religion's mythos. No one else had a logos of The Divine. Only Gliocas.

"Now examine the chawos section of the Mycenaean creation story. The Divine's fingerprints are all over it. The Divine works by combining truth and mystery. Just enough understandable to take one step forward, but not enough understandable to arrive at full truth. This is the way The Divine acts.

"Gliocas was the only person to see The Divine's fingerprints in the chawos. Is this creation story a message from The Divine? A new way to understand Him? A new way for us to grow?

"Gliocas is correct in understanding that we have not taken a 'next step' in our growth and understanding in hundreds of years. The time is ripe. Is this the next step The Divine is asking us to take?

"If Gliocas is correct, I see one hope for us. The Divine doesn't act in a period of days or years, but centuries. After the Ancients built the original The Place, He waited six hundred years before our people displaced the Ancients. It took us a hundred fifty years to build The Place we have today. Therefore, it has been six hundred years since we have taken our last step of growth of knowledge and wisdom. Notice the similarity in timing: The Divine waited six hundred years before allowing the Ancients to die out. We have had six hundred years. Is it time for The Divine to replace us? Can we act before He does? Do we have time?

"But what did we just do? By dismissing Gliocus, we have refused to listen to The Divine calling us and have turned our back on Him. Arwain, I am fearful for us."

When the council announced examination results, they invited Kikkuli for council membership evaluation. Havram's name was not on the dygsu list.

Within two years, both Arwain and Deallus had passed away. The Council elected Brysur as Arwain.

Chapter 15

INTERLUDE

Smithsonian Laboratory, Washington, DC—Present

"Yeow," the technician yelled in pain. Karen looked and found a drop of blood oozing from a finger prick.

What? she thought.

She looked at the robe she had been examining. She didn't see anything that could have poked a hole in her finger. She lightly ran the tips of her fingers over the fabric. *Yes, there's something sharp here.* She still couldn't see anything.

She rummaged in the drawer and found her magnifying glass. Carefully going over the fabric where she had been working, she barely managed to see the pointed tip of something poking up from the fabric. Getting a pair of tweezers, she tried gently lifting it out of the fabric. It wouldn't budge.

Uh, oh. she realized. *This may not be an extraneous mote to discard; it may be a part of the garment.*

Karen called for the Lab Manager, and explained what she had found.

George decided, before they did anything else, they needed to document what they had found. He called for one of the photographers with a high magnification camera. They carefully laid out the fabric and successively took closer and higher resolution images, walking them down to the offending tip protruding from the fabric.

They needed to examine the reverse side. They attached marker tapes to find the tip's position on a grid that matched the table's x-y grid. This allowed them to locate the tip. After they turned the fabric inside out, the markers allowed them to relocate the tip. The tip had wedged itself into the bottom seam attaching the inside ephod pocket to the robe.

They decided that, before trying to extract it, they would take another set of pictures, successively closer and with more magnification until the tip almost filled the picture frame.

George thought: *I'd better call David. This ephod project is his baby, and he may want to see this.*

Sure enough, David was free and definitely interested. He'd be down in ten minutes.

In the stipulated time, David entered the lab and went straight to Karen and George. They explained what had happened and showed him the pictures.

"Good job, Karen, George." David said. "If this is what I think, it's vital. George, can you please get a specimen container?"

They took David to the table and showed him the tip's base set in the robe's seam.

David examined the wedged-in tip with the magnifying glass, "Yes, yes. I think that's exactly what it is. Karen, my old hands aren't as steady as they used to be, would you please use some tweezers to extract the tip and put it into the container?"

After she removed the tip and placed it in the container, David carefully screwed on the top. He didn't want shaky hands to drop an irreplaceable item on the floor.

David used the magnifying glass to examine the tip through the clear plastic of the container, "Yes."

"George, please set up a CAT scan for this little guy. Take extra special care of him."

****

O'UR OF THE CHALL DIA

June 1749 BC

Havram locked Servant Day in memory as one of his life's most significant. The Summer Solstice day. The last day his ephod pocket would remain empty. A hundred eighty-nine started training; seventy-eight would become Servants. The Divine chose less than half. His hut started with sixteen; seven would become Servants. The Council only invited good men to Ur; only exceptional men became Servants.

Yesterday the Council told his father they had approved him as a Council member. When an opening became available, they would notify him. They had a melchizadek position—a melech (king) of zadok (priest)—for the Aramean region, and they offered that appointment. Terrah accepted.

His father would wear the melchizadek's plain silver circlet. Never in his wildest childhood dreams had he anticipated this.

His brother's continuing decline was the only detraction. Harran could no longer stand. Attendants would carry him on a stretcher to watch the ceremony.

It was the year's longest day. An hour before sunrise they assembled at the Ur pillars. Sorting themselves in order of presentation, they aligned in single file. As each reached the Pillars, the Quartermaster gave them their sign of office. For Terrah, it was a silver circlet crown. For Havram, it was his ephod. Each person accepted their sign of office, turned, and went up The Road to The Place.

Just before dawn, Arwain and the Council stood behind the Altar Stone. When the sun rose, Arwain lifted his arms in welcome and gave thanks, praise and prayer to The Divine, then he and the Council bowed. The first of the three new Melchizadeks gave his sign of office to Arwain. He lifted it to the The Divine for consecration. On consecrating the circlet, Arwain returned it. The new Melchizadek turned to face the sun, bowed, and put the circlet on his head. He became a Melchizadek. He went down the Ur-Road to town.

In turn, each person gave their sign of office to Arwain. He lifted it to The Divine for consecration, then returned it. The newly commissioned officer turned to face the sun, bowed in reverence, then left. When the day's ceremonies were complete, Arwain and the Council processed down The Road to town.

The feast that night was lavish. Coth and Sarrai outdid themselves. The best meats and vegetables; the finest mead, wine and cheese.

Havram and Sarrai had another cause for celebration. Tomorrow was their wedding day. Despite emotional highs, they got a few hours of fitful sleep in the morning's waning hours.

The morning of the wedding Havram took Lot with him and went to see Harran.

The Healer shook his head, "He is now beyond my powers to cure or delay." The Healer parted the curtain and allowed them the privacy of their last hours with Harran. He was no longer able to talk, and was conscious only fitfully. Lot began to cry and wrapped his arms around his father.

The man and boy sat and waited. When Harran gained a few minutes of wakefulness, Havram told him, "You may make your journey in peace. Your son is my son; your wealth is his wealth; he shall never be in want."

Harran smiled and fell asleep.

He passed peacefully in his sleep that night. The attendants buried him the following morning.

Terrah and Havram shattered Harran's ephod and scattered its pieces in the river Avon-on-Ur. With its destruction, they severed Harran's final ties to this world.

Since Havram was now a servant, Council Elder Arwain married Havram and Sarrai in a high ceremony.

Havram waited just outside of the pillars of the Ur Road wearing his formal white linen servant robe, but without the ephod. Arwain waited just inside the pillars on the Road wearing his linen robe and the bronze gorget symbol of office. Many villagers gathered at either side of the road to watch. Terrah, with Sarrai on his arm approached from the town. She wore a plain white linen robe and a crown of red roses in her hair. They stopped five feet from Havram.

Arwain walked past the Road's pillars, emerging from The Divine to the secular. He stood and addressed the assembly, "We gather here to witness the joining in marriage of this man and this woman."

He turned to Terrah, "Who gives this woman?"

"I do," replied Terrah. As Terrah led Sarrai forward, Havram turned to face her. Terrah reached down to lift Sarrai's right hand and placed it in Havram's right. Terrah turned and went to stand beside Coth. She was softly crying tears of joy. He put his arm around her and gave her a gentle hug. Both remembered their wedding day.

Havram devoured the sight of his betrothed. Gone was the precocious grubby tomboy with skinned knees and unreserved manner. Before him was a demure woman, confident yet nervous, radiant in beauty.

Havram and Sarrai turned to face Arwain. "Havram, will you take this woman to be your wife, to love her, cherish her, honor and keep her, in plenty and in want, in health and in sickness, from youth to old age, as long as you both shall live."

"I will."

"Sarrai, will you take this man to be your husband, to love him, cherish him, honor and keep him, in plenty and in want, in health and in sickness, from youth to old age, as long as you both shall live."

"I will."

Arwain removed the gorget from his neck, and held it between the couple. Its chest-Divine side was towards Havram, the outward-secular side towards Sarrai. "Please join your right hands." Havram and Sarrai reached out with their right hands through the gorget opening to join hands where Divine meets secular. Arwain continued, "I now pronounce you husband and wife." Turning towards Havram, "You may kiss your bride."

The newlyweds embraced. Havram leaned down and lifted her to her tiptoes. Their first kiss was a public declaration of their new status.

The assembly erupted in cheers. Arwain smiled. Sarrai burst out in tears. Havram hugged her, and she put her head against his chest. They were no longer two, but one.

Everyone left for town. The wedding party lasted two days. Food, wine, and bee's honey mead was plentiful. The honeymoon couple enjoyed a small hut. Coth left food outside the door, but it only disappeared occasionally. The couple spent their time on other appetites.

Havram had thought long and hard about what new name he would need to reflect his new character as a servant. His character would change, so his name must change. There was precedent. His Father went from his Aramean name Terah to the Ur equivalent of Terrah, the change was doubling the "r." That spelling violated Aramean grammar rules, but the Ur tongue allowed it. And, the difference wasn't easily distinguishable in spoken Aramean. Similarly, his brother went from Haran to Harran. But, that wouldn't work for Havram, his name had a different grammatical construction. Instead, he decided he would change the "v" to an equivalent "b," which again was almost indistinguishable in spoken Aramean. He would become "Habram."

He thought briefly of the Council shunning him. They invited Kikkuli instead. Had Havram succeeded or failed? He realized it was because of his honesty at his last meeting with the Council. He had offended them with his religious insight. Should he have lied by not telling the whole truth? No. If telling the truth led to the Council's human judgment error, so be it. He had never been in charge. All he could do was remain faithful. He would trust The Divine to make it right.

He resolved to be the best servant he could be. Let The Divine sort it out.

Three days after graduation, the new Servants left for their assignments. The sea voyage took them to the Rhine's mouth. From there it was up the Rhine, over the headlands to the Danube, and down the Danube to the Black Sea. An easy voyage ferried them across to the northern coast of Turkey.

From there the chariot led the caravan, with Kikkuli driving and Habram in the cab with his bow prominently displayed. This alone caused prospective robbers to think twice. News of the return of the invincible archer who had killed ten men with shields preceded the caravan. Rumors of his latest skill dissuaded even dubious bandits. He could ride a cart five times faster than a man could run and center-shot a man every time at two hundred yards. No bandit volunteered to act as target to test the rumor's veracity.

They left Kikkuli at the edge of the Hurrian Kingdom. He would face no resistance. News of his impending return had spread and well-wishers and gawkers accompanied him for the remaining miles home.

The caravan met an escort of soldiers waiting for them where the river Balikh emptied into the Euphrates. The caravan continued east towards Babylon. Terrah sent half of the soldiers to Mari to fetch their servant, Samyaza, while Terrah, Habram, and their small group accompanied their remaining escort north upriver to the city of Haran. They also met no trouble. One man with his invincible bow was a cause for concern, but there were now two of them—and an escort of armed soldiers.

As they climbed to the high plain of southern Turkey, the land changed complexion to rolling grasslands. This was Habram's homeland. No trees. Scrubby bushes no taller than a man.

This land was tailor-made for sheep and goats. Sheep and goats are ruminants. Their four stomachs contain bacteria which digest blades of grass. Even in summer's heat, the withered grass holds enough water for days at a time. Sheep and goats thrive in these lands. Whether green or brown, grass is available year-round.

Humans aren't ruminants; they can't digest blades of grass. They must eat the seeds these grasses produce. They call these grass seeds "grains." They're only available for two weeks at the end of the grass-growing season. Humans give these grasses names such as wheat and barley.

In these rolling grasslands farmers can't thrive. They are lucky to survive. In most years they can harvest a respectable crop, and occasionally a good one. But, invariably there are bad years. In bad years, farmers can not only lose their crop, they can lose their farms. The region no longer contained farmers.

This was late fall. Grass was turning emerald green from the early rains.

Beehive huts began appearing. Twelve to fifteen feet in diameter, mudbrick walls slowly curving in until they met at a point twenty feet up. Wood, even for doors, was uncommon. Most used cloth curtains.

When they arrived at Haran, King Saahdia met them at the city gate, welcoming them. He led them to the servant's home, a simple beehive hut no different in outward appearance from most huts in the city, only a few feet wider than most. He would send a courier to invite them to dinner at his palace that evening. On entering, Habram discovered the inside looked essentially like the inside of the huts in Ur. A four-foot diameter fire pit sat in the middle. An outer platform circled the outside wall halfway around, allowing space for meetings. However, its platform was wood, not mudbrick, so it didn't transfer the ground's cold. That was a status signifier. A small mudbrick chamber behind the hut contained their supply of dried grass. Habram discovered there was no wood for their cook fires. They burned dried grass or animal dung. The dried grass burned hot but fast; the dung burned slower, but had other, more pungent effects on the hut's air.

That afternoon King Saahdia sent a messenger to guide them to the palace. Palace would be a misnomer anywhere else. It was small, only five rooms. But it used all-wood construction. For Haran, that cost a fortune. The largest room was a hall barely twenty-five by forty feet, which doubled as an audience chamber and dining room.

After dinner Terrah asked the king, "I am here to serve. In what ways can I most help your kingdom?"

Terrah's words shocked the king, "Here to serve? That doesn't fit with our recent experience with Servants. They act like the masters, not servants."

"I understand. I'm here to change your opinion. Ask Nagar and Ninuwa, where I was servant. Yes, I conducted the rituals, but I also helped the community. I also never took money for my services; I supported myself."

The king smiled, "Yes, I know, I checked when I received the message from Ur about your arrival. Both cities spoke highly about you. Now let me ask a question, why weren't you sent to Mari? That's the biggest city in the Aramean region."

"Mari is one problem I intend to solve. The present servant has so enraged the king because of his arrogant behavior the Council has decided to leave the office vacant for a couple of years. Later they may reassign me there, but who can tell the future?"

"I am thankful and welcome you. We need help full-time, not occasionally. Please accept our offer of full support. We will gladly bear all the costs of your service; that is how you can best help us." King Saahdia turn to Habram. "I would like you to stay a few more days or weeks, until after the early rains and the roads harden. I will send a squad of soldiers with you to Damascus. Damascus will send soldiers with you to Salem, where you will meet your Melchizadek."

It being prudent not to travel across the upper plains in the rain, Habram gratefully accepted.

The first day Habram examined Haran's defensible fortifications. Yes, the city had a ten-foot wall. However, it was only a wall. There was no rampart for firing arrows. Its wasn't for defense. It role was stopping high wind blowing dirt and sand. Throwing a ladder against the wall would breach it.

Perhaps he should have expected that. Why fight for Haran? There was no farming to make land valuable. It was a shepherd's base. Any one featureless acre was like another. The river was Haran's only justification. However, any other location along the river would be just as valuable—or just as worthless.

Habram's latent apprehension needing a city wall to live behind returned in earnest.

A week later, Mari's servant marched in to present himself before his new Melchizadek, Terrah. His manner exuded power and authority displayed through conceit and arrogance. Terrah waited patiently, then began, "Samyaza, we meet again. You haven't changed. Just because the Council assigned you to Mari and invited you to return for council membership evaluation, you think you already have the position. Your snobbery and self-important behavior has so enraged Mari's king that he has reported your behavior to the Council. The council has verified his complaint. You have acted as if the king serves you, instead of you serving the king.

"The Council has revoked your membership invitation. You will not return to Ur. I am also reassigning you. You are no longer the Mari Servant. I am sending you to serve the town of Nagar on the Habor River, effective immediately. I have reported your reassignment to both Mari and Nagar."

"Reassigned? Nagar? Nagar is a worthless hole-in-the-wall. Terrah, you can't do this; I will appeal to the Council."

"Samyaza, the Council directed me to reassign you. You have forgotten your oath of service. Servants serve. We do not rule. Your reassignment is the result of your ego being greater than your intelligence. If you do not wish to accept the assignment, surrender your ephod. Your servant-ship will be over and your ephod destroyed.

Samyaza's mouth made the motions of "But, but . . ." but no sound came out.

"Samyaza, remember the last time we met? You mocked me for taking the assignment at lowly Nagar. You had Mari, and believed yourself destined for council membership. You judged me inferior and ridiculed me. I served Nagar and Ninuwa. The Council rewarded me for my service. You have failed to serve Mari and are reaping the rewards of your failure. Remember the old saying: Beware of the heads you step on during your climb up the ladder because you may have to kiss body parts three feet lower on your way down.

"Please note: I am not mocking you. The council advised me to strip you of your servant-ship immediately. I talked them into giving you one last chance. You have one opportunity for redemption. Serve and succeed, or completely fail. What is your choice?"

Samyaza swallowed more than his shock. The thoughts racing across his mind were obvious on his face. His pride prompted immediate refusal. However, prospects of enduring common labor were even less appealing. His face revealed his ego determined his decision, not a desire to serve.

In one last vain try, Terrah warned, "Samyaza, I will give you at most two years. Serve or you will never have another opportunity."

Samyaza's back stiffened. He said nothing, turned, and marched out. Samyaza would condescend to go to Nagar. However, the word "serve" was not in his vocabulary.

Terrah said under his breath, "I tried."

Chapter 16

Smithsonian Laboratory, Washington, DC—Present

David was in the lab for the CAT scan. If the technician needed guidance, he wanted to be there. Of course, the tech knew what to do.

After taking the scans of the tip and the ephod robe, the technician asked, "Okay, what now, Sir."

"Let's overlay the tip, robe, and ephod stone. Minimize the robe. Call up the scan of the ephod stone and assign it to layer 1. Assign the tip to layer 2. Size both one-to-one."

When both were onscreen, David continued, "Move the tip over the cracked hole." The tip floated on the screen, winding up in the hole's center. "OK, start with a twenty-to-one enlargement."

The two images shot towards the pair of men and stabilized at twenty-to-one. David looked—almost. "Let's make it twenty-five." The hole almost filled the screen, the tip floating inside.

"OK. Try rotating the tip and moving it to the missing edge of the hole."

An exact match.

"Lock the tip to the stone. Move the image center to the tip. Back to one-to-one and call up the robe on layer 3. Move layer 3 to the back." The images of the stone and tip receded, the garment appeared behind them.

"Move the stone to align with the garment pocket, switch layer three to the front, and magnify ten-to-one." The tablet floated on the screen to match the garment, the garment jumped in front, then all three enlarged. Nothing visible on the garment.

"Okay, back to one-to-one, rotate the garment ninety degrees and enlarge." Again nothing.

"Rotate again." Bingo. There was something on the garment at the tip. On screen it was just barely visible.

"Move the garment spec to align with the tip and enlarge twenty-five-to-one."

The garment spec was now plainly visible. It was a tear in the fabric.

"I don't believe this," the technician announced. "You know what this means? Whoever the guy was that was wearing this, somebody tried to waste him."

David thought, *Waste him? That was an indelicate turn of phrase.* Then he remembered: the technician was a former Marine Corps grunt. *No, Marines aren't subtle. They tended to be strictly right-at-you, in-your-face. I should've expected that.*

But the tech was correct. That fabric tear suggested someone had used a sharp weapon to try killing the person wearing the robe.

David walked over to the lab manager's office and took a chair. First he briefed him on the results of the CAT scan.

"George, who do we contract to do our FEAs?"

"FEA?"

"Yes, Finite Element Analysis."

"Oh, yeah. We use the Engineering Department at George Washington."

"Please set one up. Give them all the information: X-Rays, CAT scans, and so forth. I want the analysis to cover arrows: flint and bronze; bronze spears: thrust and thrown; and bronze sword: thrust and slashed. One hundred seventy-five pound males delivering and receiving the blows."

"Yes, David, we'll get it done."

****

PALESTINIAN LEVANT

December 1749 BC

Elshalim, the southwest Canaanite Melchizadek, greeted Habram at the Salem city gate. "Welcome, welcome to Salem of the Jebusites, I've been looking forward to seeing you. You and your wife please come to my house for a few days before we go to Hebron. I'd like to meet you. Your men and herds may graze in the nearby hills.

Elshalim was a rotund, small man of sixty, a long, scraggly beard and an enduring smile on his face. He had the pleasing disposition which made people feel comfortable. Behind the welcoming eyes was a steel-trap mind, but he wouldn't allow his mind to feel threatening to others. As they traversed the streets of Salem, it seemed everyone greeted him and he knew everyone's name. Occasionally he would stop and ask someone about their wife or child. He seemed aware of every significant city event. And, he was concerned about everyone.

Habram wondered how he could know the names of over seven hundred people, and convince each one that he cared for them as an individual. Then it stuck him: *This is what truly serving people looks like. The starting point is caring. I need to study the techniques that convinces everyone he cares for them.*

That evening at dinner he already knew Habram's history. "Tomorrow, please allow me to examine and shoot your famous longbow. I'd like to examine one of Terrah's invention arrows. I have heard stories of your chariot, and the compound bow you created. Have you brought the bow with you? Would you please go over the logic of how you solved those problems? I am glad for your father, he is a brilliant and deserving man. Putting him in charge of the Aramean Region was a wise Council decision. My condolences on the loss of your brother; he was a good man and served his city well. My condolences on your negative Council Membership evaluation. Unless mistaken, I'll bet Brysur was the one grilling you?"

Habram thought, "Why, yes, it was."

"That makes sense. He has a good mind, but he's unbending in his opinions. He believes his every thought is correct. He always did remind me of the south end of a northbound horse. But he leads a clique of half the Council. If he opposes anything, Arwain and Deallus have problems getting anything passed. No matter. Leave it to me. I need to give it four or five years and then my report will allow Arwain and Deallus to reverse the Council decision. You don't have to worry about it; just leave it to me."

The next day Elshalim took Habram with him to the city gate. The king arrived about thirty minutes later and sat in his judgment seat. The two disputants, Elyevus and Eltsiyyon, stood before the king.

Elyevus had a smug look on his face. He was friend of the king. Eltsiyyon was a poor nobody. Elyevus regarded victory in the case a bygone conclusion.

A small crowd gathered to watch the events. When the king gestured for Eltsiyyon to advance, he said simply, "Sire, my testimony is what I stated last week: someone has moved the boundary stone between our lands."

The king gestured and Elyevus approached, "Sire, I did not move the stone."

At this point Elshalim asked to speak, and the king granted it. "Elyevus, I am not disputing your testimony. However, I need to ask a question: Has someone moved the boundary stone?"

Elyevus answered, "I can only say I did not move the stone."

Elshalim turned to the king, "Sire, over thirty years ago I recorded every boundary stone's location in your kingdom. Here is this boundary stone's record." He held a papyrus in his hand. "I checked the present location against the papyrus. Eltsiyyon is correct; someone moved the stone over fifty yards. Elyevus may speak the truth when he states that he did not move the stone, because he may have paid someone else to move it. Who moved the stone is irrelevant. Elyevus is responsible for knowing his boundary stone's location. His silence to my question suggests that he is unwilling to state he knows someone moved the stone. Whoever moved the stone, the end effect is that Elyevus is responsible for stealing his neighbor's land. The penalty for unknown stealing is paying four times the amount. First, I suggest moving the stone to its original location. Next, erect a temporary boundary stone two hundred yards, four times the distance, into Elyevus' land. For the next ten years, Elyevus may only farm to the temporary boundary. Eltsiyyon may farm to the temporary boundary for the next ten years. After ten years, remove the temporary boundary and restore his farming to the permanent boundary stone. However, Sire, I have found another problem."

"What is that, Elshalim?"

"Three of the four Elyevus boundary stones are not in their original location. Someone moved two other stones more than a hundred yards into his neighbor's land. I recommend erecting temporary stones four hundred yards into his lands for the next ten years."

"You can't do that," yelled Elyevus, "That isn't enough land to farm. I'll lose my farm. I'll become a beggar."

Elshalim replied, "If you become a beggar, it's because of your own actions. Knowingly or not, you have been stealing from your neighbors. Stealing from another farmer means you have lost a farmer's honor. You now have a beggar's honor."

Elshalim turned to the king, "Sire, what is your decision?"

The king had been expecting a simple case with no evidence, only conflicting claims. He would have ruled in his friend's favor. But, the proceedings were in public and the evidence convicted his friend Elyevus. Elshalim had artfully painted him into a corner. "Elshalim's recommendation is my ruling." The king rose and left.

The proceedings shocked Habram. The Salem populace held Elshalim in high regard, even love. He began understanding how Elshalim made everyone feel cared for. Everyone knew the most common dispute was landownership and fraud was pervasive. Within the first few months of becoming the Salem Servant, Elshalim took the initiative to corroborate landownership. This went beyond his required duties. But Elshalim understood servant-ship was a job of service, and he did whatever he could to resolve community problems. The people came to see and appreciate that service. Only then did they realize his service sprang from a gift of love. That was why they began responding positively. The people gave Elshalim a form of power Habram had never experienced.

This was power he'd never considered. The power of trust. Trust wasn't a power a person had. It was power others gave. Kings should be trustworthy; but most abused power. Soldiers and judges should be trustworthy, but a few untrustworthy ones ruined everyone's reputation. Many artisans didn't fully know their trades; their declared knowledge was a sham.

A person of trust must know what they claimed, and must do what they claimed they could. In Elshalim's case, he knew the men of power in Salem and Ur. He knew their personalities, knew their strengths and weaknesses. He also knew how to make the political system work. Trustworthy people put others' welfare before their own. In short, a person of trust has to earn trust before the people will give them trust. Last, they may not succeed, but failure never results from their not trying.

Elshalim might not be able to reverse Habram's Council ruling. However, he wouldn't rest until he did.

Elshalim was trustworthy.

The next day Habram walked the city walls. The inner and outer walls were stone, but not dressed stones, cut to fit. They were irregular, jammed into place and packed with fill dirt and rubble. Only the wall's weight kept it's stones in place. A pointed battering ram could knock these from the wall, causing a domino effect, leading to wall sections collapsing. No, these walls weren't strong. Babylon with its mudbrick walls was more defensible.

On the Valley of Hinnom side the walls were thirty feet high, but at the uphill side they were no more than ten feet. This was the wall's weak section. And a well-prepared army would flow over it like a Nile flood.

No, Habram thought, this city is not safe against a determined enemy. My family would be vulnerable here.

Two days later, Elshalim took Habram, his wife Sarrai, Lot, and Habram's flocks and herds, and they headed for Hebron.

On the way Elshalim warned Habram, "Hyanaq is King over Hebron. He will not willingly welcome you. Their last servant died when his father was king and he was a teenager. He has not experienced servant-ship in a decade and sees no need for one.

"Hyanaq is an alpha male. Everyone must obey his commands. No one may question his decisions. To openly challenge him will cause everlasting ill will. You can show him he is wrong, but you can never tell him.

"He is not an intrinsically bad man. He wants his kingdom to prosper. He wants to do what's best for the kingdom. He is a smart man, but does not understand how to use his intelligence to good advantage. He sees no need for a wise man as counselor. He sees no need for a proven problem solver to help them. He sees no need for our religion; they have survived many ellipses without our help. He will admit he has made mistakes and has changed his behavior, but he must decide himself."

"Sounds like he's unwilling to consider a servant."

"Let's say he needs convincing. You'll need to wait him out. You'll also need something that will convince him he needs a servant. If you wait and take advantage of your opportunities, your chance will come. Remember, first, you will have to address his reservations; second, you must answer each question; third, answer without rancor; and last, never challenge his authority."

At nineteen miles, the journey to Hebron was an easy two-day trip. They arrived in the late evening of the second day and camped outside the walls.

The following morning, Elshalim and Habram waited outside the gate in their formal linen robes containing their ephods. About the third hour, King Hyanaq appeared on the wall beside the gate. "I see you have returned, old Troublemaker. To what do I owe the displeasure of welcoming you this time?"

Elshalim answered, "I have brought your Servant, O King. Allow me to introduce Habram." He gestured at Habram.

Habram bowed to the king.

Hyanaq continued, "I don't need a servant."

Elshalim took that question, shielding Habram, "That may be, O King. However, you have no control over the Council assigning you a servant."

"I have heard about this invincible man and his bow. I will not allow him to pass the city gate. How do I know he is not a threat?"

Habram answered, "As a candidate, I convinced the Council of my honor. You have the fact the Council appointed me. If I ever betray that trust, the Council will revoke my servant-ship. If that is inadequate, O King, my service will prove my honor."

"I will not allow you to cross the city gate."

"Then, I will serve from outside the gate."

"I will not pay you a tenth of a copper shekel."

"O King, I have my flocks and herds to support me. I do not need support. I will serve without the city's support."

Suddenly Habram felt a compulsion. He knelt on one knee, his left hand held his bow, his right hand rested over the ephod. "Before The Divine, I solemnly swear that I will be the Servant for King Hyanaq and Hebron, serving them in the name of the Council. I will be a loyal subject of Hyanaq. I will be faithful, putting Hebron's good before my good, Hebron's protection before my protection, Hebron's future before my future. Should I ever prove unfaithful, may the Council revoke my servant-ship. This oath shall last as long as the Council assigns me to Hebron."

Habram's earnest oath moved Hyanaq's heart, but not enough to overcome his reticence. "I cannot remove the Council's assigning you to me. Find a place on the mountain's far side, away from our fields, and graze your flocks and herds. But do not try to enter the gates of Hebron."

"Your wish, O King, is my command. I will not go past the city gate without your permission."

Elshalim reentered the conversation. "King Hyanaq, we will go to the Oaks of Mamre and make our encampment there. Should you need us, there you will find us."

The two men bowed to the king, turned and withdrew north towards Mamre.

Before leaving, Habram walked around the Hebron walls. These were the strongest Habram had seen in the Levant. They used large irregular dressed stones, two feet or more thick and four to eight feet long, with smaller stones filling gaps. The bed was limestone rich marl. Nowhere were the walls less than fifteen feet high, and usually twenty or more.

Yes, Habram told himself. *I want to live behind these walls. My family would be safe. I need to earn King Hyanaq's trust. But how? How?*

Habram made good use of the example Elshalim had given him. His father's old crew led by Jurael and Michel still tended his sheep and goats, leaving Habram to spend most of his time being a servant. He spent the first three months getting to know the few hundred people living in Hebron's northern region, and what their problems were.

Their most important concern was water. Only one spring fed the region. An expanding population had spread farms beyond ready access to the spring. Women often walked a mile or more each way carrying their water jars on their heads, but the limited weight they could carry forced them to make at least a trip a day. Habram's first task was buying a specially made cart carrying six amphorae jars carried upright in cutouts on the cart floor. Each jar contained almost eight gallons. A single donkey pulled the cart throughout the region daily, led by volunteer teenage boys. The cart freed women for farming tasks.

The next task also related to water scarcity. The westward-facing side of the mountain collected most of the rainfall, leaving little for the mountain's east side. The steep slope of the east side ensured that what water did fall did not linger long enough to soak into the soil.

The local farmers had tried terracing, but their inexperienced efforts merely removed the good topsoil, leaving hardscrabble unsuitable for cultivation.

Habram started by hiring a mason to cut retaining wall stones. Six months' work yielded enough for the first terrace. Habram also completed his plans for terraces. He bought drainpipes to drain excess water during heavy rainfall. He gathered a dozen local farmers and paid them a modest fee to form work crews during the hot months when crops weren't growing. This extra income, though modest, allowed them to eke out a living between harvests. For three months one crew and an oxcart brought in good loam soil from downhill. A second brought in beach sand. A third collected dried grass for fertilizer. As a fourth erected the terrace and mixed the soils, layer by layer they built a quarter-mile long terrace. When the winter rains began, they planted grapes.

Even though the mountain's backside received only a third as much rainfall as the seaside, the combination of good loam soil, sand, and plentiful grass mixed together held what water did fall. The grapes' roots sought out the soil's nutrients, allowing the roots to grow deep and produce a hardier plant.

For three years Habram bought cut stone and drainpipes. The farmers worked their way down the hillside a level each year. After the third year, the first year's grapevines were reaching maturity and the vintners presented a portion of the first productive crop to the king. They were already as good as the best grapes in the Hebron valley.

After the third year, the king decided to fund building two quarter-mile terraces a year. His tax revenue grew. The exports of his kingdom grew, bringing in added revenue, and his expanding population produced a ready labor force to work the new vines. He no longer had a pauper population draining his kingdom's coffers. Everyone benefited.

Habram ensured everyone involved received rewards in his service projects.

The donkey pulling the water cart earned immediate rewards. Many women routinely fed the donkey carrots or other vegetables to reward him for coming to their house. The donkey quickly learned which houses fed him and refused to bypass that house for any reason. He quickly became the best-cared-for animal in the territory. One donkey characteristic was their mantra: all donations will be gratefully accepted.

The two teenage boys tending the cart and donkey were volunteers, but that didn't mean there were no rewards. Yes, they were unpaid. But, if they were diligent in their duties, at the end of two years Havram appointed them as apprentices on the new grape terraces. That was a paid position, though a paltry salary. Once they served three years and experienced several growing cycles, he gave them their own terrace to manage. If that worked well, in five years he transferred terrace ownership to them. Now they could make real money growing and selling their grapes for manufacturing into wine.

After a few years, it was not surprising that the volunteer job was one of the most sought-after jobs in Mamre.

By now, Habram was a Mamre fixture. Everyone knew and greeted him on sight. He knew everyone's name. He knew what was happening in their lives.

People began bringing him their ideas about what were significant problems or what needed improvement and possible ways to help.

They displayed their trust in him.

Havram realized, *I've arrived. I'm a real servant. Making a difference in their lives. Feeling their appreciation, their thankfulness. It gives me a wash of exhilaration. I'm needed. Thank you, Elshalim.*

And the king? At least I've caught his attention. He's started to support my projects, so he knows I've improved his kingdom. That's a good start. Now maybe, just maybe, at some point he'll begin supporting me. After that, he'll trust me enough to allow me to live in the city. Then, Sarrai and I will be safe.

Chapter 17

Smithsonian, Washington, DC—Present

"Good morning, Ian. David Scortun. Got you on speaker with George, our lab manager. Got some interesting news for you."

"So everything is going as planned?"

"Yes, the project is on-track."

"Does that mean you've set a completion date?"

"No, we aren't far enough along to set a timeline yet. Now, why we're calling. We've gone over the inside of the garment with a fine-tooth comb and we've come up with some evidence. We've recovered three short hairs from the underarm portion of the robe, plus some blood and skin residue. We believe we have enough to do a PCR."

"PCR? What's that?"

"Sorry, I keep forgetting you don't know archaeologist's lingo. Polymerase chain reaction. It's a test you use when you have a small sample of DNA. PCR amplifies the sample volume for testing. We're going to send the samples for DNA analysis. We'll use half the material and reserve the balance. Back to the reason for the call. We'd like to get a sample of your DNA for comparison."

"How do you recommend I send the blood sample so it won't degrade during shipping?"

"There's no need to have blood drawn. We'll sent you a sample kit. Just follow the directions. Swipe the cotton swab along the inside of your cheek, put it into the sterile container, put that into the box, and drop it in the mail."

"That sounds simple."

"Yes, it's that simple. We want to compare your DNA to the owner of the robe. But I need to tell you that there's one problem."

"What's the problem with the test?"

"No, no problem with the test, that's straightforward. The problem is that in the garment there was human material from at least two people."

"Two?"

"Yes, two. One, you'd expect: brown underarm hair. But the inside pocket contained a woman's hair."

"Wait a minute. How can you possibly know it's a woman's?"

"How do I know it's a woman? Good question. Men in 1750 BCE didn't wear their hair almost three feet long."

"I believe that I agree with you. Three feet long sounds like a woman."

"But there's another issue . . ."

"Another?"

"Yes, the hair is red—and not just any red. Flaming red."

"But Semites didn't have red hair."

"Yes, I know; people in the Middle East didn't have red hair. But people in England may have; we know they did later in history. So, can we depend on you for a DNA sample?"

"Send me the kit. I'll drop it in the mail the same day."

"Thank you."

****

EGYPT

Early Fall, 1746 BC

Habram entered the tent, "Sarrai, pack the camp; we have to leave immediately. I sent word to have Jurael collect the animals."

Sarrai looked puzzled, "Why? What's wrong?"

"We've experienced a drop in rainfall for two years. Some streams have stopped running. We've moved the flocks more often to get good grazing. We don't know what it is in surrounding regions, but I doubt it isn't just affecting Hebron. Overnight a large band of northern people just arrived. They obviously have no food, and left their homes to find some. They have over a hundred men. They've sent scouts to survey what's here. One group is giving us a long look. The way their men talk means they may be targeting to kill us and steal our animals. We can't defeat a hundred men. We have to leave."

"Where will we go?"

"We go to Egypt. Grass is always plentiful in their northern pastures. It will cost us an entrance tax, but that's better than death."

Habram's clan was on the move before noon. Their goal was to move fifteen miles before stopping. The following day they pushed the animals to move twenty more. There were few streams on the way; the third day they reached one, allowing the sheep and goats to rest and eat for a day.

That afternoon Habram sat down with Sarrai. "Before we left, I checked with people that have gone to Egypt. The border official will ask questions. I've never explained some of our customs because Middle Easterners know them. But Egyptians are ignorant. Here's what you need to know and tell the official, if asked.

"I am an Aramean. Your mother's culture is patriarchal. That means the father is clan head. The Aramean culture is fratriarchal. The oldest brother is his age group's clan head. Before he passed away Harran, not Terrah, was clan head of our age group. As the next oldest, now I am our extended family's clan head.

"In the Aramean culture, I am allowed to marry up to seven wives. Why seven? I don't know; it just is. We joke that it means we have a different wife for every day of the week, but I doubt that's true. The important fact is the husband must choose one wife to be his favorite, and her title is sister-wife. As the only wife, you are automatically my sister-wife. When asked, in our culture we only say you are my sister; we don't say sister-wife.

"Why is this important? Sarrai, you are beautiful, even more than when I married you. There are no red-haired women in Egypt. One duty of border officials is to examine every woman entering the Pharaoh's realm. As god-king, he chooses the most beautiful women in Egypt for his harem. If she is unmarried, they take her. If she is married, they kill the husband and take her.

"If they chose to take you, I can't prevent them. But, if I am dead, I can't work to get you back. If they do take you, I will find a way to rescue you."

"But," replied Sarrai, "I am your sister."

"No, Sarrai, you are not my sister; you are my half-sister. As followers of The Divine, we may not lie. At worst, we don't tell the entire story unless they ask for it. In my culture, saying you're my sister because you're my favorite wife is completely true. We cannot tell a half-truth."

"This makes no sense."

"No, Sarrai, it may make no sense to you, but it does to someone of my culture. Because it's true, it's what you must say."

"If there is a high risk going to Egypt, should we return to Hebron?"

"The return risk is death. Which is worse?"

"It seems we have little choice, do we?"

"We can depend on The Divine to protect us. We may endure trials. But if we remain faithful, The Divine will be faithful."

The Egyptian border official was a small man of stature, but believed himself seven feet tall in importance. "Next," he called out.

Habram moved to the head of the line and said in Semitic, "Habram, of Hebron, requesting to provide lambs and goats for sale, and to graze our herds in the eastern delta."

"Number of animals?"

"876 sheep, 74 goats."

"Permission granted. Tax is thirty sheep and two goats." He gestured to two of his assistants who selected the best-looking animals and herded them to a holding enclosure.

"Number of people?"

"Seven men, one woman, and a boy."

"The boy your son?"

"No, he is my brother's son. My brother died and I'm raising him."

"Who is the woman?"

"She's my sister."

"Come here, woman." As Sarrai approached, the astonished look on his face proclaimed he'd never seen anyone with red hair. Blue eyes, though rare, he had seen in people from eastern Turkey. But, never red hair. Never freckles on her face. She was beautiful. It took no more than five seconds to decide. He asked Sarrai, "You are his sister?"

"Yes," she replied.

He turned to the exchequer, and speaking in Egyptian, "Count out two hundred silver shekels."

"Two hundred," the exchequer gasped, amazed by the extravagant amount.

"Yes." he answered, "She is one of the most beautiful women I have ever seen. She is worth two hundred. Adding her to his harem will please the Pharaoh."

The exchequer counted out the money, put it into a bag, and gave the bag to Habram.

The official turned back to Habram, continuing in Semitic, "This is for your sister. We are taking her to Pharaoh's harem."

Sarrai burst into tears and ran to Habram's arms. Habram hugged her for a minute, then looked into her eyes and spoke gently, "Sarrai, we must." He took her hand and led her to the soldier who would guard her.

They continuing looking at each other as Habram slowly led his men and herds down the road. Heartbreak, fear, worry, determination, anxiety, and longing chased themselves across both faces.

Her last glimpse of Habram gave her some comfort. His face promised, "This will not be forever." Her final thought before she lost sight of him: *I must believe. I must trust. Habram will find a way. The Divine will not abandon us.*

When Sarrai arrived at the harem in Itj-Towy, they assigned a Semitic middle-aged slave woman to care for her. Nahat's first task was to quiet Sarrai's fears. "My lady, what is your name?"

"Sarrai."

"Don't worry. Here are Egypt's most pampered women. You look young, how old are you?"

"Two hands plus four."

"You are beautiful. Especially your red hair and freckles. They selected you at the border?"

"Yes."

"Let me quiet your fears. Pharaoh Imyremeshaw is a kind, old man, but he's usually unable to mate. The harem has almost three hundred women. Over half will never see him. Most others never see him twice. Of those who do spend a night, nothing will happen.

"How long before you are ready? It will take three months to prepare you, perhaps more. First, learning Egyptian will take two months or more. Then you need to learn proper court decorum."

Nahat looked Sarrai over from head to toe. "Because of summer heat, most women shave their hair. I would recommend we leave yours. Your red hair will be your signature look."

Yes, Nahat cared for Sarrai, but she realized that Sarrai needed more than a slave; she needed a friend. She became Sarrai's friend and surrogate mother.

The officials assigned Habram an eastern delta fertile grazing ground. But his mind wasn't on his flocks, it was on his wife.

Two days after arriving at Tanis, Jurael and Michel approached Habram and Jurael put his hand on Habram's shoulder. "Sarrai is our concern. It takes two of us minding animals and two more tending camp. That gives you two men to help. Make a plan to rescue her. Then tell us what you want us to do."

Habram put one hand on each of the two men's shoulders and his voice was a little husky, "Thank you. You two are real comrades. I'll tell you what I need to learn.

"First, the background. Here's what I have discovered. The pharaoh's capital is Itj-towy. Pharaoh's harem is there, so that's where Sarrai must be. Pharaoh Imyremeshaw is a figurehead; he doesn't rule Egypt. He's an old man and never leaves the capital. Itj-Towy is about forty miles south of Memphis, just over a hundred miles from here. Worse still, its on the west side of the Nile—we will have to cross the river to escape. Memphis is the administrative capital of Egypt. Ankhu is the djat there; we would call him a vizier. He's the real ruler of Egypt. He's mentally sharp, physically vigorous, and a capable ruler.

"Second, we face difficult problems. Ankhu only allows Egyptians in Itj-towy. I'll identify harem buildings from the western hills. I'll have to guess the number and disposition of guards from movement patterns. It's unlikely there's more than thirty, split between the Pharaoh's quarters and the harem. Why? Because the town is far from the river and there's no governmental function there. So, there's no reason for a large force. We may have a good chance of rescuing her from the harem.

"The real difficulty is escape. First we have to cross the Nile. Then it's a long way to the Egyptian border, and no matter how fast we go, the runners are faster. The entire border guard will be on alert, looking for us. Sarrai's red hair would be a dead giveaway.

"The key is skirting the delta and finding a route through the eastern mountains to the Red Sea. After we round the top of the Red Sea, we'll have to go south, then cut through the Sinai peninsula and north to Hebron. I'll need to scout and mark the trail to the Red Sea. I'll have to stash food and water along the route for us. Figure preparation will require at least two months.

"Before we escape, we'll have to move the herds out of Egypt. Once we rescue Sarrai, they'll shut the border. So, we can't escape before the early rains start in two months. The herd will need the greening of grass. So we'll plan for a late moon rising in two and a half months. That will give us darkness to rescue her and moonlight for our escape."

Six weeks later, Habram gathered Jurael and Michel in a tent and showed them his plans. On the floor, he had constructed a clay replica of the Itj-Towy compound. Michel was especially intrigued with the exactness of the layout.

Havram began the briefing with an overview. "The compound is laid out in a north-south-east-west axis. All roads are either north-south or east-west and all buildings are on the same rectangular axis. That makes it much easier to get your bearings. Once you understand where things are, there is no way to get lost once you get inside. The compound is enclosed by a ten-foot-high wall, but that's all it is—a wall. It's designed to keep out blowing dust, not an enemy. There are no ramparts, towers, or other defensive positions. Once you scale the wall, you're in the compound.

"The main gate is on the center of the east wall. There are two men on-duty at all times. No matter what happens inside the compound, they never leave their post, so we don't have to kill them. The Pharaoh's building is this one on the northeast corner. Again, there are two men always on duty, but they can't leave their post, so we can dismiss them also.

"Just behind the king's quarters on the north wall is the harem. It's the building with the large rectangular front and three wings oriented east-west, like three fingers pointing off a hand. The women's rooms are along the fingers. There are three guards on duty during the day, but only two at night. We'll have to kill them to gain access to the harem.

"Just behind the harem is guest quarters on the northwest side of the compound. It's usually unoccupied and there are no guards. That section of the wall is where we go in and out.

"This building on the southwest corner is the kitchen and bakery. They serve the entire compound, so it runs continuously and people are constantly going back and forth for food. Stay well away from here. If anyone spots you, it is the fastest way to alert the entire compound.

"The guard shack is this one just south of the main gate and against the east wall. There are two guards on duty at all times. I also suspect there is one superior on duty inside the building. The guard's sleeping quarters are in the back.

"The rest of the buildings are offices and living quarters for functionaries and people who support the court. They don't count because, by the time they're awakened by the ruckus, we'll be gone.

"Okay. That's the compound. What do we have to do? We go in where I have the clay ladder against the wall. We hoist the second ladder and put it against the wall on the inside to get out. Then we split up. Jurael and Michel, you go the harem's front door. Count to one thousand. Then each one of you take one of the guards and put an arrow center chest. You have five minutes to run through the women's quarters calling for Sarrai. Get her out the door, over the wall and go one quarter-mile due north. I've sunk a ten-foot-tall pole in the ground—I'll show you when we get there. We stash her clothes there and she can change. We leave her Egyptian clothes there, so any search party who finds them will think we kept going north.

"I'll hold off the guards for ten minutes to allow you time to get her into traveling clothes and join you there. Then we head west to a cave I'll show you in the foothills. It's the last direction they'll look to follow. We hole up for two days. The search parties will keep going away from Itj-Towy and we'll sneak out behind them. Then we go south about thirty miles to where I bought and hid a rowboat. We can't cross the Nile from Itj-Towy because there are only foothills to the east. First, we can't get lost in foothills, and second, that's the first place the searchers will look because that's the easiest way to escape. No, we have to cross south of Itj-Towy through the mountains. That's a harder way, but they won't be looking for us there. We cross the Nile and head into the mountains for the Red Sea. I've stashed food and water skins along the way.

"If everything goes well, we will pull off a clean exit and only have to kill four or five men. Questions?"

They were quite a few, but after several hours, all three men had their part of the escape plan down pat.

The day before they were to move the herd out of Egypt, an official and four soldiers from the border guard approached them. The official spoke flawless Semitic. He went straight towards their flock.

"I'm looking for Habram from Hebron."

"I'm Habram."

"I'm a translator. Please come with us; we need to bring you to a hearing in Tanis."

"A hearing?"

"You'll know more when we arrive."

Two hours later they entered the open doors of an imposing building. The guards told them to wait in the antechamber. Various people came and went from the inner chamber; Habram understood no Egyptian and had no idea what was happening.

When the last group before them entered the inner chamber, the translator came to Habram, "We're next. When we go in, watch me. When I stop and bow before Ankhu, you stop and bow as deeply as you see me do."

"At the word 'Ankhu,' Habram's heart skipped a beat. Ankhu was Egypt's djat. Why would such a high-ranking official want to see him? Habram's anxïety level skyrocketed. His mind was screaming. *I'll walk in. Will they give me the chance to walk out? Have they discovered our plans? If they had, wouldn't they have just executed me? What is happening?* He had many questions and no answers.

When the doors opened, the translator told Habram, "Follow me," and headed through the doors. Habram followed and attendants closed the doors behind him.

Ankhu sat on a throne on a dais. He looked down on those gathered before him. Habram recognized that the short official they had met at the border was also in the room.

Ankhu said something in Egyptian and the translator turned and spoke to Habram, "Tell us what happened at the border when this official stopped you."

As Habram began speaking, the translator repeated his words in Egyptian to Ankhu. "The official asked me why we were seeking to come into Egypt. I told him to graze and sell animals from our herd. He asked me how many people we had, and I told him seven men, one boy, and one woman. He asked if the boy was my son and I told him no, the boy was my dead brother's son and I was raising him. He asked me who the woman was and I told him she was my sister. He turned to Sarrai and asked if she was my sister, and Sarrai said yes. Then he told us he was taking Sarrai for the Pharaoh's harem, gave us some money, and told us to go on."

The translator turned to the border official and said something in Egyptian. At its conclusion, the translator told Habram the official corroborated everything Habram had said.

The translator asked Habram, "Is the woman your sister?"

"Yes."

"Is the woman your wife?"

"Yes, she is my sister-wife."

The translator turned to Ankhu and continued in Egyptian. Habram could not understand, but the translator told Ankhu that Habram had told the truth. The translator pinched Habram's robe and told Ankhu that anyone could recognize from his clothes that he was Aramean. In Aramean a "sister" was the man's favorite wife, not a biological sister. Habram was just a poor, dumb shepherd. They couldn't expect him to understand what the border official wanted. He answered truthfully for his language and customs. Similarly, Sarrai had answered truthfully. He pointed to Habram. "There's no fault here." Then he continued, "But you expect your border officials to be more than simply skillful in foreign languages. They should know what the foreigners are saying, which means they need to know the foreigner's customs, or at least to be smart enough to ask additional questions. The border official did neither. Therefore, he was at fault."

Ankhu thought for a minute, then turned to the border official and pronounced judgment. The translator gave the Semitic equivalent to Habram. "You have heard the evidence. Why this hearing? Not two weeks after you took this man's wife for the Pharaoh's harem a cattle disease started. Disease has claimed a quarter of Egypt's cattle. Three weeks later there was an earthquake in upper Egypt. The quake leveled four towns and left seventeen hundred dead. You have offended the gods by your ignorance and stupidity, and caused ruin on Egypt. Don't you realize that only virgins may enter the harem? You didn't ask if this woman had laid with a man. Your failure to ask basic questions is the cause of the god's anger. The kingdom has not lost seventeen hundred dead; it has now lost seventeen hundred and one." Turning to the soldiers, he ordered, "Take him away." Six soldiers grabbed the border official and led him through a side door and out of the chamber.

Ankhu turned to the other side, "Release the woman."

An attendant opened a door on the chamber's far side, and Sarrai tentatively stepped through the door. On catching sight of Habram, she ran into his arms, sobbing with relief and joy. Habram wrapped his arms around her.

Ankhu faced Habram and began speaking again. The translator gave the Semitic equivalent, "Habram, you have been unjustly accused of lying. You have been unjustly separated from your wife. Egypt has unknowingly caused you harm since you arrived. Your suffering has reached the ears of the gods, and they have cried out for justice. Egypt has heard their cries. We cannot restore the three months you have suffered, but we need to show the gods that we will compensate and offer sacrifices for the sins we have committed. We are offering you a cart, an ox to pull it, and five hundred deben of gold for the harm we have caused. We ask that you accept this gift and leave Egypt so there will no longer be any ill will of the gods towards us."

Habram bowed and said, "I accept, O Lord."

The translator give Habram's answer in Egyptian. Ankhu nodded his head, rose and left the chamber through the back door.

On the return trip from Egypt, the whirlwind events settled in Habram's mind.

First, he was now rich beyond dreams. His first act would be to give Elshalim, his Melchizadek, one tenth—a tithe—of what he had received.

Second, he had the wherewithal to fund every planned improvement project to make Hebron a vibrant success.

Third, he had the money to order thirty Ur bows. He also had the money to buy a dozen herds from current down-on-their-luck owners. He'd retain the former owners to manage them. By coordinating, they could avoid undercutting each other's prices. By cooperating, they could earn more. By banding together, no thugs could threaten them.

Forth, he didn't need to assault the Pharaoh's harem, killing innocent guards. The Divine stopped the plan. In other words, The Divine had chosen him as worthy of personal care.

Last, what he'd heard about border officials killing the husband and taking the wife was false. The translator had said that they only took virgins. Since Sarrai was no longer a virgin, she had been in no danger. It was their carefully schemed plan to trick the border officials that had backfired and caused Sarrai to be taken.

He asked himself questions he could not answer. *Did The Divine only rescue them after they had gotten into trouble? Did The Divine know in advance what they would do and, after they had gotten into trouble, only then cause the events that would rescue them? Did The Divine cause everything, including their scheming at the border? In other words, did The Divine only react to events as they happened? Or, did The Divine cause everything, including causing Habram and Sarrai to plot their scheme?*

Habram couldn't tell.

Had The Divine always been faithful because that was His nature? In other words, The Divine was the initiator of faithfulness. Or, had The Divine been faithful to them because they had first been faithful? In other words, was The Divine's faithfulness a reaction to their first being faithful.

Habram couldn't tell. He only knew that The Divine *had been* faithful to them. Habram couldn't tell which possibility was true.

What did Habram know? The Divine would do enough to *prompt* and *enable* you to have faith, but not so much that you were *forced* to have faith. Reworded, you maintained your free-will; you could chose to believe or disbelieve in The Divine. The Divine always remained in that in-between state between giving you evidence of His acting in history, but not forcing you to believe it was Him and not fate that was acting.

Habram shook his head. *I will make my decision. As for me and my house, we will follow The Divine.*

On the long trip back to Hebron, Habram asked himself one additional question. He'd always searched for what he wanted in life. What should be his occupation? What should be his life goals? What would make him happy? Now he questioned his whole life approach.

Before he became a servant, everything he'd wanted was for himself. "What's in it for me?" That had proved selfish. And, selfishness had proved unsatisfying.

He reviewed what he'd done since becoming a servant. He'd worked for the good of the community. Like Elshalim, his community had rewarded him with their trust. There was no wealth or worldly power in that, but it felt infinitely more rewarding.

Like the morning mist disappearing, suddenly his world solidified into a clear picture. During his whole life, The Divine had been preparing him as a servant. Not just having an ephod stone in his tunic, but being a real servant.

This was late fall. Grass was turning emerald green from the early rains. This land was tailor-made for sheep and goats. What did he want now? He wanted precisely what The Divine had given him.

Going forward, what should he do now? He should strive to discover what The Divine wanted him to do. Where The Divine was leading him. Then, desire and work for that. The Divine would reward him.

Habram shook his head and gave up his questioning. He would probably never know everything he wanted to know about The Divine. That was just The Divine being The Divine. The Divine granted his worshipers just enough insight to enable them to have faith, but not so much that full knowledge forced faith on them.

That was enough. He had experienced The Divine's favor. He now had experience-knowledge from the heart, not just deduced-knowledge from the head. The Divine did act in the world. Knowing you were in The Divine's good graces was the most important fact.

Chapter 18

Smithsonian, Washington, DC—Present

"David?" asked the phone. "Professor Carter here at the George Washington Engineering Lab. Got the results of your set of FEAs. Thought I'd give you a call to talk through the lab report in case you have any questions."

"Yes, thank you, you always go above and beyond what's required."

"I know, but not everyone can interpret data. Anyway . . .

"The FEA eliminates bronze point objects: arrow head, sword, and spear. All tips would have deformed at impact, creating a significant tear. I know you didn't ask, but we also modeled a flint-tipped spear. Both thrust and thrown spears produce so much force the stone would shatter, not crack. The weapon accounting for all data is a flint-tipped arrow.

"Next, force analysis suggests the arrow traveled eighteen yards distance if fired on a level, or fifteen yards if fired from a city wall to ground. The shorter distance accounts for the force of gravity amplifying the force vector.

"So, someone fired a flint-tipped arrow at whoever was wearing that garment. Any questions?"

David thought for a minute, "No. I think your summary accounts for all variables. Thank you again."

"No problem. Call us again if you need anything. Bye."

They both hung up.

David mused. *Now I know what happened. But why? How does this fit into the overall picture?*

****

HEBRON

Early Spring 1744 BC

A year later, Habram was integrating his new sheep flocks and goat herds. He now controlled seventy-eight men and multiple thousands of animals. With women and children, his people numbered three hundred and eighteen. His territory stretched from just East of Salem, around south to the mid-point of the Dead Sea on its east side.

He took Lot to a promontory overlooking the Dead Sea valley. "Lot, I promised your father that I would look after you, and that I would never take anything from you. We have so many flocks and herds we need to separate your animals from mine. From here you can see the entire valley. Choose which half of the valley you wish for your animals and I will take the rest."

"Uncle Habram, I know I am of age to be a man, but I'm not ready to manage that many men and animals. I need to become more mature. Would you manage them for me until I am three hands plus one? I will choose the southern valley in the Sodom and Gomorrah region. I don't need half of the valley because the southern plain is lush and fertile. That's enough. Until then, I'll live in Sodom."

"Lot, you have made a wise decision. Buy a house in Sodom and live there. I will manage your animals; they are yours whenever you're ready. I will visit. If you need anything, let me know."

Each put their right hand on the other's shoulder, hugged, and parted.

There was no warning. Elshalim was walking with Salem's king. In mid-stride his left leg gave way and he flopped on his right side in the middle of the road. The king grabbed his left arm to pull him upright. The arm was limp. Elshalim tried to raise himself with his right arm and leg, but only succeeded in thrashing about. The left leg was immobile. He tried talking, but the left side of his mouth wouldn't work. His words came out garbled and unintelligible. For a couple of minutes he struggled for breath, then stopped. A peaceful calm settled on his face, and he was gone.

The king sent runners to the stewards in the Southwest Canaanite Region.

Habram found out a week later when he returned to camp. His first thought was sadness for Elshalim.

His next was realizing that he would never see him again, never have a chance to learn more from him.

Then it hit him. With Elshalim gone, there would be no letter sent to the Council to make them reconsider their decision. He would probably never have a chance to earn a seat on the Council. *Oh, well,* he thought, *there's plenty to do in Hebron. I don't need to sit on the Council. I don't need to become a melchizadek. With The Divine looking after me, I don't need to worry. I will do whatever The Divine puts in front of me to do.*

Sarrai looked up at her husband putting his ephod in his white linen garment's chest pocket. "Habram, what are you doing?"

"Since this year is a danger year, I've been paying close attention to sunrise and moon fall. The two are growing closer. In about two days we will have moon fall at sunrise. That is a possible eclipse signal. So, it's time to warn Hebron of the danger."

"But Habram, they've already told you they don't want you to bother them. So why are you warning them?"

"It doesn't matter what they think or how they act. My faithfulness is all that matters. I will call a solemn fast. If they refuse, as I expect, I will hold it on their behalf."

"Since you know they won't pay attention, why not just hold the fast without even telling them?"

"Because I'm a servant. Whether they listen or whether they don't is between them and The Divine. My duty is calling. If I do not, I give them no chance to respond. If I call, perhaps some will listen."

"Habram, sometimes I just don't understand you."

Habram thought, *I know you don't understand. Only someone fully committed to The Divine can understand.* But, he said nothing.

Habram finished donning his robe and left for the trip to Hebron.

As he approached Hebron's city gate, a watchman called out from above the gate, "O troublemaker, what mischief would you cause today?"

"I've come to call a solemn fast. There is significant chance of an eclipse within the next few days. We need to ask The Divine to restore the sun and moon to their proper balance."

An archer on the rampart had heard too much. "Heretic," he yelled, "There is no 'The Divine'. You deserve death like the rest of the Servants." In one smooth motion, he pulled an arrow from his quiver, strung it, aimed and let fly. It flew straight and true toward Habram's chest.

The arrow struck with a loud crack. Its force thrust Habram to the ground. To everyone's amazement, despite Habram receiving an arrow in center-chest, he rose to his feet. He stretched his arm and pointed at the archer on the wall, and commanded, "Kill him, and throw his body over the wall."

A soldier drew his dagger and plunged it into the archer's heart. He dumped the body over the wall, sprawling on the ground below.

Habram shifted his arm to point at the Watchman, "Call the King; I will wait." He crossed his arms over his chest.

Fifteen minutes later the king appeared on the wall, "O mischief-maker, what brings you to my gate today?"

"I have come to call a solemn fast. There is an eclipse possibility within the next few days."

"Why did you order my archer killed?"

"I am unarmed. He tried to kill me. Only you, O King, have that authority. Without your authority, it's called murder. Murder is punishable by death."

"Why are you still alive?"

"The Divine protects me."

"The Divine didn't protect all the other Servants. So, why are you still alive?

"Sire, what do you mean: all the other Servants?"

"You haven't heard?" It was a statement; not a question. He answered it anyway. "Every servant in Canaan is dead. Bethlehem's was the last. Every servant. Their family. Their staff. Everyone."

"Every servant? Why?"

"The Servants were impostors. They lied. They stole money from their cities to live in luxury. Our cities have supported thieves for generations.

"'The Egyptians cracked the 'fod-ef' code. It was long and complicated. But, not magic. The length made decipherment difficult. It's a repeating cycle of seventeen hundred days. A 'fod-ef' isn't needed to predict eclipses. You can count the days on a papyrus scroll. It's as regular as spring-summer-fall-winter. A never-ending, repeating cycle. There is no magic to calculate eclipses. There is no servant religion. It's all a sham.

"The news has enraged every city in Canaan. If you'd been here last week, I would have killed you. There are only two men in Canaan that faithfully served their city: Elshalim and you. And Elshalim has passed on peacefully. If I had any other servant, I would still kill you. But, you deserve respect.

"As for your eclipse, let it come. It will pass without prayers, without solemn fasts, without intervention. Because it is part of the sun and moon's natural cycle. We cannot make it happen. We cannot prevent it from happening.

"For everything you have done for Hebron, you deserve my respect. But your heretic religion does not deserve any respect. Go away." He turned and left the wall.

Habram ran the three miles to camp.

As he burst into camp, he yelled, "Michel."

Michel came running, "Yes, Habram."

"Grab your bow. Fetch six skins; three for each of us. One each of water, fresh goat's milk and grains. I'll get two travel baskets of bread and six quivers, two of flint arrows and one of square bronze each. We're leaving in fifteen minutes."

"Fifteen minutes? Where are we going?"

"Mari."

"Mari? That's a long way from here. Why are we going to Mari?"

"Three months ago the Council transferred Terrah from Haran to Mari. He's in danger. Canaan began killing their Servants a week to a week and a half ago. I expect runners are on their way to Mari. We have to outrun them."

Habram ducked into their tent and let Sarrai know he was going to Mari to rescue their father and mother before the Egyptian news reached Mari. He stripped off his ephod garment and donned his working robe. "I have to leave immediately. I'll be back in six weeks."

The first four days the two men made fifty miles a day traveling four miles an hour, twelve to fourteen hours a day, alternating between fast walking and slow jogging. The constant travel took a toll on their bodies, and after that they could only travel forty miles at best. They also had to stop every few days long enough to refill their bread, grains, and milk. Their milk goatskins were fresh. There was enough rennet left to curdle the milk. By conserving their cheese for eating and whey for soaking the grains, they made each goat-stomach-full last for three days between refills.

A normal travel time to Mari took three and a half weeks to travel the five hundred miles. Habram calculated the runners had a week's head start. They needed to make the trip in twelve days to ensure they could beat the runners.

Habram had no way to know the news of the Egyptian code decipherment hadn't gone from Egypt, through the Levant, to the Tigris-Euphrates river basin. The news had gone to Stonehenge. Then south along the trade routes to Babylon. Then west to the Levant.

The two weary travelers appeared at the gates of Mari twelve days later, their garments dirt and grime encrusted, their hair sweat and dust entangled, smelling like three day-old dead fish. A guard stopped them at the gate. "Reason for entry?"

"I'd like to visit my father, Terrah, the Melchizadek."

The guard delivered the news with unfeeling distain, "You've wasted your trip. We executed the heretic almost a month ago."

Habram felt his heart go cold, and his stomach tighten into a hard knot. "Executed?"

"Yes. Those bandits preyed on us to support them. They'll never lord it over us again. We've cleaned out their dens from the city they call Ur in the north to Ur in the south. We've not left a single Melchizadek or servant alive. We killed Terrah and his wife. I'm sorry about your loss of your mother, but your father deserved his death. We hung Terrah's body on the city wall for a week. We broke his fod-ef stone in little pieces and used it to weight his body down in the middle of the river. He deserved it; he and all of his thieving, lying kind."

"What of my brother Nahor."

"Since he's not yet a man, I don't believe they killed him. I expect you'll find him in the orphan's home."

"Is there an inn where we can stay the night? We need to bathe and have a meal. We'll return to our home in the morning."

The guard gave them directions. Before they left, Havram looked out on a calm, placid Euphrates. His world was anything but. His father's bones were somewhere out there. They had executed him, the last Melchizadek. Hung his body on the city wall for a week, then used his shattered stone to weight his body down and let the fish finish him off. The Melchizadeks, the Servants, Ur itself—slaughtered, gone. He was the killing frenzy's sole survivor. He surrendered to the weight of his emotions. His shoulders sank. His forehead fell. His eyes drooped to ask his hands "Why?" A long, sorrowful sigh escaped his lips.

But he knew. *I must return. Will they leave a sandal for Sarrai to mark my grave? No; no grave. For me, it will be buzzards.*

The innkeeper had one of his assistants lead them to the orphan's home where they found Nahor. He and Habram had a joyful reunion. Nahor had lost all hope—his only future was to be sold as a slave when he became of age to be a man. Habram had rescued him.

The next day the two men and Nahor prepared to join a party traveling to Sidon.

The Mari journey had been frenetic. The return was lethargic. The slaughter of Terrah and Coth shattered all their hopes. The men didn't know what would await them. They hardly talked. Putting one foot in front of the other was a chore. They had to return.

Chapter 19

Yale University, New Haven, Connecticut—Present

"Professor Clyster, thank you for agreeing to see me," Doctor Scortun began. "You are one of four expert historians of Ancient Middle Eastern history. I have an archaeology riddle to solve." He gave Professor Clyster pictures of the tablet, the first five names, and the garment. "The garment has been carbon-14 dated to 1750 BCE and bears pollen samples consistent with Stonehenge in England. The tablet stone came from the Preseli Quarry in Wales, the same bluestone used at Stonehenge. The cuneiform writings date from 1800 to 1700 BCE. The first five names are Havram (likely Abraham's original name), Abraham, Isaac, Jacob, and Israel. All Aramean names. Our problem is understanding events in England and the Middle East that could explain a tie between them. I realize I'm stretching, but are you aware of any lines of evidence to verify or refute a working theory?"

"Stonehenge and the Middle East? That's interesting. There are no written records documenting a connection, but that means little. This was before most civilizations used writing for anything but lists of goods. Few kept written history. A theory based on negative evidence is unverifiable.

"Stonehenge. Well, we know the inhabitants abandoned Stonehenge sometime around BCE 1700–1750."

"Abandoned?" asked Doctor Scortun.

"Yes, just that, abandoned. Actively flourishing one day; lay fallow from then on. Towards its life's end there is archaeological evidence of people visiting from as far as Switzerland or southern Germany. The Amesbury Archer, you know, came from there. Buried at Amesbury, a few miles from Stonehenge. Then there were those twin children, probably brother and sister, although I can't recall where they came from. Not local, that's for sure. But I don't know of any direct connection to the Middle East itself. There are stone circles which could be Stonehenge mimics, but it's impossible to confirm cause and effect. No evidence has withstood scientific scrutiny.

"The Middle East. 1750. Several come to mind. First, the Tigris-Euphrates was calm until shortly after the death of Hammurabi in 1750. His son, Samsu-Iluna, briefly expanded his empire by forced conscription of troops from tribute countries, but they proved unreliable. He overextended the resources of Babylon. In 1742 Rim-Sin II of Larsa led a revolt which almost resulted in the downfall of Babylon. The city survived, but lost most of its kingdom and never recovered. Assyria was the eventual winner. So figure ten years after Hammurabi's death, the rebellion effectively erased Babylon from the map.

"We know that around 1750 the Hurrians invented the modern chariot. We don't have written records, but we do have a picture carved in stone. It had small wheels with four spokes. Two horses lashed to a single axle hovering between them pulled it. A driver and an archer wielding a short compound bow operated it. Hints in written records—but the pictures are unrevealing—suggest leather tires circled their wheels. I'd say that occurred sometime between 1750 and 1740 BCE.

"By the way, many scholars believe the Hurrians formed the battle core of Hyksos that invaded and conquered Egypt a hundred years later. The only advancement was a larger six-spoke wheel with brass fittings replacing the smaller four-spoke ones.

"The Mycenaeans also invented the chariot within ten years of the Hurrians. Seemingly they did this independently, because the Mycenaean chariot was unusual. Again we have no surviving chariot in the archaeological record, but by the surviving pottery images had a small four-spoke wheel. It also sported the most unusual axle imaginable. A single horse pulled this chariot. Just behind the mane was something like a modern ball and hitch. The axle bent up, over the horse's back, and rested on the hitch. This axle was fragile. The Mycenaeans only used it to ferry high status nobles to the battle, after which they dismounted and fought on foot. It appears that this chariot remained the same for four or five hundred years, for Homer's *Iliad* reports Agamemnon rode one to battle.

"I admit it's odd that Mycenaeans and Hurrians developed chariots at the same time, despite being a thousand miles apart with no known contact.

"That's all I can think of. I trust I've helped?"

"I believe so, sir." replied Doctor Scortun. "If our investigation proves publishable, we'll add your name to the report. Thank you for your assistance."

****

FROM MARI TO THE PALESTINIAN LEVANT

1744 BC

Meaningless hours stretched into meaningless days, each empty, void of significance. Habram's face was vacant; his thoughts mindless. His body lived on, but he wasn't alive. He existed to place one footstep in front of another. A black cloud enveloped him; his mind no longer active; he was a semiautomatic walking machine.

Everything he had believed in, worked for, hoped for: gone. The Council, the Dygsu, the candidates, the melchizadeks, the servants, all gone. O'ur of the Chall Dia—its people driven from their homes; the city burned to the ground—silent. Abandoned. The voice of The Divine banished. Only he remained. He was alone.

Habram couldn't see beyond his own feet.

Man is a creature of hope. Without hope, there is no thriving, only mere existence. And, Habram wasn't sure he even existed.

Habram stopped living to eat; now he ate merely to live.

One night deep into their second travel week, Habram was asleep on his back with his head resting on a rock. Suddenly his eyes were open and he felt a deep thought resonate in his mind. The thought said, "Habram, look toward heaven, and number the stars, if you are able to number them. So shall your descendants be." The thought had no words, Habram had to supply those. The thought was one flash of all-encompassing completeness. He knew with a qualitative surety through his entire being—this came from The Divine. He had never experienced anything like this. It thrilled him to the core, yet also scared him. He was aware of an all-pervasive presence in the thought. Powerful yet caring. Its supernatural character, transcending this transient world, humbled him.

As he had earlier suspected, what The Divine told him meant The Divine could see the future. It also meant The Divine had a plan. In some manner He caused that plan to happen.

And Havram believed The Divine. The Divine cared for him, so The Divine's plan was good enough for him. He didn't need to control his world. The Divine could take care of it. Habram was at peace. He would trust The Divine. He would be faithful.

And The Divine reckoned Habram's faithfulness as righteousness.

In response, another thought flooded into Habram's mind. Like before, Habram had to translate the thought into his own words. "Go from your kindred and your father's land to the land that I have prepared for you. And I will make of you a great nation. I will bless you, and make your name great, so you will be a blessing. I will bless those who bless you, and him who curses you I will curse; and by you, all the families of the earth shall bless themselves."

Habram knew with a surety beyond doubt that he was acting in response to The Divine's commands. A peace he had never before experienced, a peace beyond understanding, enveloped him. All was well. He closed his eyes and slept the sleep of refreshment for the first time since leaving Hebron.

The next morning Habram was his normal self. He could think clearly. Put events into their proper perspective. Connect individual facts and form patterns.

He thought: *What happened? Of all The Divine's believers, only he had survived. That meant he was different. How?*

First, with only a few exceptions, like his father and Elshalim, he served selflessly. Assumed entitlement had run rampant throughout the ranks of the Servants, resulting in arrogant behavior. That created resentment. Which accumulated. The pent-up hatred only needed a spark for release as righteous rage. The Egyptian discovery was the spark.

But I wasn't killed. And, why now? Why me? Something's missing.

He racked his brain for anything he had done, and came up empty. He had done nothing that his father and Elshalim had not done.

Then he realized the difference. *It wasn't what he'd done. It was his beliefs.*

The Council always asked two questions. "What had you invented" was the first question. It occupied everyone's attention. "What have you learned about The Divine" was more important. No one concentrated on it.

Until Habram. That made Habram different. Habram identified The Divine in the Mycenaean creation story. The Mycenaeans paid attention starting after the first phrase: on the gods, starting with Gaia. But, the first phrase was the critical part. The chawos part came from The Divine, the rest was mankind's invention. Only Habram recognized its importance.

What happened? Did The Divine cause the Servants' slaughter? No, that didn't fit with how The Divine worked. No, the slaughter was the Servants' own fault. Through their arrogance, they had created a worldwide resentment against them. The Divine had only prevented the slaughter until

Habram arrived. When He released his protective hand over the Servants, that's when the slaughter happened.

Suddenly the image of the Ancients came to his mind. That happened to them! The Divine had prevented disease from killing them until the Servants arrived. This meant The Divine doesn't cause harm, He merely delays the harm already there from happening. He enables good to result from evil. The Ancients prevented new insights until the Servants. The Servants prevented new insights until Habram.

Brysur. Brysur prevented anyone from listening and learning from Habram. Brysur caused Habram's exile to the most remote place possible. But, in reality, Brysur "the man" wasn't important. Brysur merely represented what the Servants had become.

But, Brysur had failed.

Brysur's exile protected Habram from the impending slaughter. Habram was a shepherd, so he wasn't at Hebron for the early killing fervor. Then his community improvement projects and his never receiving monetary support made the king realize he had added to, not leached on, the king's coffers.

He suddenly realized his frustration at the king for refusing to allow him to live inside Hebron's city walls was The Divine protecting him. The stone walls wouldn't have kept him safe by repelling external invaders. It would have kept him inside the city and vulnerable to his real enemy— built-up rage of the citizens.

But his father had served selflessly, so why had The Divine removed his protective hand from him? Suddenly he knew. Habram wanted to do what The Divine wanted done. Father chose what to do what *he* considered in The Divine's benefit. In effect, Havram was the horse pulling The Divine's cart who obeyed the guidance of the bit and bridal. Father took the bit in his mouth and pulled The Divine's cart where Father wanted it to go. He insisted on making the decisions *for* The Divine. He wanted to be on the council for his own glory and aggrandizement, not because The Divine desired it. In effect, he put himself first and The Divine second.

Havram's head drooped. Father had come so close. But, he hadn't taken the last step of asking The Divine what He wanted done.

Habram considered his thought's effects. What was wrong about the Servants' methods which required change to better align with how The Divine acted? Habram realized The Divine never forced people to believe in Him. God always stayed in the margins between seen and unseen, belief and unbelief. He gave his worshipers enough evidence to enable them to have faith, but not so much that belief was forced upon them.

The Servants imposed belief in The Divine. Imposing creates resentment. That didn't align with how The Divine acted. The Divine hinted; He invited; He called. He never forced; He never cajoled; He never scolded. That means that Habram must call, must invite. He must never force. Belief needs to be voluntary.

The next realization was that he could never use the words ef-fod, fod-ef, or The Divine again. The Servants had built up so much anger in the population at large that those words would have a negative connotation for decades, if not centuries. They were toxic. He would never be able to restore those words to a positive connotation in his lifetime.

Suddenly it struck him. When a man changes his character, he needs to assume a new name. It was the same for The Divine. The Divine needed to assume a changed character, therefore He needed a new name. Habram needed to find another name for The Divine. Suddenly the new name was obvious. "Ephod" was a Semitic parody of Ur's "fod ef"—"he is." The Semitic language equivalent was "Yahweh" (YHWH). Habram would rename The Divine YHWH. As a pseudonym, he would call YHWH "the LORD."

Last, he realized he also needed a new name. He was no longer a servant; there were Servants no longer. Habram needed to become a different person. That required a new name. On thinking about it, the loud crack that resulted from the arrow hitting his ephod meant it had shattered, breaking his original contract with The Divine. His broken ephod sundered his old relationship. Suddenly the thought came: YHWH had already renamed him. YHWH said he would be the father of a multitude. He would become Abraham. Likewise, if he were a new person, his wife must become one also. She could no longer be Sarrai, an Ur name, but she would become Sarai, an Aramean name.

When he returned home, he withdrew his ephod from the robe. True to his anticipation, it was in three pieces. Yes, he was no longer a servant. Yes, the broken stone was a sign that his old life was gone. But, the stone was a part of who he was, like the parent always carries the child within them. He couldn't just discard it, like the shepherd's bowl on the plains of history. He resolved to repurpose it; with its Urim and Thumim, he encased it in a clay tablet and incised his Havram signet ring onto it. After he had an Abraham ring made, he would add that. He would have a box made, and place the ephod tablet on his folded-up robe inside the box. YHWH had said that he would be the father of generations. He would bequeath it to his descendants. It would forever be part of who we are.

The news that Mari had executed her father and mother devastated Sarai. She withdrew to her tent for the better part of a week, but finally allowed her duties to reclaim her attention. It was several years before she could put her loss and grieving behind her.

Several days after his return, Abraham received another message from YHWH. "Bring me a heifer three years old, a she-goat three years old, a ram three years old, a turtledove, and a young pigeon." He brought the animals, cut them in two, and laid each half over against the other, making a pathway between halves. He did not cut the birds in two, but laid a carcass on each side of the path. When birds of prey came down on the carcasses, Abraham drove them away.

When the sun had gone down and it was dark, a smoking fire pot and a flaming torch passed between these pieces, as if carried by an invisible being. The thought message came to Abraham, "To your descendants I give this land."

This astounded Abraham. This was a vassal's Fealty Pledge Ceremony. The vassal passed between the animal halves. It proclaimed to the vassal's lord: "I pledge my loyalty. If I break this pledge, may it be to me as the animals; may my body be severed in two."

But, Abraham did not pass between the animals. YHWH the LORD made the pledge to Abraham the vassal. By this, Abraham knew YHWH would never change his pledge. And, Abraham pledged to himself: *No matter what YHWH asked of him, he would obey. He would remain faithful.*

Where YHWH directs me to go, I will go. What YHWH gives me to do, I will do. What YHWH wants of me, I will want for me.

But by now, Abraham also knew that YHWH did not make pledges lightly. Something would happen that would tax his faithfulness.

Chapter 20

Smithsonian, Washington, DC—Present

"Good morning, Ian. David Scortun. We have the results of the DNA analysis. Got thirty minutes? And you may want to get your wife Alice with you on speaker. . . .

"Okay. We were correct. There's DNA samples from two people, one male and the other female."

"Two?"

"Right, the female is the redhead. The female is a Celt, or I guess we need to say a proto-Celt, because the Celts didn't arrive in England until about 800 BCE. However, this woman is genetically indistinguishable from Celts.

"The male is a Jew; but not just any Jew. If you compare his Y chromosome DNA to that of the world's Jews, you could say he's the Jewish father.

"Now for your DNA. Your Y chromosome matches his. Exactly, gene for gene. In more than one hundred eighty generations, you'd think there'd be a mutation. No. You are an *exact* match. You are a Jew."

"No, I'm a Christian."

"Sorry, I wasn't specific. There are at least three different ways you can define a Jew. First, by where you live, in today's case Israel. Second, by your religion: the Jewish religion. Last, a people or race. This is genetic. On this category, you are the quintessential Jew. From your Y chromosome, you might have fathered the Jewish nation. Abraham could have been your immediate father, instead of more than one hundred eighty generations back. Or, you could have been his father. You are a Jew."

"Hold on, let me get my jaw off the floor. If I'm a genetic Jew, it means every tablet name must be genuine?"

"Exactly. Some names are likely brothers or uncles, but all—every last one—must be from Abraham's line.

"Next. Are you braced? Abraham's mother was a blonde and he had blue eyes."

"Blue eyes? How does a Semite get blue eyes?"

"That's just it; he doesn't. Unless his father had a blue eye recessive gene and his mother had blue eyes."

"So you're telling me . . . ."

"Yes, Not only did Abraham go to Stonehenge, but his father and probably grandfather did also, and both father and grandfather married blue-eyed women. In this family, Stonehenge wasn't a one-time event. It was a tradition. That, plus the evidence of the stone in the tablet, likely means they were priests of a religion whose center was Stonehenge. Stonehenge was where they were consecrated. Stonehenge was where they met and married their wives. Can we prove this? No, but the evidence fits. Abraham did not have black or even dark brown hair. His hair was light brown."

"Wait a minute. The woman. You said she had red hair, right?"

"Flaming red, yes."

"That means, if the hair comes from Abraham's wife, that's a third generation of intermarriage with Celts."

"Ian, the intermarriage issue is more convoluted than that. Abraham's son, Isaac, married Rebecca, who was the sister of Laban, related to Abraham's wife. Isaac's son Esau had red hair and was his favorite son. That may be another tie suggesting that his red hair reminded Isaac of his mother's red hair. That is four generations straight of blonde or red hair, resulting in a red-haired Esau. And Esau's brother Jacob went back to Laban again and married his two daughters. That's now five generations straight. Now you have enough recessive genes floating in this family that you will periodically have red hair pop up seemingly out of the blue. It's in your family tree."

"I have red hair and red hair does run in our family—at least periodically. We always thought it was the fault of the women we married. Now you're saying the men carry it."

"Yes, both men and women carry it."

"Wait a minute. If I'm a direct descendant of Abraham, that means my family was Middle Eastern who traveled to England to marry. How did my family get back to England hundreds of years later?"

"Ian, your genes are a clue it did happen, but they can't tell you why. Perhaps if you looked into the names on the ephod tablet, they might contain a clue."

****

The news that travels fastest is always bad. The news raced down the King's Road on the east side of the Sea of Chinnereth, to the Jordan and the Dead Sea. A Sumerian army was coming. It numbered twelve hundred men. One hundred were swordsmen with shields and cattle-hide chest armor. Six hundred swordsmen wore bronze plate or cattle-hide chest armor. Four hundred light infantry carried spears. Fifty archers and fifty slingers formed the auxiliaries.

They proclaimed they simply wanted food and leave to pass through.

The King of Damascus didn't believe them. The invaders slaughtered his army, not 20 percent escaped. But the Sumerians didn't pursue the remnants of the army. The Damascus populace retreated into the city. The invaders bypassed it.

The King of Bashan provided a small herd of cattle for food. They passed through in peace.

The King of Ammon led his army to meet them. The invaders smashed it, remnants fleeing to the surrounding hills. Again, the invaders did not follow. Again, they bypassed Ammon.

The invaders were methodical. They marched twenty-five miles a day, slowing or pausing only if impeded. Scouts ensured no one could catch them unawares. Their mission was supreme. Speed was the priority. They brought no carts for food or spoils. Oxen pulled at two miles an hour. Oxen would have slowed them down. Spoils without carts would mean extra weight on a soldier's back. Extra weight meant slower pace. They took no prisoners or captives. They left both sides wounded on the battlefield. Speed of advance trumped all else.

An army marches on its stomach, and sheep and goats were their first choice for meat. The meat is succulent, quick to prepare, and easy to digest. Its meat lasted several days before spoiling. A man could carry a carcass for two days, then cook it. Its meat would last three days more.

The light infantry foraged for food, never wandering more than five miles afield. To go further would entail falling behind the march. Scouts confiscated available food from unprotected villages. It meant a lower grade of food, and occasionally several days without any. Their deadline demanded it.

The army did not stray from the King's Road. They couldn't risk revealing their goal. Their mission might fail. They could lose the impending war.

They were confident of success. They believed themselves invincible to everything except distractions.

Abraham's men led their flocks and herds to high mountain valleys fifteen miles out of the army's path.

Abraham moved a tent to a hill overlooking the Dead Sea Valley. It gave excellent vantage for everything happening on the far-side.

Once at Ammon, halfway down the Jordan River, the Sumerian army's advance pattern changed. The main army continued their speed-march south, but auxiliaries began collecting oxcarts. They emptied each and followed the army, littering the King's Road, collectively moving south.

The oxcarts were Abraham's final clue. It revealed their mission.

1. Collecting oxcarts only now meant: first, they were nearing their final destination, and second, they would need to haul massive amounts of material for their return trip.

2. Only the Gulf of Aqaba and the Red Sea were south of the Dead Sea plain. So, they were heading for Sodom and Gomorrah.

3. Bitumen was the Dead Sea Plain's only commodity. The southern marshlands of Sumer were the only other source.

4. Bitumen only had two uses: first, for cosmetics and medicines, and second, to waterproof goofas. Sodom and Gomorrah earned their wealth from selling bitumen. But, cosmetics only used small amounts. If the invaders wanted cosmetics, they'd buy it. But they sent an army to confiscate it.

5. An army sent to confiscate bitumen meant that their own supply was inadequate for their needs. That meant they were building an excessive number of ghoofas. That meant an army which needed to cross rivers.

6. The excessive number of oxcarts meant that they intended to return with all the bitumen they could collect.

7. Hammurabi had died a few years ago. His son had extended the boundaries of his father's kingdom, but only by conscripting subject kingdom armies and using these unreliable troops in other kingdom's regions. That created resentment in both subject populations. It signaled a weak Babylonia. That invited rebellion.

8. A successful rebellion would need multiple subjects banding together. The Babylonians were still too strong for one subject kingdom.

9. If multiple subject kingdoms had formed a conspiracy, their different types of armor would show it.

Abraham examined the invading army more closely. Yes, his evaluation was accurate. There were four distinct groups of people:

1. The men carrying shields all wore cattle-hide chest armor. They were Sumerians. Their swords were light, thin-bladed and four feet long. Their shields were two feet in diameter, reaching from their shoulders down to their waist. Their weapons were designed for fast, six-foot distance between lines, sword-against-sword battle. Only Sumerian marshes could provide enough river reeds for an army's shields. They also wore cattle hides for chest armor.

2. The swordsmen wearing bronze had individual two-inch by four-inch bronze plates sewn to a cloth backing. Their swords were only three feet long, but thick and heavy, designed for slow but powerful blows at close-in distance. These were Iranian Elamites. They had ready supplies of bronze.

3. The swordsmen wearing cattle-hide chest armor were a Babylonian subject state like Mari. They had no uniformity of weapons. Their weapons were not issued to them by their cities, but purchased by the men carrying them.

4. The archers and slingers formed a fourth group, probably from smaller Babylonian subject states.

He checked the marching order. Yes, the bronze and cattle-hide chest armored were in separate groups. They marched separately. That confirmed distinct groups.

Who commanded? Sumerians led the column.

Realization dawned on Abraham. The Sumerians had learned of Terrah's armor-piercing arrows. They carried shields and wore cattle-hide chest armor. Terrah's arrows could not penetrate both. Infantry defense had caught up with archery offense. This was a problem.

Abraham needed to report this news to King Hyanaq.

Abraham had just arrived at Hebron and asked the gate guards to tell the king, when King Hyanaq appeared leading his fifty picked men arrayed for battle.

"What do you want, O Troublemaker. What ill news have you brought this time? Why do you only appear at the worst of times?"

"O King, there is an army approaching the Dead Sea plain. It contains Sumerians, Elamites, Mari, and other small kingdoms. There is no danger to Hebron. They are after the Dead Sea bitumen."

The king stopped in his tracks and gawked, "How do you know that? Never mind, I haven't time. I need to meet with the Beersheba King. We're joining forces with the five cities of the valley."

"But sire, there is no need. The invaders aren't coming here."

"I don't believe you."

"Then may I offer myself and my archers to augment your force?"

"No, I don't trust you any more than I believe you. Why should I trust you?"

"Because I have sworn an oath of loyalty to you, Sire."

"I remember, but I don't trust oaths of loyalty from shepherds. Now go; we need to join forces for battle." He marched past Abraham, never looking back, his picked men behind him.

Abraham lowered his head and shook it in disbelief.

Two days later Abraham was standing on the promontory east of Hebron offering the best observation of the Dead Sea plains stretched out below. The two armies looked like small stick figures. The Five Cities Army blocked the King's Highway where it ended at the plain, sixteen hundred men strong. The Sumerian army was down to eleven hundred from their earlier battle losses. Both side's battle lines were roughly equal length, but the Five Cities army was heavier at three ranks deep while the Sumerian was two deep. The Sumerians had a reserve unit behind the left side of their line consisting of a hundred swordsmen plus their archers and slingers. Fifty yards back was a single line of spearmen. The Five Cities army had no reserve.

The two sides approached each other and the Sumerians halted at a hundred yards separation. Commanders on both sides went down the line encouraging their men. Then the Sumerian line continued their advance. The last twenty yards the Sumerians ran into the Five Cities Army line.

In the initial melee, neither line gave ground.

At the two minute mark the sound of a shofar horn rose above the fray. The Sumerians turned and retreated at a run. The Five Cities Army initially paused, then their general lifted his sword. It was too far for sound to be heard, but his command was obvious—he had yelled, "Charge!" The Five Cities Army line broke into a running assault, chasing the fleeing Sumerians.

But the Sumerians weren't fleeing. They retreated to the line of spearmen, stopped and reformed their battle line facing the Five Cities Army, swordsmen interlaced with spearmen. The spears protruding eight feet forward from the Sumerian lines gave the Five Cities Army pause. The Sumerian army had repeatedly practiced this maneuver. They preserved unit integrity and balance. The Five Cities Army had never experienced this and did not preserve their integrity. They lost their balance. Parts of their line plowed directly into a prepared defender, other parts hesitated and reacted timidly. They were no longer a cohesive force.

The Sumerians seized the initiative.

The Sumerian reserve force ran from behind their retreating line, then forward, wheeled and faced the charging Five Cities Army's right flank. Fifty of the Sumerian swordsmen flanked the Five Cities Army, wheeled and attacked. The balance of the Sumerian archers, slingers, and fifty swordsmen to support them continued to the Five Cities Army rear. The rightmost unit of the Five Cities Army had enemy to their front, side and rear. They had never practiced a wheel maneuver to be able to face the enemy attacking from their flank or rear; they broke and fled. The Sumerian flanking force advanced to face another unit of the Five Cities Army, which also broke and ran. And another. And another.

The Sumerians never lost unit integrity. They reacted as a whole army, not disjoint units.

Yes, the Five Cities Army had the advantage in numbers of men. But they hadn't fought on the battlefield as an army. They hadn't practiced maneuvers. They never developed the ability to react with speed as a unit. When they lost their balance, they lost the power of their units. The Five Cities Army was no longer an army, it had splintered into small individual groups of men.

It was no longer battle; it had become slaughter.

When the Five Cities Army units fell apart and their men tried to flee, they found archers and slingers reinforced by swordsmen confronted them. The Sumerians forced them back on other unit's rear, where they piled up in a disjointed mass. No cohesion. No unit control.

After thirty minutes, the shofar blew twice. The Sumerian army backed away from the Five Cities Army. Abraham saw a man step into the gap between the armies. The enemy spokesman told the men of the Five Cities Army that they could kill them all, but didn't want to. They offered them a choice. They could fight to the last man, facing certain death. Or they could surrender. The Sumerians would take them to Tyre and sell them on the slave market. Their choice. At least a slave had some measure of hope. There would be no hope if they chose death.

The Five Cities Army took off their armor and dropped their weapons.

The Sumerians sent emissaries to the five cities. They offered surrender or death. All chose surrender. They herded the citizens with the men.

They executed everyone who would slow their march to Tyre, anyone who wouldn't bring a significant price on the slave market. Everyone less than six years old, older than forty-five, the injured and lame.

They confiscated every cart, every wagon. They gathered every amphora, every jug, every jar able to carry bitumen.

They collected every skin able to carry water. They marshaled every container of nonperishable food.

They rounded up all gold and silver.

Then they burned the cities to the ground. Abraham was glad he couldn't hear the screams of the few who tried to hide.

They filled every container the carts could carry with bitumen from the pits.

Then began the ten-day march to Tyre.

Abraham didn't wait for the Sumerians to leave Sodom and Gomorrah. Their plans were clear. They would take the captives to Tyre or Sidon and sell them on the slave market. The question was whether they would keep their force together, taking the slow wagons, or split their force and send the slow wagons ahead, saving that much time for the trip.

For time's sake, the smart move was to split their forces. Their mission was bitumen, not slave money. If they marched so fast to get to the Dead Sea bitumen pits, speed delivering the bitumen came first. Yes, if he were their commander, he would split their forces.

But, for safety's sake, the bitumen was so important that he wouldn't blame the commander if he didn't split their forces. Returning the bitumen safely was more important than returning quickly.

In the end, he decided it didn't affect what he needed to do. With Sodom's citizens, they'd likely taken Lot captive. It was likely King Hyanaq was also captive. The king's force was on the Five City Army left, where there was little fighting. The fierce fighting was on the battle line's right side. Abraham's duty was to Lot and King Hyanaq. He had given his oath to his brother Harran to raise and protect his son Lot, and he had sworn an oath of loyalty to Hyanaq. Those were his only honor duties. The bitumen was irrelevant.

The problem was they must defeat the Sumerians in battle to rescue Lot and King Hyanaq. That wouldn't be easy. The Sumerian commander was crafty. And he knew about Terrah's armor-piercing arrows. His front rank of men with chest armor and shields were impervious to armor-piercing arrows.

How could he do it? He'd have to think on it. He had a few days before he needed to join battle.

But, winning was only half the goal. The other half was winning without causing the enemy commander to execute their prisoners. What motivation would convince the enemy commander it was in his best interest to free the captives?

First, Abraham needed to gather his forces. He had seventy-eight men. He needed to keep two three-hand old men with each of the five flocks. They would need four two-hand men for each flock. That would give him sixty-eight for the battle. He sent runners to each flock and the main camp at the Oaks of Mamre. The older men would meet at the Jordan River ford to Salem of the Jebusites on the west side in three days.

Second task. He called for Jurael. "I need you to take two men on a rapid scouting expedition. The Sumerians have taken my nephew Lot captive, and probably King Hyanaq as well. They will be going up the King's Highway to the east of the Dead Sea and Jordan valley. They'll cross west north of the Sea of Chinnereth, going to either Tyre or Sidon. They plan on selling their captives. They would prefer going through the Hazor mountain pass. We need to make that pass look like a death trap."

"Abraham, wait a minute. How do you know all this?"

"It's not difficult; think like their general. He has two routes to get north of the Sea of Chinnereth: up the Jordan's west or east side. The west is heavily populated. He would face four or five battles from city-states. After taking captives at Sodom and Gomorrah, they wouldn't trust his word to innocently pass through their territory. On the east side, he's already defeated Damascus and Ammon, and Bashan meekly surrendered. No one will oppose him. Going north, his train will move slowly, so his scouts can scavenge further afield for food. Bashan will feed him again. He has no choice but the King's Road."

Jurael was following the explanation. He began nodding his head in agreement.

"Okay," Abraham continued, "he's now north of the Sea of Chinnereth. The closer city is Tyre. There are two ways to go. The shorter and faster way is through the Hazor mountain pass to the sea-plain. The problem for their general is the pass is narrow and he can't deploy his forces in the cramped confines. We must make that path look like the men of Hazor are resisting his advance and traversing the pass would be a death trap.

"That makes no sense. He has armored men with shields. He can force his way through."

"No, he can't. His armored men aren't the problem. Cities pay soldiers a small fixed pay no matter if they sit in barracks in peacetime or fight to the death in wartime. Soldiers only reap the benefits of soldiering after they win battles. They rob the loser of their valuables—called the spoils of war—and sell the losers into slavery. Their captives are from a place hundreds of miles away from Hazor. The men of Hazor could care less about them. The Hazor men would kill all the captives. The Sumerian army would have no one to sell. No captives; no money. They would also set the bitumen carts on fire. That would mean a failed mission. They might be executed on their return. Therefore, if it looks like Hazor will defend the pass, they can't risk going through. Now do you understand?"

Jurael followed the logic. Now it did make sense. "So they're going up the river to Laish?"

"Right. At Laish they turn left at the Litani river and follow it west until it empties into the plains between Tyre and Sidon. Once they come out of the mountains, they could go either way. Or more likely split their force and take half their captives to each city. That way they get money from both."

"Okay, I understand what they're doing. What do we have to do?"

"First, they're not going to give up their captives willingly; the captives are their ticket to wealth. We'll have to fight them and win. But we can't kill them all. If they knew they were facing certain death, they'd kill the captives first. We must win just enough to convince them to give up their captives."

"Now I don't understand."

"Neither do I. Yet. I need to think on it. But I do know we can't just fight the battle anywhere. That Sumerian general is wily; he will try to out-flank us, like he did against the Five Cities Army. If he can outflank us, he'll surround and kill us. No; we have to choose the battlefield and force him to fight on our terms."

"You've lost me. That's all right; you're the brains of this outfit; I'll trust you. Just tell me what you need me to do."

"We need to constrain the width of the battlefield. You remember a long time ago, before I went to become a servant, we fought the twenty-eight villagers in the wadi? They couldn't spread out to surround us because the wadi walls wouldn't let them. You need to scout their path to Laish. Find a location where the road closes to a hundred yards. The river on one side and a steep hill on the other. Force them to come through the narrows. Then they have to come straight at us, not from the side. If you can find a constricted location, we can win this battle. Otherwise, we may lose."

"No problem, Abraham, trust me. I'll find one." And he left to head north.

Third. He called Michel. "I've got an important task for you. First, we need to whittle down the enemy force before we join battle with them.

Second, we've got to make them angry. Angry enough so they don't think clearly. Take two men with you. Here's what you need to do.

"First: we need an ambush party. You have eight nights before the Sumerians reach the Laish road. On four nights I want you to infiltrate close enough to their camp for each of you to fire two to four arrows at point blank range. Shoot to kill, but wounds are enough. Shoot quickly, then escape and scatter. Don't all exit in the same direction.

"Here's what's important. Infiltrate the Sumerian area, no one else. Why? Because the Sumerians carry wicker shields and wear cattle chest armor. Terrah's arrows will pierce the shield, but won't also penetrate the chest armor. So, your ambush needs to kill Sumerians. At night they won't be wearing chest armor, so only take flint arrowheads with you. Also, take only normal bows. We can't let the enemy know we have special bows until the battle. By then it will be too late to adapt new tactics.

"In your ambushes, never use the same tactics twice. Vary your infiltration routes. That way the enemy can't detect patterns, so they won't adapt."

"Any questions?"

"No, Abraham. You can count on us."

Last task, Abraham loaded two money sacks with three hundred silver shekels each, and two more with a hundred shekels each. He grabbed his longbow and four quivers of arrows, and led his men to the Jordan River crossing.

It is human nature not to ask questions.

Michel had never been bright. But, Abraham was faithful to his men.

When you don't understand why someone gives you specific instructions, it is natural to hear only what you understand, and forget what you do not. Michel remembered to ambush on four nights and forgot the instruction to vary what he did. He carried out the ambush on the first, the third and the fifth nights. When he returned on the seventh, the Sumerian general had figured out his pattern. He always used the east side so he could run to the mountains.

He was successful the first night. The three men killed two enemy each. The second ambush they killed or wounded three each. The third ambush they killed or wounded four each. They had accounted for twenty-seven men. All Sumerians.

The fourth ambush they wanted to play it safe; they would leave after three each.

Michel fired his first arrow from twenty yards away. The arrow bouncing off the man's chest shocked him. He was wearing chest armor. A second arrow met the same fate. He suddenly realized something was terribly wrong. He turned and fled—straight out.

A shadow rose before him. Michel felt a pain in his gut. He tried to rise on his tiptoes to get off the blade in his stomach, but his tiptoes were too short. The knife plunged the rest of the way up his stomach and into his heart.

Michel gulped twice, collapsed onto the knife hilt, and was still.

One of the three escaped by running sideways and out at the Elamite zone. The following morning he witnessed two severed heads mounted on spears stuck into the ground. He slipped past the Sumerians the next night and reported to Abraham.

True to prediction, when the Sumerians reached the north shore of the Sea of Chinnereth, instead of marching east and back home, they turned west. They were going to Tyre.

When they reached the north road to Laish, their column stopped. The advance scouts kept marching west. They were planning on taking the road to Hazor.

The Sumerian general was cagey. His scouts were a full two hours march ahead of the main column. The local guides he had hired told him the key to the Hazor road was a pass only twenty-five yards wide. A line-abreast of swordsmen could only fit eight men wide through that narrow confine. It didn't matter how many men he had. He could only fit eight at a time. A defending force of twenty-five swordsmen could prevent him from forcing his way through. Yes, he had almost a thousand warriors, but all but eight at a time were ineffectual; he couldn't bring their power to bear on the enemy. His column of warriors would stretch almost a half-mile back, not counting his captives. He could only fit one bitumen ox-cart at a time. If the defenders used fire-arrows on the carts, the bitumen cart would burn for three days. Only then could they push the burned hulk aside and continue marching. No, he could not force his way through the pass. His only choice was to convince the Hazor king to allow him to pass.

When his scouts reached the pass, they noted twenty or more archers in the hills above the pass. They saw no swordsmen, but they could be just around the bend. On an alert signal, they could defend the pass within minutes.

The captain leading the scouts removed his sword and gave it to another soldier. Unarmed he advanced fifty yards ahead. His outstretched arms, holding no weapons, announced that he wanted to talk, not fight.

"Men of Hazor," he shouted, "I come in peace. I lead the scouts for a Sumerian army of a thousand men, but we have no quarrel with Hazor. Our destination is Tyre. We ask permission to pass peacefully past Hazor to the shore. Will you allow me to talk to your leader so we can discuss how we can guarantee our peaceful intent?"

Four arrows landed in the pass twenty-five yards in front of him. The defenders never spoke; the arrows delivered the message.

The captain turned and retraced his steps to his men. They withdrew a hundred yards and set up a defensive position. All archers had disappeared. But, they were still there.

With no words spoken, the local guides couldn't detect the defender's accents were from Hebron, not Hazor.

The captain sent two runners to report they had failed to achieve permission to pass through peacefully.

The Sumerian general realized it was time for Plan B: the road to Laish. He recalled the scouts and sent them north.

Chapter 21

Smithsonian, Washington, DC—Present

"Good morning, Ian. David Scortun. We're completing arrangements, getting ready for opening day. We've contacted some local news agencies on background . . ."

"Yes, I know, Fox TV has already called me."

"They've already contacted you? They're not supposed to do that. Thank you for letting us know who to never contact again. We've made some tentative decisions about what to present to the public. We first thought to have the tablet resting in the original box, just as you brought it to us, but we now believe that might not be a wise choice."

"Why not? I wanted to display the entire artifact."

"I understand why you would want that, but we evaluated that as a bad idea at this time."

"I don't understand. Why not?"

"Why? Because we couldn't hide the fact we aren't revealing everything. Even a first-year archaeology student would perform tests we aren't presenting. The fact we weren't presenting all the evidence would raise eyebrows and prompt questions we aren't ready to answer. That this specimen contains the name 'Abraham' has excited the news media to a feverish pitch. If we even mentioned the word 'ephod' or connected the word to either the tablet or garment, questions would be raised. Remember, the word 'ephod' doesn't occur in the Bible until Moses and the Israelites went to Mount Sinai. To have an ephod garment show up five hundred years before it occurs in the Bible would have the religious community storming our doors. This is 'everything or nothing.' And we have too many half-answered questions.

"I propose we only present the names on the tablet. Over the next couple of years, we'll present more results, but we'll do it in scholarly, peer-reviewed articles. That way the leaks can trickle out rather than hit the news as a tsunami."

"I see. That's disappointing, but you're probably right. I'll trust your judgement."

"Thank you, Ian. We'll do our best to earn that trust."

****

PALESTINIAN LEVANT

1742 BC

At twilight the Captain reported, "O my Lord, fifty of the southern Canaanites following us have set up a blocking position on the Laish road. They are all bowmen with no other visible support.

Fifty men, the general thought. *That isn't a problem. We outnumber them twenty to one. Arrows are useless against armored infantrymen with shields; we'll sweep them aside.* He spoke, "Show me what the terrain looks like," and knelt down so the captain could draw a map in the dirt.

The captain used his finger, "Here on the left side are steep mountains ending in almost sheer cliffs at the river. The water here is narrow and deep, and flows fast. There is no nearby ford, so the river precludes a left flanking. The right side does offer an opportunity. The pass is usually a hundred fifty yards or more wide, but here the mountains have pushed a spur halfway to the river, reducing the pass to seventy-five yards. They set up fifty yards back on their side of the spur. If we also set up fifty yards back, we'll be beyond their effective arrow range. This mountain spur is steep, but not impassible. It's two hundred yards high and rocky. It's difficult but not impossible to scale. Archers can climb it. We'd fire down on their position."

"Good job, Captain. We'll do exactly that. When we get close to their position, we'll stop, feinting getting organized for battle. Meanwhile, our archers move out of sight to the promontory's side and scale the heights."

In the morning the Sumerians advanced to Abraham's blocking force, arriving an hour after daybreak.

At first, the Sumerians saw only five men facing them. But as they approached, six men who had been standing behind each of the front five emerged and all stood in line abreast, thirty-one strong. Abraham and thirty men with longbows faced the enemy. The Sumerians, never having seen a longbow, didn't realize the difference. They didn't understand the danger.

When they saw the archer's placement, the Sumerians stopped and feinted getting organized.

In twenty minutes the archers scaling the mountain discovered Abraham's remaining archers were already on the mountain spur's top, preventing their advance. They sought instructions. The general surveyed the placement. They had twenty archers on the spur.

You are wily as well as smart. The general thought about his counterpart. *I'll grant you that. Your twenty men have stopped me from flanking you. But, you're not smart enough. You don't understand warfare. You've split your force, a tactical blunder, and now you have only thirty men left to face me in the pass. That will prove your undoing. I'll force you to keep those twenty men on the mountaintop. They're too far away to provide support during the battle.*

He turned to the captain of his spearmen, "Take sixty men and relieve the archers on the hill. Approach no closer than one hundred yards. Remind your men: their arrows have a greater range when fired downhill, but no better accuracy. Don't close unless you see them start leaving. Your job isn't fighting, but convincing those archers to stay there."

Turning to the captain of his archers, "As soon as the spearmen relieve you, bring your archers down and join us at the front of the advance."

When the archers arrived at the front lines, the general advised how he wanted them placed, "Men, we need to pound on their will to fight. Let's whittle down their numbers and their courage.

"Sumerians, this is a job for the archers, your turn to shine in battle glory will come later. We will pair one archer with one Sumerian. The Sumerian's job is to use his shield to protect his archer. An armor-piercing arrow won't penetrate the shield until twenty yards' range. So, keep your shield in front of your archer. Remember, your protection is your chest armor. Close to seventy-five yards from the enemy. Archers, stay close to your Sumerian. Remain behind his shield until you are ready to fire. Once ready, step outside the shield just long enough to lose your arrow and duck back behind the shield to reload. You have only twenty-five men. The rest of your comrades guard the captives. Brave is different from brash. Normal arrows won't penetrate shields. Even the new armor-piercing arrows won't penetrate beyond twenty yards. Stay behind your Sumerian's shield."

Abraham was watching the enemy archers and Sumerians pair up. The enemy tactics were obvious. "Men, remember, they know about the armor-piercing arrows. However, they have no knowledge of our longbows. Don't let them find out too soon. Make their first experience count. Our greatest threat is the Sumerians with shields and armor. Our arrows will penetrate one. Not both. If you have a straight shot at a Sumerian outside his shield, take it. Otherwise aim for the archer. Your arrow will penetrate the shield and take down the archer. I'll let them get to one hundred yards before giving the commence-fire order. May YHWH protect us."

The general gave the order to advance and the Sumerian-archer teams spread out into twenty-five pairs in line abreast formation and began to move forward. Abraham let them advance from a hundred twenty-five to a hundred yards, then gave the order. "Begin fire, fire at will."

Abraham's men were now on hair-trigger alert. No sooner had Abraham spoke the first syllable, "Be," than the first arrow headed downrange. But adrenaline doesn't preclude being nervous, and nervous creates jittery muscle control. Despite normal target practice of 75 percent hits at a hundred yards, only half the first volley produced casualties.

But 50 percent casualties created shock and unbelief among the Sumerian-archer pairs. They stood in disbelief while Abraham's men fired a second volley. All but three archers fell, with four Sumerians also down. The survivors ran behind the spur.

The general stood in shock, but he stopped a Sumerian who had an arrow protruding through his shield. He took the shield and examined it, gasping in astonishment. The bows his men used couldn't do this beyond twenty yards. What he saw was impossible. But the impossible was real; the enemy had slaughtered his archers. His dead and wounded were irrefutable testimony to the power of his enemy's weapons.

The Sumerian general needed to reduce the power of Abraham's force before he would launch the main attack by his infantry. A slinger could hurl a stone up to four hundred fifty yards. He gathered his twenty-five slingers—the rest were guarding the captives. "Men," he began, "The enemy has bows and arrows that can pierce our shields. We need to pound on them, wound or kill some of them, reduce their numbers and their will to fight. I want you to retreat well beyond the normal bow range of a hundred twenty-five yards. Yes, it will be too far for accurate fire, but we'll get enough hits to pound them into submission."

He directed his slingers to form a line abreast two hundred yards downrange from their enemy.

But Abraham did not give the slingers a chance. No sooner had they unfurled their slings and started choosing stones, than he gave the order to fire. With thirty arrows aimed at twenty-five slingers, the first volley took down thirteen, the second volley had thirty arrows aimed at twelve men, and eight more fell. The four left ran for cover, but only two made it.

The loss of his slingers shocked and embarrassed the general. By now, caustic anger consumed him. No upstart archer was going to stop him!

The general called for one massive hammer stroke. Two Sumerian ranks of twenty-five shield-men each led eight ranks of Babylonian rebels. Everyone wore chest armor.

Like a juggernaut, the mass of men formed behind their side of the mountain spur and marched out to face Abraham's men. The first two ranks of twenty-five were the Sumerians wearing chest armor and holding shields. Terrah's arrows could pierce the shields of the Sumerians, but they would then bounce off their chest armor.

But this time, Abraham's men were not firing Terrah arrows, nor were they aiming for a chest shot. For every group of three archers, two knelt down while the third remained upright. The two kneeling aimed just above the Sumerians knees. The Sumerian shields were only two-feet in diameter. Light, but strong, they were designed for speedy maneuverability in a fast-paced sword fight. They didn't reach below the waist, so they didn't protect the legs. It didn't matter if Abraham's arrows hit the first rank. If the arrow missed, it would pass through to the second rank, or third, eventually hitting someone. They fired flint tipped arrows, designed to cut arteries. If they didn't find an artery, killing the men by bleeding them out, they cut leg muscles or tendons connecting muscles to the knee. Men began falling, unable to rise. Every third man of Abraham's archers aimed for a Sumerian's head. The head is a small target, so most didn't hit their mark. But, the arrows continued flying. Many hit someone, but even with those arrows which missed, the sight of them flying by their face unnerved the Sumerian force.

The Sumerian ranks grouped tight, a man every three feet. Every fallen man disrupted the rank behind; they had to step over his body. The long-bows decimated the first two ranks of Sumerians. Most were still alive, flat on the ground, flailing in pain from leg wounds, unable to rise. The battle-lines lost rank cohesion. The battlefield became a quagmire.

With the Sumerians removed, the remaining soldiers bore no shields. Abraham's men switched to armor-piercing arrows. These pierced the Babylonian rebels' chest armor, killing most by penetrating lungs. In fifteen minutes the following ranks couldn't advance through the field of bodies on the ground.

The general stood aghast. He'd lost a third his fighting force in twenty minutes without a single enemy fallen.

Abraham sounded their shofar. Arrows stopped flying; men on the battlefield halted in place. Abraham stepped forward ten paces, "I call a pause to the battle. Is there a leader to parley?"

The general climbed through the morass of bodies and stopped ten paces before Abraham. "I command the army," he said.

"Leader, this battle is over. This has become slaughter. There is no honor in slaughter. We could continue to butcher your men, but life is precious. We ask your surrender. Allow your men to live."

"What are your terms?"

"To begin, stop in place and free the captives. Pick twenty-five of your best men. Arm them with swords and shields. Select fifty men to carry spears. Pile the remaining weapons here. Your men may leave and return home."

Abraham removed a bag of silver from his belt and held it up before him. "Note that your force will carry enough weapons to ensure no bandits will rob you, but isn't strong enough to force any city to give you food. You will buy your food. Three hundred silver shekels will buy enough food for your return trip." He placed the bag on the ground and stepped back.

"Next, you came for bitumen, and if you return empty-handed, your king may execute you. I will give you one-third of the bitumen with their carts and oxen. I can't give it all to you, because you have burned our cities. We need to sell the rest of the bitumen in Egypt to get the money to begin rebuilding."

Abraham continued, "If there are any who don't want to return, we have much work that needs done. You will be free men. We will hire you as free men. We have cities to rebuild. After we rebuild, if any man still needs a job, I will hire him as one of my shepherds. No one will become a pauper."

The general thought for a minute, "What of my wounded?"

Abraham responded, "You may take anyone possible back with you. I am sorry, but we can spare you no additional carts for the wounded." He held up a bag of a hundred shekels, "We will pay Laish to tend the wounded. I will guarantee we will try to save them. Some will have lost use of a leg. No matter; I will still hire them. They can watch sheep with one good leg and a crutch. I repeat: no one will become a pauper."

The general was in disbelief, "These terms are more generous than I have ever heard. Why do you do this?"

"Leader," said Abraham, "We worship a God we call 'Yahweh.' Everyone is his creation, and he cares for each person. If he cares for you and your men, then we must also."

The general needed no more time. "I accept your terms."

Carrying out ideas is never as simple as conceiving them. But, over the next few hours, the two sides organized themselves.

The invaders began their long march home.

Sodom and Gomorrah's kings choose a delegation to transport two-thirds of the bitumen to Egypt to sell. Havram gave them the last hundred-shekel bag to fund their trip.

Abraham arranged for Laisha doctors to care for the wounded. With the primitive medical knowledge, recovery rates were predictably low. Most of those who did recover elected to follow Abraham and join him in Hebron.

The freed captives were overjoyed. Everyone began their trek south on the west side of the Jordan. Cities gladly sold them food in exchange for the three hundred shekels in the last bag of silver Abraham carried.

Before they left the battle scene, Abraham surveyed the carnage. He asked himself: *My men and I defeated an army of over nine hundred. Did I just make history?* That question forced him to mentally review his life. *No. I didn't make history, YHWH did. It was his plan from the beginning. He shaped me for this purpose. Like a sword is forged and then beaten and honed to a razor sharpness, YHWH prepared me for this task. Why did father invent his armor-piercing arrows? It was just in time for me to defeat the ten men with shields on the way to Ur. Why was Klymenos lactose tolerant and put into my hut? So I could learn of the Mycenaean creation myth, and then the Council assigned me to Hebron. Why was Sarrai chosen at the border and why was this followed by the disasters? So I would have the money to buy the other herds and have the thirty men and bows on hand when I needed them.*

No. I didn't make history. YHWH prepared me to carry out His plan for history. I have often wondered why I had to go to Stonehenge and back. Why couldn't YHWH have just done His will without dragging me over half of the entire world? Because He doesn't act that way. God won't do things Himself. He uses us to do what He wants done. Why? Because if we don't do it, we won't grow. What it means is that, without God, we can't do His will, and without us, God won't do it. Abraham nodded to himself. *Finally, I understand.*

What did I actually do? All I did was say yes when He called. And that understanding was followed by an emotional flood of overwhelming humility and gratitude.

When his world had calmed down to normal, Abraham considered the meaning of his life. *Fundamentally, the world hasn't changed; it's still dangerous. But I've changed. What have I achieved in the last ten years? I've gotten nothing I'd longed for; everything I'd hoped for. I no longer need to be in control; I now want what YHWH wants for me.*

On the long journey home, King Hyanaq sought out Abraham. "Abraham, I have grievously mistreated you. You swore loyalty to me and I refused to accept you as a loyal subject.

"You used your money to buy a cart to provide needed water to the people of Mamre. You built terraces to expand agricultural production and provide jobs. I should have done that, but I was not as wise as you. I did not consider my people's needs like I should have. I have seen how the people of Mamre respect you. They should respect me, but they don't. Instead, they respect you.

"When you met me at the city gate and told me what was happening, I refused to believe you. I was wrong. I refused your offer of archers. I was wrong again. You defeated an army thirty times your size. I couldn't have done that.

"You convinced the Sumerian Commander to free us. I expected to be executed. But you prevented it.

"I never repaid you for what you have already done for my kingdom. I was wrong. That money should have come from my coffers. I would like to repay you for everything you have done."

"All you asked was a house inside my walls, and I denied that to you. I never once gave you even a word of respect. Abraham, I was wrong. As king, there should be no one who has greater honor—but you do. I offer you any house in Hebron, even my palace.

"Abraham, you are wise beyond any man I have ever met. For the sake of my kingdom, I need you on my council. I need you to teach me what I should know as king, but don't."

It was Abraham's turn being flabbergasted. "Thank you, O King, I accept your offer to be one of your councilors. However, I would suggest we spend our money helping our neighbors rebuild. As for your offer of a house: for the better part of my life, I have wanted the safety and security offered by strong city walls. However, I have come to understand a shepherd's place is not inside city walls, but with his flocks and herds. I have also come to understand city walls do not provide the safety and security I had believed. Safety and security come from the strong right arm and blessing of God. YHWH is my city wall, my strength and my shield. I need no other."

POSTLUDE

Smithsonian Anteroom to the Abraham Tablet Exhibit, Washington, DC—Present

"Good morning, Ian. Glad you're here. I must admit, you look magnificent in your uniform."

"Thank you, David. I may be medically retired, but I'm still entitled to wear the uniform. I thought it would help advertise the display."

"Thank you for coming and meeting with the reporters."

"I hate reporters; but I'll do it. After all, uniforms make good background shots for photographers."

"It can't hurt." David paused, "You have to realize I'm a civilian. I see the wings; were you a pilot?

"No, look between the wings. See the parachute in the middle? I was a paratrooper."

"What are the medals for?"

"I was in World War II. Most of them are for being somewhere so someone could shoot at me. They simply mean I was there. Some were for meritorious service, meaning my boss thought I did a good job. A few were for bravery."

"Really? You were a hero?"

"Define hero."

"Never mind, that was a dumb question. What's the highest ranking one you earned?"

Ian pointed to the top ribbon. "This?

David nodded.

"The Army Distinguished Service Cross."

"How'd you earn that?"

Ian got a faraway look in his eyes. The question took him back to waist-deep snows of the Ardennes Forest, December, 1944. "The 505 was outside Rheims, France, on December 17th, when the Germans attacked at the Battle of the Bulge. The following morning they trucked us a hundred fifty miles in twenty-four hours and we went straight into the lines. We crossed the Salm River to the high ground at Haute-Bodeaux facing the First SS Panzer Division. They pushed us back to the river, but we held. It was all the 82nd could do to hold the Trois-Ponts to Grand Halleaux line. Finally on Christmas Eve General Gavin realized, with our casualties, we were overextended and had to pull back to shorten the lines. They left my company to cover the strategic retreat. We had three platoon positions. The Ninth Panzer Division's Storm Troopers assaulted, yelling and firing rifles.

They expected us to break and run, like most battles they'd experienced. We held our ground. One squad passed by us without realizing, and swung back. There were seven Germans. I dropped six with my Colt and was out of bullets. Their last man was also out of ammunition. He ran at me with his bayonet. He made a mistake, aiming low for the gut instead of the chest. I took the blow through my arm, deflecting it past me and decapitated him with my kukri. I wrapped the wound and used a tourniquet to stop the bleeding. We held, but when Patton's men broke the blockade and I saw a doctor three days later, it was too late to save the arm."

"Didn't the Germans know where you were?"

Ian's eyes narrowed slightly, his lips took on a crooked grin, and his face turned to steel. "No, they didn't. Both sides were firing. Let them yell and scream. We'll let our bullets do the barking. The crack of fire will sound in their ear just after the round hits their chest. Why let them know where we are and spoil the surprise?"

Now David was surprised. The affable, pleasant Ian he thought he knew was only a veneer. Underneath was a granite mountain of a man. David had heard the expression before, but it was enacted before his eyes. "You can't tell a warrior by the look of his face, but you can by the look on his face." David thought, *With a gun in my hand and Ian with bare knuckles, I wouldn't want to face him.* And then he realized what Robert Heinlein's expression meant: "There are no dangerous weapons, only dangerous men."

David reached out his hand and Ian took it. "Thank you for your service."

The warrior vanished and Ian's pleasant self reappeared.

Then David remembered what Ian had said, "Decapitated him with a kukri? What's a kukri?"

"The standard sidearm of a Gurka soldier. An eighteen-inch long cousin of a Bowie knife. Been carried into battle for seven generations of Maccleiths. My son was the last to use it; he's a retired Marine General. My grandson carries it now."

"You said you hated reporters. Why?"

"After they took my arm off, a Stars and Stripes reporter interviewed me. Asked me 'How do you feel?' Idiot, how do you think I feel?"

David thought, *Wow. The answer's vehemence revealed a hidden depth in Ian. In his world, there were warriors and wimps, and it was obvious which category he thought reporters belonged in.*

David almost apologized, "I'm sorry, but there are about twenty photographers and fifty reporters who want to ask you about the display. I didn't realize I was putting you into a bad spot."

Ian took a deep breath. "I'm ready."

"You're ready to face the reporters?"

Ian's face took on a hint of a smile, "I'd rather face the Germans. At least the brass let me shoot the Germans."

David opened the door and Ian started through.

A dozen flashbulbs popped. Several reporters called out, "Mister Maccleith . . ."